Attraction

a novel by

JAMES MANLOW

Attraction

a novel by

JAMES MANLOW

MacAdam/Cage

MacAdam/Cage
155 Sansome Street, Suite 550
San Francisco, CA 94104
www.macadamcage.com

Library of Congress Cataloging-in-Publication Data

Manlow, James, 1978—
    Attraction / by James Manlow.
        p. cm.
    ISBN 1-931561-83-4 (alk. paper)
    I. Title
    PR6113.A54A94 2004
    823'.92—dc22

                                                2004014842
                    Manufactured in the United States of America.
10 9 8 7 6 5 4 3 2 1

Book and jacket design by Dorothy Carico Smith.

For my mother and father

1

Why wonder at a sunset? The sky is blue light scattered as the Earth turns, leaving it redder in the morning and redder at night, until the moon takes over, throwing its cold reflection on everything. Above the smog, the dead and dying stars have never seemed so far away.

Tonight stretches before me like a spool of tape. This is my last chance to go back, to remember once and for all, to decide one way or the other. Funny what power I have. Funny how, in the end, everything depends on something so underlying and unstable, fleeting yet all-encompassing, something I once thought I knew but have lost my way in. What to do? Forgive or condemn? It depends, you see, on love.

Granted, that's quite an enigma to try and fathom in less than ten hours, but ten hours are all I have. Then they'll come and wake me and take me back to the commissariat. You'll have arrived from England, Maguire, ready to inform them all. I must have things clear in my mind.

It's dark in here. I've left the curtains open so that the light from Rennes is just enough to see by. The room is simple and clean, small, with a high ceiling. There are two doors at one end – one for the corridor outside, one connecting to a bathroom – and a balcony at the other, though with barely enough room to put out a chair, if there was one: there is only a green armchair, squeezed in at the foot of the bed, whose cushions smelt of smoke and coughed up dust when I sat down to remove my shoes. From where I lie, fully clothed upon this, hardly, double bed, it looks in the moonlight as though someone could be sitting in that armchair, with my coat over its shoulders and my shoes beneath.

But I am alone, more now, maybe, than I've ever been, and I feel it acutely tonight, remembering, silently dictating to these off-white walls the past weeks of my life.

If only the French knew! I'd be locked in a cell now, not here in this waning hotel room, with its deep mahoganies and bleached wallpaper, and just the one gendarme on the door outside.

If I keep still, from time to time I can hear him smoking in the corridor – a sigh, a sharp intake of breath. I know he is out there, awake, alert. It almost makes me feel safe, as if he were here rather for my protection. I do not know his name. He accompanied me with the detective, Jouette, having travelled in the car with us. Like Jouette, he is armed, I noticed. He has a sizeable St Christopher around his neck and sports a wristwatch with a purple Velcro strap, the specifications of which, despite his explanations in the car, I failed to understand. My French isn't good enough. Better than I've been pretending, but still not good enough.

The lobby appeared to have changed little from when the hotel first opened in 1912, as the plaque above the reception desk explains. On our arrival, a young man in a red uniform complete with cap, who clearly knew that we were coming, plucked a set of keys from the rack and handed them to Jouette. The two men spoke in unusual soft tones, the attendant pointing to an elderly lady sitting in one of the three armchairs lining one side of the room.

She was reading by the light from a lamp fixed above the only painting on the wall – a landscape depicting some woods and a river. Jouette took the attendant's meaning – discretion, I assumed – and nodded his understanding.

I was escorted to the lift at the far end of the lobby. Inside, the panels were mirrored, and as we rode up Jouette's reflection flashed at me in full profile. His blue eyes were wide, yet there were bags under them, and although he stared ahead, his mind appeared elsewhere. He seemed a good officer, Maguire, like you, but quieter somehow, no less keen, but vulnerable. There's a sad subtleness about him. He looked like he had done all this before. The gendarme with the St Christopher was trying to act cheerfully. I wondered if this was an expensive hotel, if the Rennes police force were trying to impress me. Or perhaps all this was for you, Maguire.

When we reached the fourth floor and the lift doors opened, Jouette caught me looking at him and blinked away. He directed me down a maroon-carpeted corridor. There was another painting on the wall – a horse without a rider in some trees. When we reached room thirty-nine, Jouette unlocked the door and we went inside.

'This is your room, Monsieur.'

He spoke as if I were on holiday here, but there was no sarcasm in his voice. When he went outside to check the balcony – its old-building lack of fire escape, its height above the street, busy enough – he looked as if he were assessing the possibilities for himself. I stood in the middle of the room, if you can say this room has a middle, sweating in my coat, my hands in my pockets.

Jouette turned to face me through the open door. 'You

will not jump,' he stated in English, so there could be no confusion.

He came back in. For a moment he stood in front of me, holding my gaze. His tie was tight in the light blue collar of his shirt. Then he signalled to the other gendarme that they were leaving.

'He will stand outside,' Jouette said.

And this gendarme is standing outside now, as good as his boss's word, in the maroon corridor, smoking and shuffling, sometimes talking French into a mobile phone – his wife or girlfriend, I guess. He won't be home to sleep tonight. None of us will.

I think of my own wife. I think of our wedding ring, soon to become evidence in a court of law. My Anne-Marie, whom I swore, three years ago, to love, until death do us part.

There is a Bible on the shelf above the headboard of the bed. I bring the leatherbound brick down, run my fingertip along the gold embossing stamped into the spine, and flick through a thousand frail pages. I remember verses being read to me during school assembly. I imagine I found it comforting then, as a child, first thing in the morning, to have the world explained so confidently. I haven't read it in years, not properly, only in order to make a reference for some academic paper or other. I leaf through, every word in French, pages of text I can't understand. Anne-Marie would know some of these verses by heart, no doubt, the way I have parts of the English edition filed away for ever. In the beginning God created heaven and earth. And the earth was without form and void.

And perhaps this is where I should start. At the beginning.

2

'Stone' is my mother's name. I have never known my father, never even seen him, except in photographs: he upped and left my already pregnant mother three weeks before their wedding. She has rarely talked about it.

'Didn't even tell her to her face!' my grandmother informed me, when I was eight.

I can picture my grandmother clearly, turning to fill the kettle or passing me flowers from the sink so I could cut their stems. I had lived with her and my mother all my life at number twenty-three Woolrych Street, a red-brick terrace house no different from the others, except that ours had a new white-framed door, with a glass panel, and matching double-glazed windows, the front ones going in first, then the back ones a year later. It was the year I was eight and began to understand what 'budgeting' meant, and how some of the other mothers didn't have two jobs, one at Woolworth's and one working for Mr Giles at Pen and Ink, and that at some point something very sad had happened to my mother. The year I also began to demand a father.

'Upped and left her, he did. Just like that,' my grandmother said.

We were in the kitchen as usual. It was early Saturday morning, seven o'clock, and we were making up the bunches of flowers for the special-offer bin. My mother was still sleeping upstairs. I never knew what time she got up on

Saturdays. 'That's your mother's time,' my grandmother would say, as we drove through the empty streets into town, with the back seat blooming. But my mother was always up and cooking omelettes by the time I returned, bringing her a bunch of something I delighted each week in choosing.

'Darling, you're an angel!' she would say, squeezing a giggle out of me, taking the flowers and trailing her signature of cigarette smoke through the back room to the kitchen, where those omelettes would be lightly frying. This would be my time, this hour with her, when I'd devour my lunch from a large yellow plate on the foldaway table, while she smoked and read the paper, asking my opinion of the stories there, and I in turn told her all about the market that morning. Then, with exquisite timing, at half past one precisely, she would crush out her cigarette and say, 'Right! Your gran must be starving!' and we would take the dishes to the kitchen, where she'd make her mother a sandwich while I packed away the table. Then we'd dash around each room, emptying the ashtrays, checking the new windows were closed, the back door locked, and leave the house as if we were beginning the day all over again.

From two 'til six each Saturday my mother worked for Mr Giles at Pen and Ink, the stationery shop. She would walk me into town and then, when we reached the fountain, carry on up to Sadler Gate, while I walked in the opposite direction across the cobbles to the market.

'You star!' my grandmother would say, not unlike my mother, when I brought her her sandwiches. And I'd mind the stall while she ate, sitting on her stool a little behind me, to let me think that I was minding the stall, and I'd shout, 'One day only! Chrysanthemums! Two pound a bunch!' holding up the flowers we'd wrapped that morning in the still, dripping silence of the kitchen.

The morning I remember asking about my father there were other silences in that kitchen. My grandmother believed in telling things straight, exactly how she saw them. As a child, Maguire, I was never spared anything, which generally I think I'm grateful for. And, bless her, that morning my grandmother was trying.

'Just left her a note, if you can believe that!'

'What did it say?'

'It said he wasn't coming back, that's what it said. Broke your poor mother's heart, it did. Broke it right in two.'

I pictured my mother's heart, a heart from a textbook at school, left alone like a jelly on the kitchen table, torn into two pieces that would never quite fit back together. I didn't understand.

'It's a crying shame. Your mother, she loved him with all her heart she did. It's terrible, what human beings can do to each other.' My grandmother always pronounced 'beings' like 'beans.'

We finished wrapping the flowers and laid them in the back of the car, where they rustled in their papers as we drove through town. That morning my grandmother had been more open with me than I'd expected, but when it was time for me to leave the stall, to go home for my lunch and collect her sandwiches, she made me promise that I wouldn't question my mother. 'Not this morning, love. Do you understand?'

'Yes, Gran.'

But I didn't understand. I didn't understand about my mother's heart and I didn't understand why I shouldn't ask about my father. Other boys had fathers. Where was mine?

It was a colder day than the previous one. The radio had forecast rain for the afternoon; the clouds had threatened it all morning, but had so far held off. By the time I reached home I'd worked myself up into such a state that I couldn't remember my walk from the market. I stood outside our white-framed front door, the glass panel steamed over. My breath rose in front of me. I rang the doorbell.

No answer.

I lifted the letterbox and peered into the empty front room. There was no light on. The door to the back room was closed. There was no sound of omelettes frying or the smell of herbs and eggs meandering through the house from the kitchen.

I rummaged in my duffel-coat pocket for my key, which I'd carried for a year but, so far, never used. The door slipped open easily; I stepped into the front room, closing it behind me. The clock ticked on the dresser.

A sudden panic seized me. 'Mum!'

I bolted for the door to the back room and threw it open. No light on here, no table laid with yellow plates.

'Prentis! What is it?'

'Mum!'

She was coming down the stairs, folding her floral dressing-gown around her. I clambered up the first few steps on my hands and knees, meeting her half-way. She sat down and I hurled my arms round her.

'What's the matter, darling?'

'Mum, are you okay?'

'Of course I am, course I am. Come here.'

Then she understood. 'I'm sorry about lunch, I was feeling unwell. Here, we'll go down and make some together. How does that sound?'

But I didn't move. I didn't want to let go, because then I knew the questions I'd been harbouring would leapfrog out.

She gently disentangled me.

'Mum?'

'Yes, sweetheart.'

'Where's Dad?'

Now it was her turn to cling to me. She was so warm from bed that, held against her, I started to sweat. She was shaking. Then I realised she was crying. My mother, whom I'd never heard cry before. I listened to that sound for the first time – a full, steady sobbing. She kissed my hair and let me go. She took my hands in hers. Her eyes were full and red. My mother, whom I'd never seen cry before. There was a crease on her cheek from the pillow.

'Your father's in America, darling. He lives in Chicago now. He works for a company called Sansom. They make parts for cars.'

These words etched themselves into my memory. I knew what they meant, regardless of what explanations would follow, and they would grow to take on profound meaning.

I asked my question only once, there on the stairs, meeting my mother's red eyes with my own, like a mirror held up to both of us.

'Is he coming back?'

She shook her head.

We looked into one another.

She forced her voice: 'No, darling, he isn't coming back.'

Again I waited as the words sank in, as if my body had

been expecting them for a long time. There was no mis-understanding.

'I love you, Mum.'

'I love you, too, sweetheart.' She hugged me hard again. 'Would you like to see a picture? Would you like to see your father?'

'Yes.'

'Come on, let's go upstairs.'

We sat together on my mother's too big bed. She'd dragged back the curtains to let in some light and slipped open the window, for the air swirled with cigarette smoke. There was a shoebox on the bed. It was filled with photographs. Some of the pictures were of me, some of people I didn't know.

She rummaged for a moment, then drew out a photo-graph and handed it to me. 'This is Matthew,' she said, 'your father. Today is the anniversary . . . Well, today, a long time ago, we were going to get married.'

I took the print from her, and stared, unable to take in the image of this man, unable for a while to say anything.

'You keep that, darling,' my mother said, 'and anything you want to ask me, you ask me.'

She disappeared into the bathroom to shower. She was late for work.

When it was time to leave, I folded the photograph in two and placed it carefully in my coat pocket.

'Your gran will just have to fend for herself today,' my mother said as she locked the front door, 'She can get something from the market. Are you okay, darling? Do you want me to take you all the way?'

I nodded, then shook my head: I was okay.

We walked, hand in hand, into town. All the way the

picture of my father burned in my pocket, but I said nothing. My mother didn't intrude on my silence.

We reached the fountain.

'Are you sure?' she asked.

'I'm all right. I'll see you later, Mum.'

'Absolutely, darling. And remember, you just ask me.'

'I will, Mum.'

She hugged me tightly, too tightly for the street, I felt, then left on her way up the hill.

'Where have you been?' my grandmother asked, when I materialised. She was looking at me expectantly: she was hungry.

Instead of her sandwiches, I gave her the photograph of my father.

She sighed, nodded, understood. 'Help me shut the stall,' she said. 'Come on, I'm going to get a cob.'

We sat on the steps of the war memorial outside the Assembly Rooms, while my grandmother ate her cheese-salad cob and told me about a man called Matthew Saunders, whom once upon a time my mother had loved and was going to marry. Who had left her without an explanation to go and work in America. Who was my father.

When I was five years old he had sent a postcard, explaining how he was working for the car-part manufacturer, that he was well and was wondering about me. He wanted to know my name, but gave no address.

I have never seen this postcard.

But I have the photo with me now, Maguire. My mother said I was to keep it, and I have for twenty years. These days it is here, folded in the back of my wallet. Sometimes I'll go through phases where I take it out and study it, as if I sense it's time for it to impart some meaning. I haven't looked at it for a while. And I have never been to America.

After the conversation with my grandmother on the memorial steps, I never asked about my father again. All I allowed myself to know of him was what I could deduce from this single black-and-white photograph. 'Skegness, 1969,' it says on the back, in handwriting that looks like my mother's. My father is in his work trousers and shirt-sleeves, standing by himself on a pier. He's holding a cigarette casually in his right hand, the way people do in photographs from the time. His hand with the cigarette rests by his side as he leans back on the railings with the other, his hair ruffled by the breeze blowing in off the sea. When my mother knew him, he worked at the Rolls-Royce factory. In the photo he has a mischievous grin showing the tips of his crooked front teeth, and large eyes – blue like a baby's, my grandmother once said. But in the picture his face has sharp features, as if the skin's been stretched too tightly over them.

Looking at the photograph of my father always made me wonder what name he would have chosen for me.

I was baptised 'Prentis.' My mother had named me (it's one of her best-loved stories) after the naval-officer hero, Jack Prentis, in her favourite novel *On Wings of Love* by Jane Adcock, although, growing up, I never told anyone this. We lived in New Normanton and I went to Hardwick Infants, then Hardwick Junior School, where I never liked my name because I got picked on for it. I have vague recollections of standing at break-time with a girl called Paula, apart from the groups of other children, and I remember

Stuart Green – 'Green Stew' – calling me a girl in an English lesson Mrs Longley gave us on the origin of names.

It's funny, Maguire, how we reimagine our childhood. I don't think about mine often, and have few specific memories, except that day with my mother. Perhaps I was picked on more than I remember. My name certainly bothered me enough that, during the summer holidays between leaving Hardwick Junior and starting secondary school, I changed it to Jack. Jack as in Jack Prentis, so I felt I wasn't being disrespectful to my mother. I explained this to her very seriously one Saturday morning.

'Well, if it's important to you, darling, and you've obviously thought about it, I think it's a brave decision. Jack it is,' she said.

But my mother has never once, as far as I can remember, in the twenty years since, called me Jack. I've never held it against her, and rather enjoy it, these days.

So from then on I was Jack, or 'Stone' at school, though I continued to be Prentis at home, and occasionally, though less frequently through my teenage years, an 'Angel' or a 'Star.'

Who knows? It might well have been these early names that stirred my first interest in the cosmos. In Dooley's, where my mother would drink each Saturday after work, on the wall by the cigarette machine, there used to be a poster of Irish writers. The face of an old man with round-rimmed spectacles, who looked for all the world like he was trying to hold on to a straight and serious expression, but might burst out into the widest of smiles at any moment, intrigued me. I now know, through Anne-Marie, that this was Sean O'Casey. Underneath his picture it said,

An' as it blowed an' blowed
I often looked up at the sky
an' assed meself the question,
what is the stars, what is the stars?

What I do know, looking back, what seems as clear to
me now as a night sky at Solstice, is that when it was
understood I was not to have a father, I began to replace
my questions about him with questions about the stars.
And these were a lot easier to accommodate in our house.
My mother bought me books, and my grandmother, who
had always been devoted to reading her 'stars' in the daily
paper, complemented my new interest with her own
passion for astrology. My mother, who had her reasons,
was less interested in this, although at night she liked to
look up at the Milky Way with me. As for astrology, it
was left to my grandmother and me to map out our futures.
I was more interested in a career as an astronaut then,
than in women, especially the girls at school, who hadn't
yet begun to bulge and curve the way the women in the
newspaper did (which had, I admitted privately to myself,
indeed begun to interest me). Even so, my grandmother
would predict the future of my love life. What intrigues
me now, Maguire, is not the who, for she would pick a
different type of woman each week, but her emphatic
belief, not so much that it was possible to predict future
events (although as a question for physics I would later
find this enthralling) but that there was actually someone
out there, or rather down here, one person on Earth for
each of us, whom we were meant for.

3

St Patrick's Day. Anne-Marie had just turned twenty; she was a second-year undergraduate, and I was standing in the middle of her room, naked.

Through the window I could feel the sunlight warm on my shoulders, and if I looked down I could see thin streaks of it reach across the carpet to Anne-Marie's boots, where she stood facing me with her back to the door. But I was trying not to look at her boots, for she'd asked me to look straight ahead. Which was fine, only now she was looking into my eyes, and straight ahead meant looking into hers.

Her room in the student halls on Belgrave Road was box shape, twelve feet by eight – wardrobe, desk, washbasin, bed. There was a noticeboard on the wall by the bed, which she'd covered with a copy of her university timetable and a print of Waterhouse's *The Lady of Shalott*. On the desk an uncompleted jigsaw depicted a forest and the beginnings of a lake.

'You have good eyes,' she said.

It reminded me of the way my grandmother used to inform me that I had good teeth. There was something about Anne-Marie's own eyes that made me realise, if I didn't do something soon about my nakedness, I was going to embarrass myself.

'Can I get dressed now?'

'Yes. We'll take another break.'

She left the room and went through to the kitchen to make coffee, while I caught my foot in the bottom of my trousers, relieved she couldn't see me. She returned with a mug steaming in each hand, opening the door with her foot, letting it swing slowly closed behind her.

We sat on the edge of the bed, sipping our coffee carefully.

Before, when I'd stood naked and self-conscious in the sunshine, I had felt Anne-Marie looking at me, as if I was somehow being assessed. Yet she'd also seemed utterly unaware of my presence, and this in turn had had a similar effect on me, until she became merely a figure moving at the outskirts of my vision. Now she was finding it hard to look at me at all.

'You're a good model,' she said finally.

I asked her if I could see the painting.

'Not yet. It isn't finished.'

'It's interesting to watch you work.'

This amused her.

We'd only met twice before, once at a party, once drunk on her twentieth birthday, and now here I was, loving her near-perfect English, the way she laughed, throwing her whole head back. She was wearing denim jeans and a T-shirt from a band I'd never heard of, which she'd tied in a knot across her midriff.

She untied her hair. 'Every time I paint, I want a haircut,' she said. 'I hate it like this.'

'No, you don't. It's beautiful.'

'Yes, I suppose you think it's Pre-Raphaelite or something.'

'Is that what your father says?'

'What do you know about my father?'

She eyed me suspiciously. The smile had drained from

her face; her expression now bordered on defiance.

'I just know he's a writer. That he lives in Paris.' Where I also knew he lectured on nineteenth-century literature. But I didn't want her to know I'd been asking about her for three days now, digging for any information that might help some fantasy I had of seducing her.

She was studying my face intensely.

Thinking back, this may have been the crucial moment, the point when she decided to take me into her life, her confidence, and that our wedding vows five years later were merely a confirmation of this second in her room. She told me about her childhood in Paris, her convent school in Arcueil. She was fourteen when her parents were divorced and her mother brought her to England. Her father had remained in Paris.

'He's written a book,' she said, 'on King Arthur.'

Then she smiled. And this is still the smile I think of when I imagine Anne-Marie smiling.

How fitting her father's themes were!

I realise now, not for the first time, how at some point between those early days and these last years, the very topics we studied at university, all that philosophy of life, has merged into my own life experience somehow, has become entangled there and irretrievable, the way, in a sense, Anne-Marie and I have become entangled and irretrievable from one another. Which, I suppose, is what all this is about. Which is why what happened happened.

I see her now, twenty years old, sitting cross-legged on her bed at Belgrave Road.

'Are you finished?'

She meant the coffee. She left the room to return the

mugs to the kitchen. What was she thinking, as she rinsed those two mugs in the sink then placed them to drain? About me? This young bookworm sitting on her bed, a little pathetic, but not unintelligent and perhaps cute in a way. Did she decide then to take me to her, to come back into the room, the way she did, beginning at once to arrange her brushes without looking up?

'Come here.' How did I ever have such bravado?

But she came, stepping around the easel to stand in front of me.

'We don't have to do any more today,' she said, 'It's not that good anyway, the painting. We don't have to—'

I kissed her. That first kiss, fresh, even now, in my memory, while the sun on our faces kept us there by the window and slowly I became aware I was no longer kissing her, but she was kissing me. She began to undress me.

It wasn't a large bed. (A bit like the one I'm lying on now.) We made the most of it, her turquoise duvet pleasant on the skin and warmed by the sun. Anne-Marie's thighs warm. She leant forward and wrapped herself around me, and we remained that way long after we'd finished making love. Even then she wouldn't let go.

I ran my finger along the inside of her arm.

'That's what I get for living here,' she said. 'Whenever I go back to France everyone's brown. "Tanned"?'

'Tanned.'

'It takes me a long time to get like that now. And when I come back to England it just goes.'

She brushed her arm with her other hand, as if dismissing the whole thing. It's the sort of gesture I've learnt well. I told her that if she was English they'd call her an English rose. I remember her repeating this softly to herself. I remember asking her what she liked about me.

'I like your thoughts. Your face. You're fun to talk to.'

'That's it? My face? What about this wonderful physique, this great body?'

'I like your sense of humour.'

It was late in the afternoon. Playful and sleepy, we were still lying wrapped up in each other beneath the turquoise duvet, the bed as warm as a nest and smelling faintly of the frisson of our bodies. The last of the sunlight slid in through the window. Anne-Marie's flatmates were out, so all was still, the kind of stillness you sometimes sense before an event, before time seems to begin again, like the seconds in which a stopped clock is being wound.

Suddenly I started. Anne-Marie giggled.

It sounded as though something had just hurled itself against her door.

Something had.

The thud was followed by a light scratching.

'That's Keats,' she explained, 'Natasha's new kitten.'

'You're kidding.'

'Nope. He followed her home from the Blue Note on Saturday night. She must have left her door propped open.'

'Won't she get found out? I mean, won't the cleaners come in and see it – him?'

'Probably.'

Thud.

'I don't think she's thought that far.'

Anne-Marie threw off the duvet.

'Hey!'

I admired her bare back as she wove to the door and

opened it a fraction. Keats bolted in, pivoted in the middle of the carpet, and purred. He was a classic black-and-white picture-book kitten, and seemed utterly aware of it. Anne-Marie closed the door. 'Come here, fuzzball.' She bent to scoop him up, then carried him back to the bed and set him down between us. She slipped beneath the duvet.

'Jesus, your feet are freezing!'

'Sssh. Come here.'

At first I thought she was talking to me, then she turned the kitten in her arms.

'So you're Keats,' I said.

'Don't tell me, Tash should have picked a scientist.'

'There are animals connected with scientists. Heard of Pavlov's dog?'

'Yes.'

'How about Schrödinger's cat?'

'I have, actually.'

'And?'

'No idea.' She nuzzled up to me, cradling the kitten between my side and her breasts. 'You tell me. Tell me and Keats about Shrodginger . . .'

'Schrödinger.'

'About Schrödinger's cat.'

She was gazing at me, the pupils in her brown eyes so large I could see my face in them.

I kissed her.

'No. I'm serious.'

'Okay.'

I leant back and propped my head on my hand. 'Schrödinger was concerned about light,' I said.

'He was a German?'

'Austrian. He was born in Vienna.'

'What was his first name?'

'Erwin.'

'Was he married?'

'I don't know. Anyway, along with others, people like Paul Dirac and Werner Heisenberg, Schrödinger helped formulate quantum mechanics. He was interested in wave-particle duality – that there is strong evidence for light being both particles and waves.'

'You mean waves like water waves?'

'Exactly like water waves.' I grinned.

'But how can they be both?'

'That's the paradox. On the one hand we can measure distinct particles at distinct points, but on the other hand these particles behave like waves: they can pass through each other, rather than collide, and are spread out infinitely over space. What quantum mechanics does is to propose that before you measure the position of a particle it doesn't have a definite position: it is in all possible places. In the world of quantum mechanics we talk about where the particle *might* appear *if* we measured its position, how fast it *might* be going *if* we measured its speed. Particles can even exist and not exist at the same time.'

'We did that at school,' Anne-Marie said. 'You're talking about, how do you say? Wave . . . purpose?'

'Wave functions. That's right. Or wave probabilities.'

'And what do they have to do with Keats here?'

'Well, Schrödinger's cat is a thought experiment, so don't worry, no one's ever actually tried this.'

Keats purred and glared up at me: he didn't seem convinced.

'It is an experiment set up to measure a quantity in a particle that scientists call spin. Spin is a property of sub-atomic particles, and is generally said to be 'up' or 'down'. But in quantum mechanics the likelihood of it being up or down is governed by a wave function. That is, until you measure the spin of the particle, its spin is neither up nor down. It is undefined, except in terms of probabilities. So in quantum mechanics you might say that the spin of a particle is thirty per cent up and seventy per cent down.'

'We're with you. Aren't we, Keats?'

'Well, in Schrödinger's experiment he is measuring the spin of just one particle, an electron. The spin-detector machine is hooked up to a box with Keats – with a cat in it. If the detector detects that the spin is down, it releases cyanide into the box. If the spin is up, it doesn't release the cyanide. And that's the problem. If our particle – the electron – cannot be said to be spin up or down, but is only a probability wave that will determine what will happen if we use the detector to measure its spin, then the cat itself—'

'Himself.'

'The cat himself must also be a probability wave, which is neither dead nor alive, but both.'

'Both?'

'Dead and alive at the same time.'

Anne-Marie and Keats pulled identical faces. 'Sounds ridiculous to me,' she whispered into the kitten's ear. 'What do you think? You're not dead, are you?'

Keats scrambled to his feet between us on the bed, and leapt on to the headboard.

'Yes! You're very much alive, aren't you?' Anne-Marie

laughed, then turned her head towards me on the pillow. 'What if you opened the box?'

I smiled at her. She was making fun of me in the most marvellous Anne-Marie way. I snatched her by the waist and lifted her against me. Keats yelped and dived, and I heard him land on the floor somewhere. 'If *you* opened the box, Mademoiselle, we'd all be in trouble!'

Anne-Marie giggled, then disentangled herself. She frowned. 'I don't understand. How can a particle only have a probability of being real? I'm made of particles.'

'Each with their own probability wave.'

She took my hand from her face and placed it on her breast. She held it there. 'Is this real?'

'*This* is made up of a millions of particles all with their own probability waves, all added up and taken into account.'

'You sure?'

I looked down at our hands on her breast.

She swam on to me and began rocking until I was inside her.

'You sure you're sure?'

I sat up and fastened my arms round her, tipping us backwards until we hovered on the point of unbalance.

'You dare,' she said.

One hard kiss and I let gravity take us over, pitching her on to her back, and we tumbled clean off the bed, upsetting the rug and sending her easel crashing to the floor.

Keats launched himself at the door, then changed his mind and hopped back up on to the vacant bed.

'Don't move,' she said.

We lay tangled on the cold floor, listening to our breathing return to normal. I rested my cheek on her chest.

I could see the bottom of the curtain lifting in the breeze. The temperature had dropped.

'Still think I'm not real?' she whispered.

'I never said that. How do you know I'm real?'

She took my face in both her hands. 'Because I can see you. I can feel you.'

I sprang off her.

'Hey!'

'Okay,' I said, playfully, stepping over her, so confident I had her all figured out. I crossed the room and righted the easel. It had a magpie carved into its side.

When I looked back, she was battling Keats for the bed-clothes. She won, dragging them to the floor and pulling them up to her chin. Now she was looking at me over them like a guilty child.

'Let's see how you see me!' I said.

Only at the last moment did I realise there was something I couldn't quite place in Anne-Marie's eyes. But it was too late. I turned the easel around.

The canvas was blank.

4

It's a resourcefulness of Anne-Marie's I've never understood. Over eight years I've attributed it to many things –
the convent school, her father, her parents' divorce. I've
never been able to place it, this element in her nature, not
devious but an ability there all the same for manipulation
and cool calculation. Although maybe now, by going back
like this, I can begin to understand it.

That first year flew so fast for us. I had my finals to do.
Anne-Marie had her literature degree and her paintings. In
the mornings it was her who set the day rolling: she was
always first out of bed. I'd lie back and watch her rushing
around, organising her college things. Eventually she'd
remember she had no clothes on – she'd shiver or become
aware of me watching her – then go to her underwear
drawer. To compensate for this, as if it was an unspoken
pact between us, when I finally got up and showered, she'd
watch me shave.

'Can I do it?' she asked, one day.

I was standing in front of the mirror in her room, a towel
around my middle, having worked the foam into a lather on
my face. I was about to make the first stroke. 'No,' I said.

She looked hurt. 'I won't cut you.'

'Yes, you will. You don't know what you're doing.'

'Do you think women automatically have smooth legs
and armpits?'

'It's not the same.'

'Why not?'

'It's my face. I know the shape of it.'

'And I don't?'

There it was again, that something going on behind her eyes, a place to which I had no access, like a basement I was forbidden to enter. What would it mean to her if I let her? What would happen if I didn't?

So I said, 'All right. There you go. But I guarantee you'll cut me.'

'I won't cut you. Look ahead.'

I stared at myself in the mirror while she took the razor to my right cheek and made a stroke. Then another. As she became more confident she lowered the razor to my throat. I took her hand and turned the razor around. She carried on, fascinated. After a while, I relaxed. And I was just playing out a scenario in my head – whereby the next time we bathed together I'd ask her if she'd let me shave her legs – when she cut me. By accident. Which proved I was right.

But that wasn't the point. To her, the point was trust. I'd trusted her to do it. I'd trusted her not to cut me. In a way, I sacrificed myself, my blood. Because that, too, appealed to her. The blood seeping from my skin, the blood on the blade. Trust.

Maguire, you ask me, do I love my wife, my Anne-Marie? I know I loved her then, when we were students. I know the first moment I loved her.

It was only a week or so after I'd done the modelling in her room. Since then we'd barely been apart. I can't remember what day it was exactly, but it had been raining that morning, and by the time I was walking back from town the sun was out, drying the pavements; raindrops glittered in the trees. I'd been doing some food shopping while Anne-Marie was finishing off an essay.

Swinging a carrier-bag in each hand, I breezed into the courtyard of Belgrave Road Halls of Residence. I was thinking of rainbows and light refraction, of Anne-Marie, of Keats, the kitten, and the man (the kitten had indeed been discovered and handed over to the RSPCA); thinking, very unscientifically, that if you could bottle a moment, I mean really scoop one up in a vial and pop a stopper on, then for me, that moment, standing on the grass outside the door to rooms 32–48 Belgrave Road, would be one of them.

To save me buzzing up to her Anne-Marie had lent me her key, so I let myself in and traipsed up the flight of stairs to the second floor. There was no one in the kitchen or on the landing, although someone had been frying bacon; the smell had strayed through to the stairs. I knew Natasha was in her room: behind her door I could hear her radio playing, and she had a hairdryer going.

Anne-Marie's room was at the end of the corridor. I strolled down with the carrier-bags, but she didn't hear me approach.

She had propped her door open with a tennis racket, and was sitting alone by the window. At first I thought she was writing her essay, but then I saw her notes and textbooks piled on the bed behind her, and realised, deliciously, that she was completing a jigsaw. Nothing significant about that, only I'd never seen someone of our age doing this before, and there was suddenly something fascinating about this young woman, who was surprising me day by day, sitting by the window, working on her jigsaw.

She was sitting with her back to me, at her desk, which she would drag, as was her habit, to the window whenever she needed to write. All her painting materials were packed away, the canvases stacked under her bed, her easel and paints stored in the bottom of her wardrobe. She was in what she called 'degree mode.'

Yet it seemed that she was also done with English literature that afternoon, abandoning Thomas Hardy for a 1000-piece puzzle. I couldn't see the picture properly from where I stood, just the back of Anne-Marie – my girlfriend, I mused – with her thick brown hair gathered in a ponytail and tied with a red ribbon left over from one of her birthday presents. She was wearing a pair of faded jeans I hadn't seen before and a green woollen jumper that was far too big for her. The sleeve on the arm I could see covered her hand so that only the tip of her forefinger and thumb were visible when she held up the piece she was trying to place, the light from outside reflecting off it, the way it fell all over the ribbon and her hair, flinging coloured fragments on the wall.

That was the first moment I loved her.

I didn't know it then, of course, though I often thought about it.

And why that moment? Why not the day we bought our rings from the French pedlar and I proposed to her, or the night we made love, room to room in our new house on Peach Street; Anne-Marie in her white dress at the Sagrada Familia; Anne-Marie burning cheese on toast barefoot at two in the morning; Anne-Marie on the platform at Dieppe as the French trains came through?

Because it is only now that I am able to see. And I choose that moment: I choose the twenty-year-old Annie-Marie sitting in the sunlight by her window on Belgrave Road, after a morning of rain, quietly piecing together her jigsaw.

Because we seemed innocent then, and because the sheer togetherness of us both, the fact we were a couple, would become a part of the fusion that was our final time as under-graduates. We had our friends, parties to go to, papers to write and a world to talk about changing. Because it was a precise time that, even then, I knew would never be the same again. We were students, believers in books, assured of answers if only we could ask the right questions.

Books were the beginning of things for me. Although you must not think, Maguire, that I had always been merely some bookworm curled up in the corner with Einstein and Newton. In the beginning I was a creature of quite a differ-ent kind, of Anne-Marie's and her parents' variety. I, too, was a student of literature. Of drama. I've got imagination. You'd do well to remember that, Maguire. Yes, I, too, might have been an artist.

When I was fourteen, while Anne-Marie was being weaned on copies of Dickens by Sister Agatha at St Mary's, I was being encouraged by my own English teacher, Miss Reed, who, when I was in the third year, took our class to see *Hamlet*. Twenty-five thirteen- and fourteen-year-olds, bored and excited, a day out in London. I sat with my friends on the cramped seats, textbooks in front of us, hoping for a naked Ophelia. We wanted to be out on the streets, anywhere but here, Miss . . . Why are we studying this? This isn't even English, Miss. This . . . The house-lights dimmed: the theatre plunged into darkness. Hush. A drum roll.

'Who's there?'

'Nay, answer me. Stand and unfold yourself!'

'Long live the King!' And we were hooked.

That summer I ploughed my way through a *Complete Works* borrowed from the school library – not the *Tempest*s and the *Twelfth Night*s Anne-Marie would later introduce me to, but the histories and the tragedies, *King Lear* and *Macbeth*, and the Prince himself, that great adolescent role model.

So is it any wonder I went on to marry someone like Anne-Marie, with her parents' passion for literature, who even worked in a theatre, enabling me to see enough free productions to rekindle my old interest? Only once has she ever asked me why. Why science? Why abandon my earlier pursuits? You may ask the same question, Maguire, and the answer is simple.

Because science is the greatest story of them all.

In my eyes I wasn't abandoning the arts, I was embracing them, just as I was embracing the new languages and tech-nologies of the sciences; to take their questions to the absolute limit, to render, if you like, the ultimate story. I set out (a conscious decision at sixteen) to satisfy the curiosities imbued by my love of literature – the why, why, why of the classics. I began to pay less and less attention in English and more and more in the labs. At first it was the immediacy of biology and chemistry that enthralled me – 'What a piece of work is a man' – but it was to be physics where my real interest lay and physics my choice for university. I wanted the whys of the universe, ultimate truths, the kind of thing modern literature seemed to be giving up on. Science had already tracked the beginnings of the universe down to its first nanosecond. I wanted the ultimate answer, the ultimate truth, the Big Bang, the Big Story. 'To be or not to be.' How desperate I was then, my first years as an undergraduate, before I met Anne-Marie, eager to go straight into the research labs and do some 'real' work, to attend symposia of the great theoretical minds, to get my hands on mankind's latest piece of kit, the tool of the day, a particle accelerator.

But something happened when I met her.

When I was sixteen, my mother had saved for months (I know, because I saw the coffee jar she kept for the purpose, under the sink) to buy me a telescope. A hundred billion stars in the Milky Way and our galaxy but one of a hundred billion others.

Yes, something happened with Anne-Marie. A new wonder, a new shifting of the cosmos.

A light year, my A-level physics teacher, the apt Mr Bolt, explained, is the distance light travels in a year moving at 186,000 miles per second; it is a fixed and fundamental property of the universe. The furthest stars we can see with the aid of the most powerful telescopes are several billion light years away. And out of all those stars, all that matter rushing through space, all that chance of life, there we were, Anne-Marie and I, sitting on the edge of her bed in her room on Belgrave Road. And it was as if nothing else existed before or after the first time I had seen her laugh, that first smile breaking on her lips, throwing her head right back, her T-shirt riding up, her deliberate hand reaching behind her, unclasping a clip there and letting loose her hair.

And what is it I had said to her, what remark of daring and sophistication? That her eyes were like sapphires? That I thought they had the sea in them? No. I had explained how a cat can be said to be both alive and dead at the same time, in different versions of the universe.

I was the perfect Casanova.

Yet afterwards this was how I came to think of my life with Anne-Marie, as if two separate versions of the world running parallel had been set in motion and I inhabited both simultaneously. There was my professional life, well, what was left of it, the part of me that still wanted to make my mark in the world, wanted to study again and take my MSc, and then there was my life with Anne-Marie, in which I couldn't care less who had made anything, let alone the purpose of my place in it, only that it existed, she existed, and we were together. There was the outside world, the one I was so at pains to thrive in, and then there was this inner world too, of our own making.

I'd go on drawing parallels between our relationship and my work. I remember the afternoon Anne-Marie first told me she loved me. It was a few weeks after the day I saw her doing her jigsaw. I'd finished my finals and had, that morning, moved into a flat on Colville Street. Anne-Marie still had another year of her BA to go, and was delighted that she would now have somewhere to retreat, when needed, to escape life in halls.

My belongings were in fact still at home in Woolrych

Street, where I'd lived throughout university, unable to justify the expense of renting somewhere else in the city, and it would be another two days before I would be able to use my mother's car to move them. But I'd been dying to show Anne-Marie the flat and she'd been as keen to see it.

'It's not much,' I said, turning my new key in my new door. I pushed it open, and she followed me inside, heading straight across the wooden floor to the window, under which stood the only piece of furniture in the room – a small wooden table that my new landlady, Mrs Friedrich, had explained had been left by the previous tenant. There was a double bed with mattress in the adjoining bedroom, and that was it, except for the kitchen and a small bathroom. The kitchen had a two-ring cooker with oven and grill and plenty of cupboards. Anne-Marie went to investigate.

'There's not much room in there,' I called after her, but she had disappeared into the bathroom.

'It's tiny!' she squealed.

'I know, I know.'

She returned to the living room, where I still stood, not quite believing the place was mine. She kissed me.

'Well?'

'I think it's lovely. Don't you think so?'

I looked around. Yes, I did. 'I just think it's going to be so nice to have another room to walk into,' I said.

'Show me the bedroom.'

We lay, fully clothed, on the double bed, staring up at the smoke-stained ceiling. And it was in that empty, un-furnished room that I first showed Anne-Marie the picture of my father by the pier; I told her about growing up with my mother and grandmother, of the market and the flower stall, of my grandmother's passion for horoscopes and my own first stirrings for the stars.

'Our sun,' I was saying, 'is just a regular yellow star on one of the outer arms of the Milky Way, formed five billion years ago from a cloud of rotating gas from a supernova explosion, caused by another dying star. Some of the heavier elements from this explosion bonded together to form the planets, like the Earth. So we really do come from the stars. We really are made of stardust.'

'I love you.'

I looked at her, lying on her back in her jeans and green leather jacket, boots still on, her head tilted towards me.

For a second, she looked worried. She turned back to face the ceiling.

We lay, silent, side by side on the bed.

'We're like the first two atoms that existed in the universe,' she said, 'What were they?'

'Hydrogen and helium.'

'Yes, hydrogen and helium.'

Later, Maguire, I often thought of the nuclei of those first atoms, formed one hundred seconds after the Big Bang, soaring together through the river of space, whose temperature had then dropped to a cool one thousand million degrees, one having come from the other, motivated only by a single willingness to be.

5

Yes, maybe now, by going back like this, I'm beginning to understand Anne-Marie better. She is like a puzzle I'm having somehow to piece together.

I spent that April, Maguire, to- and froing between my new flat and the indoor shopping centre, carrying cans of knocked-down emulsion and floor lacquer; I toured the city for second-hand furniture, and for the next two months I worked packing floor tiles at Quicksmart, while Anne-Marie studied for her exams. The Friday she finished her last paper we booked ourselves flights to Nantes.

Our plan was to start in the south-west of France and spend a couple of months making our way back north. I'd not known Anne-Marie so excited: there were so many places, she said, that she wanted me to see.

We sat on my bed in Colville Street and on paper pooled what was left of our student loans. Our flights had been cheap, although they meant we had to fly from London. That weekend we both phoned home.

'That's wonderful, darling,' my mother chirped. 'You have a fantastic time. Make sure you look after her, won't you?'

'I will.'

'And get me some of that perfume. Hold on, I'll find the name of it.'

'Yes, Mum.'

I didn't say I thought it more likely Anne-Marie would be looking after me.

Anne-Marie's mother said that she was in London for a few days. She was due to see her publisher that Monday but would meet us first for lunch. Gina Dufeur was a translator of new French literature.

'She wants to check me out,' I said.

'Of course she does.' Anne-Marie giggled. 'You'd better have a shave.'

So that Monday morning, clean-shaven, wearing hiking boots, jeans and a faded Chili Peppers T-shirt (with the shirt I had planned to wear tied around my waist, having sweltered on the tube the one stop from St Pancras) I extended my hand to Gina Dufeur, glad to have Anne-Marie beside me, buoyant on my arm. Outside Bellini's, her mother pulled us both towards her for complementary kisses on each cheek.

'It's so lovely to meet you, Jack.'

'And you, Madame.'

She laughed an Anne-Marie laugh. I met her dark eyes, and smiled.

Gina squeezed her daughter's hand. 'Ravie de te voir, ma chérie. Shall we go in? I've booked a table.'

It was so wonderful to watch them together, Maguire. Gina was a beautiful middle-aged Anne-Marie. That day she was wearing a tailored khaki suit, with a white blouse open at the neck and a green silk scarf. She was forty-five, I worked out later. And she was stunning.

'Order what you like, Jack. No excuses,' she said.

Anne-Marie squeezed my arm.

We ate a light pasta lunch. Gina was known at Bellini's,

I think, for the service was remarkably fast. When I asked about her work she spoke of the book on French heroines she was translating. She enquired about my new flat, which Anne-Marie had told her about, my physics degree and plans for the future. Then she and Anne-Marie talked about French literature and a new exhibition in Paris – paintings by an artist called le Doaré that, according to Gina, we had to go and see. 'You *are* going to Paris?'

I glanced sideways at Anne-Marie. In all our planning we hadn't discussed this. Henry Parrot, Anne-Marie's father, had remained in Paris for the past twelve years, since his and Gina's divorce. I'd guessed Anne-Marie didn't want to see him.

'Perhaps,' she said.

'Have you been to Paris, Jack?'

'Once, on a school trip, when I was fifteen. We saw the Eiffel Tower, but then it was time to go back.'

'Does he know you're coming?' Gina asked her daughter.

Throughout the conversation she only ever referred to her ex-husband as 'he.'

Anne-Marie stirred her coffee. We'd finished our meal and her mother had signalled for the bill.

'To France, I mean.'

Anne-Marie shook her head. I took her hand under the table.

'I should tell him, I suppose,' she said. 'We'll see.'

She squeezed my hand.

'Actually, we'd better go, Anne-Marie,' I said. I glanced at Gina, and found her smiling at me.

'What time's your flight?' she asked.

The waiter brought the bill. She gave him a credit card.

'Three-thirty. We've got to check in at Heathrow by half past two.'

'That's perfect. I've got to be in Vauxhall then. We can all go together.'

And so we did, Maguire, Anne-Marie and I lugging our packs onto the tube, which was beginning to crowd again for the lunchtime mayhem, Gina with us, the opposite of awkward, carrying only her brown leather satchel. When we got to Green Park, she placed a card in her daughter's hand.

'Call that number if you need anything,' she said, 'and have a wonderful time. It's a pleasure to meet you, Jack.'

'And you.'

She kissed us both.

'Take care, Maman.'

'You too, chérie. And, well, if you see him, give him my regards.'

'I will.'

We stepped down onto the platform, which had suddenly become swamped with people wielding carrier-bags and pre-packed sandwiches.

'She's lovely,' I said, hoisting my pack on, 'I'm sorry it was so brief. We could have come earlier, I guess.'

Anne-Marie sighed. 'There'll be another time.'

We thought we owned time then.

She turned to the departing train. Gina waved from her carriage, her green scarf flapping in a draught, and then she was gone.

When we left Heathrow, Maguire, when the wheels finally eased off the runway, I felt a sudden, colossal sense of freedom. I hadn't expected this, hadn't realised I had felt the opposite of free, whatever that was – not trapped exactly, but circumscribed, I suppose. At last in the air, I experienced an incredible release. We would soon be in another country, and here was Anne-Marie sound asleep in the seat beside me, her head heavy, so very *there* on my shoulder.

That sense of freedom lasted our whole trip, which seems strange looking back on it now, having travelled since, having revisited some of the same cities even. That summer somehow was different. Viewing it now is like gazing through the wrong end of a lens, or an eight-week kaleidoscope of shape and colour. We have the photographs, of course, at home – Vannes, St-Brieuc, St Malo, Bayeux, Le Havre, Dieppe, Rouen, Paris – but I've always found them inadequate. The couple in those photographs, whether they are standing on the steps outside the Palais des Arts or sitting in a bar off a cobbled street somewhere, are too young, too happy-looking to be us. What I see, when I close my eyes, is Anne-Marie's face coming clear out of the colours now and then, suntanned and grinning, to tease a lens, or take me firmly by the hand to show me something – the sunset from the old bridge between Lanvallay and Dinan, lobsters in a pot at a village market somewhere south of Rouen.

I remember that first night in Nantes. We landed at four-thirty in the afternoon and took a bus from the aéroport into town, where we headed straight for the river, walking along the quai de la Fosse. Since it was our first night in France, we treated ourselves to a room at the Hôtel d'Arbre, Anne-Marie having charmed the owner, a Monsieur Toutain, with a flirtatious tale of poverty and studentship.

'You could never do that in England,' I said, as we stood on our first-floor balcony overlooking the Loire, where a three-mast sailing-ship was anchoring amid a spatter of motorboats.

Anne-Marie laughed.

'Does it feel good to be home?'

'Oui.'

That night we strolled again along the lamplit quayside, admiring the eighteenth-century houses, built, according to Monsieur Toutain, by the local ship-owners. He had found it highly amusing that we could not afford his restaurant at the hotel and he recommended us a crêperie further down the quayside, not far from another house with ornate balconies, which, he explained, had once been the offices of the former East India Company.

The crêperie was small, but busy, run by a local couple. We ate two courses and Anne-Marie had some kind of flambé that burned gas blue.

She looked at me across our little table, bathing in candlelight. 'This is perfect,' she said.

And it was, Maguire. She was.

We stayed in hostels mostly, or booked ourselves on overnight trains, making nests in wooden compartments and waking to the sound of the wheels on the tracks. We made love in a sleeper carriage between St Malo and Bayeux, and were disturbed by a German man, throwing open the door, looking for his wife. Drunk, we yelled, 'Je t'aime, tu sais! Je t'aime, tu sais!' from the back of a ferry-boat on a day-trip out from Le Havre.

Only once during those two months did Anne-Marie

frighten me – a clear memory I have of that summer, set apart from the haze. I saw her turning towards me on the platform at Dieppe. She was dressed in her green combats and light grey sweatshirt and wearing her Derby Duck cap, her rucksack on her shoulders. Her face looked tired and pale: for a second her cheeks had lost their colour, and her eyes were wide and questioning. This is one of the few images of Anne-Marie that stays with me, I mean really stays with me, clearer than any photograph, one I can call up anywhere when I'm away from her, like the image of her sitting by her window doing her jigsaw. It is an effigy I don't like thinking about, one that returns to me whenever I feel doubt.

I've thought a lot about it recently, Maguire.

I attributed it then to the fact that we were low on funds and that we were beginning to approach the question of Paris, and Henry. It is from about this point – the station at Dieppe – through Rouen to Paris, that I can recall things more distinctly.

My memory of Anne-Marie at the station was the morning we arrived in Dieppe, where we stayed in a rather rundown hostel, a dormitory overlooking the industrial end of the twenty-four-hour port. The first night we slept right through, exhausted from the journey, but the second night we were kept awake by the sound of trucks and cranes setting down containers in the docks.

It was a mixed dormitory, and not very busy. We lay side by side in single beds, our two rucksacks on the floor between us. There was another couple at the far end of the room, braver than us, who had crept into a single bed and after some soft commotion now slept soundly.

When I'd had enough of the grinding and clanking outside I reached for my watch and tilted it in the half-light. 'Anne-Marie, are you awake?'

'Yes.'

'It's five o'clock. Do you want to get up? We could go for a walk.'

'Okay.'

We dressed in silence, grinning at one another in the semi-darkness, then tiptoed out.

Our hostel was on a side-street that led directly to the port. We headed that way for the sake of the sea. It was dawn and the sky was beginning to burn a spectacular red-orange. The trucks kept coming along the quai Duquesne and the cranes carried on with their tilting and turning.

'Do you want to go to Rouen?' she asked, as we walked.

'I think the question is more do you want to go to Paris?'

She took my hand. 'I'd like to take you to Paris. Rouen's nice, too, they say. I haven't been before.'

'We don't have to see your father, you know, if you don't want to.'

'Oh, I know. We will, though. It's stupid not to.' She squeezed my hand. 'It's just that he can be a bit over-bearing sometimes.'

We reached a stone wall, beyond which sprawled the sea.

'It will be all right,' she said.

'Course it will. Anyway, I'm the one who should be worried, right? New boyfriend and everything.'

Anne-Marie smiled and then laughed, as if she hadn't thought of that. She kissed me. She walked over to the wall and stood looking out towards England.

I joined her and put my arms round her. Together, we gazed at the Channel, which was rough that morning, rising and falling. I could feel Anne-Marie's heart beating beneath her fleece.

'We could always just get a ferry,' I whispered. 'You can almost see Newhaven from here.'

She followed my gaze out across the water, then turned and began walking towards the town with her back to the sea. I caught her up, and we strolled with our arms around each other's waist, through the ceaseless clamour of the port, which seemed to rise with the sun.

'Let's get out of here,' she said.

That evening we were in Rouen.

We stayed for three days, lodging at a small hostel on the rue St Vivien, where we paid an extra two hundred francs for a room of our own. There was a firework display on the river that first night, a Saturday, and we made our way down through the crowded streets so I could get my first proper look at the Seine. A mock eighteenth-century flagship had been towed into the harbour area and was launching fireworks in the direction of a group of locals, dressed as soldiers, on the far bank, enacting a battle Anne-Marie had never heard of. It was spectacular. But Anne-Marie was distracted. The explosions caused her to start, and her face, caught repeatedly under each umbrella of fire, was wide and white, and far off somewhere.

During the days we visited the galleries and museums laid out in a local guidebook almost reluctantly. I think we were becoming tired of the endless histories of cities, and every church looked like another.

On the second day Anne-Marie called her father. She used the payphone in the lobby of a nearby hotel, while I waited at a table in the empty bar area, nursing a coffee.

She returned too quickly.

'Well?'

'He's not in. I got the cleaner. Or she said she was the cleaner.'

She looked out of the window. It was ten o'clock, and the street outside was beginning to fill with shoppers.

'I left your mobile number, I hope you don't mind. Otherwise this could take all day,' she said.

'That's fine.'

We'd only taken one phone with us, which I'd put on a tariff to use abroad. I got up and hugged her. 'Where to?'

That morning we spent at a local art gallery, where we saw an exhibition by artists still working in Rouen. Anne-Marie fell for a set of portraits of street dogs by a local woman. We were in the gift shop, trying to find a print of one of them, when Henry rang.

I fumbled in my pocket for the phone. A few customers in the shop tutted at the interruption. Anne-Marie was over at the till, paying for a Renoir postcard, having given up on the dogs.

'Hello?'

'Anne-Marie?'

'Oh, hello. I'm Jack, I expect—'

'Pourrais-je parler à Anne-Marie, s'il vous plaît?'

'I'm sorry—'

'Pourrais-je parler à Anne-Marie, s'il vous plaît?'

Henry's voice was higher pitched than I'd expected, but direct.

I walked the phone over to Anne-Marie, shrugging my shoulders. She rolled her eyes. She handed me the post-card and we swapped places. Taking the phone, she headed for the door.

'Papa, c'est moi, Anne-Marie. Comment vas-tu? C'était Jack au téléphone.'

I considered the Renoir in my hand, then dug in my pockets for change, watching Anne-Marie through the glass double-doors, pacing up and down in the gallery foyer. I tried to picture Henry from his voice, but couldn't.

'Puis-je vous aider, Monsieur?'

I'd reached the front of the queue.

'Pardon, Madame.'

I barely had ten francs on me, but managed to pay in the end, amid an array of smiles and nods from the other customers. The attendant thanked me in English and wished me a nice day.

I went out to find Anne-Marie, but the foyer was empty. Then I saw her coming out of the ladies' toilet.

'Hey.'

'Hey. You all right?'

'Yeah.'

'Sure?' Her eyes were a little red.

'I'm fine.'

She took my hand with both of hers, and we guided one another to a wooden bench outside the gift shop.

'God, that man can be hard work,' she said, when we'd sat down.

'I don't think he knew who I was.'

'Yes, he did. I'm sorry about that. It's just his way of putting you down. He knows you don't speak French.'

Great, I thought. I was suddenly not looking forward to Paris after all. 'So, what's the plan?'

She patted my hand, and I watched her force a smile.

'We're going to meet him tomorrow. I'll ring when we've got a train time and he'll meet us at the station. What's that?'

'Your Renoir.'

We booked the cheapest tickets for a slow train departing at noon the next day, then Anne-Marie phoned Henry and left a message on his answer-machine, asking to be picked up at five o'clock.

She handed me back my mobile, looking relieved.

'Well, at least we're all sorted,' I said. 'Now, what shall we do for the rest of the day?'

'What time is it?'

'Almost two.'

'Do you fancy a drink?'

We found a restaurant in town on the boulevard des Belges and ate moules-frites and drank a bottle of white wine. Then we went to a bar along the quayside and drank another bottle. The sun had stayed out and in its presence the afternoon was warm, so warm that Anne-Marie removed her fleece, unsteadily as we navigated the cobbles. I lunged for her waist as she tried to tie the fleece round it. She resisted, then gave in, giggling, kissing me hard in the open square. There was a market on. We went to say hello to Joan of Arc, but she was too dull, being a statue, so we floated, arm in arm, between the coloured stalls. Then Anne-Marie steadied us to a tabac and bought a pack of Gauloises. Neither of us had smoked since we were teenagers. Before the shops closed we bought some bread and cheese from a bakery and wolfed them down, then strolled more steadily towards the pier, to find another bar.

'To Rouen,' I said, raising a glass of Loire-Valley wine.

'To travelling,' she said, raising a glass of Pernod at the Restaurant Reymond.

'To us,' I said, raising another glass of Pernod at a bar at Pont Fluvial.

'To us,' she said.

Drunkenly, she reached for my wrist and turned it in her small hand. Nine o'clock.

'To dancing?'

I met her eyes. She was wearing a very Anne-Marie expression. 'Why not?' I said. 'To dancing.' I drained my glass.

She ordered two tequilas.

And we danced that last summer night into autumn at the Hôtel St Jeanne, riding white crests of alcohol and jazz.

6

Paris was awful.

We woke late on our last morning in Rouen. With a crashing hangover, I perched on the edge of the single bed Anne-Marie and I had tumbled into and felt like vomiting.

Madame Gérôme, with whom we'd had to argue our way back inside the building only a few hours earlier (the hostel having locked its doors at midnight), hammered on the door.

'Il est onze heures. Vous êtes en retard.'

'What?'

'She's saying we're late,' Anne-Marie said slowly, also sitting up. She stared at her toes. 'We should have been out by nine.'

I noticed I still had my watch on. 'Shit. It's eleven o'clock.'

'C'est quand vous voulez . . .'

'Merci, Madame!' Anne-Marie called, then said something in French. I didn't ask for a translation: I was too busy trying to stand.

Anne-Marie looked so unlike herself it was laughable.

'Shall we just pay up and go?' she said. Her voice was husky.

I looked around the room. The sun slopped in through the curtains. 'Absolutely.'

We reached the station ten minutes before our train, panting and sweating with our packs.

'Have you got the tickets?'

'Didn't you have them in your bag?'

We searched frantically.

'Here. They're here. My fault,' I said, retrieving them from the side pockets of the combats I was wearing, which I realised I'd also slept in. 'God, I need a shower.'

'I need everything,' Anne-Marie said, beaming.

'Well, I'm glad you're feeling better.'

'We need to find a noticeboard. Some water. And some food. Come on. I'll sort the platform, you get us something to eat from that kiosk. We'll sleep on the train.'

And we did. Or I did, anyway, waking two hours later to find Anne-Marie opposite me, a novel in her hand, which she wasn't reading.

'All right, sleepy?' she said.

'No. I feel terrible.'

'You'd better have something to eat.'

I reached for the bread and croissants, the orange-juice carton and the bottle of Evian, and attempted to have some of everything at once. 'How do *you* feel?' I asked, amazed at how relaxed she seemed.

'Awful. Good night, though.'

'Yeah.' I grinned. My first smile of the day. 'I haven't kissed you yet.'

'I don't think I want you to.'

She laughed, then winced.

Good, I thought, she *was* feeling awful.

'Try a couple of these.' She tossed me a strip of paracetamol.

'Do they work?'

'No.'

I swallowed them with the Evian.

'We'll be there soon,' she said. 'About twenty minutes, I reckon.'

I sat back and gazed out of the window. More houses were beginning to pop up across the farmland. We passed a power station. I breathed steadily, hoping the croissant would be good and stay down. The only thing that stopped me doing what I really wanted – close my eyes and fold myself back into sleep – was the knowledge that I was about to meet Henry. I desperately needed a shower, and all I could taste was alcohol and the stale stench of cigarettes – I swear I could actually taste the smell of the Gauloises Anne-Marie had bought in her inebriated twinkling of nostalgia.

Our train arrived in the capital at precisely 17.00 according to the digital clock at the end of our platform. Anne-Marie met my eyes as our carriage shuddered to a standstill. 'Relax,' she said. She leant over and kissed me. She smelt faintly of sweat and smoke.

'I'm fine,' I lied. 'You okay?'

She sighed. 'Yeah. Let's go and see if we can find him.'

We stepped off onto the platform with our packs, and joined the stream of passengers heading for the concourse up ahead. The station, with its glass skylights and white floors, was sunlit and immaculate. The air was stale and warm. It seemed like a hot day out there, and walking towards the string of boutiques and coffee shops, I was looking forward to some fresh air.

'Over there,' Anne-Marie said, pointing, then waving to a man standing beside a news-stand, who, seeing us, raised his newspaper in acknowledgement. We paced over as Henry began what seemed like a long walk towards us.

He was shorter than I'd expected, a thin, but healthy-looking man, with sharp blue eyes. His beard was clipped and greying, but his hair was still Anne-Marie's dark brown in places. He looked like a mathematics teacher. He was wearing a single-breasted black suit, white shirt, but no tie. He had a black suit-carrier, slung over one shoulder, and a red and white sports holdall in the hand without the newspaper.

'Papa.'

Anne-Marie stepped up for a kiss. Her father put the bag down and hugged her, a little awkwardly, as she still had her pack on. I stood behind them.

'Anne-Marie, you are beautiful. Let me look at you. Yes, yes, you are. We're speaking in English?'

'Yes.'

'That's my fault, I'm afraid.' I stepped up beside her.

'Ah, yes,' Henry said. 'Jack.'

'Pleased to meet you.' I put out my hand.

He took it. 'Yes, pleased to meet you.'

He might not have been living in France all these years: his native English was still spoken with a Kensington accent.

He looked me up and down, while Anne-Marie clutched my arm. I tried to picture how we must have appeared: it wasn't pretty.

'It's very kind of you to let us stay,' I said.

'Not at all. How could I turn down a chance to see my daughter? Did you have a good journey?'

'Fine.'

I looked around. The station was busy but not over-crowded.

'Have you got the car?' Anne-Marie asked.

'Yes. There's not much time, actually.'

Henry took out a set of keys and handed them to his daughter. Anne-Marie looked puzzled. 'You're not coming with us?'

I glanced at the suit-carrier on her father's shoulder.

Then she realised. 'You're going away, aren't you?'

'I've got to go to Chartres for two days, I'm afraid. A teaching conference. My train's at five forty-five.'

Anne-Marie's face was deadpan.

Henry looked at me. 'I'll be back on Thursday. We'll have dinner. Meanwhile, help yourselves to anything you need. Michelle will be around, if you have any problems.'

'Fine,' Anne-Marie said. 'So what are you going to do for the next, what, forty minutes?'

'I thought I'd buy us all something to eat.'

'That's very thoughtful of you.'

He looked at her, then me, then her again.

'Great,' I said.

We ate at a street café opposite the station on the rue de Chalon. It was indeed a hot day, and being so close to the station, the café was packed, its round tables and wicker chairs all taken and spilling out into the street. Luckily a couple was leaving as we arrived. Anne-Marie and I sat down, setting our packs back to back beside us, while Henry disappeared inside the restaurant. He returned with a waiter, who handed us each a menu.

'Drinks?' Henry asked.

'I'll have a glass of water,' Anne-Marie said.

'What, no wine? Ah, come on, we can have a drink, can't we? It's not often I get to see my daughter. Jack, you'll have a glass of wine with us, won't you?'

'Well, I—'

'Wonderful.'

He looked at his daughter.

'A glass of water.'

Henry ordered some water and a bottle of red wine I'd never heard of, then sat back in his wicker seat, sighing contentedly. He glanced at his watch.

'I'll have the paella,' Anne-Marie declared.

I didn't want anything, least of all a glass of red wine, but when the waiter returned with the water, I ordered the same as Anne-Marie.

'So,' Henry said, 'you're a scientist, Jack.'

'Yes. Well, I've just completed a physics degree.'

'And what are your plans?'

'I'm thinking of doing some postgraduate work, but I haven't decided yet.'

Henry laughed. 'Don't worry, I'm not vetting you. I'm not one of those fathers.'

Anne-Marie turned her head sharply.

The waiter brought the wine. 'Mademoiselle?'

She shook her head. The waiter poured two glasses and I sampled whatever Henry had chosen. 'Perfect,' I said in English, appreciating nothing: with my hangover anything would have tasted like poison.

'And what about you, Anne-Marie?' Henry said, 'What are you going to do now?'

'I've still got another year to go, Papa.'

The food came quickly and we ate in a mixture of silence and sporadic talk about various sights to see in Paris and student life in general.

'Gina said we should go and see the – what was his

name, Anne-Marie, le Doaré?'

I said this without thinking, and the word 'Gina' floated above the empty dinner plates, until the waiter came and removed them. He asked if we would like anything else.

Henry looked at his watch. 'No time for me, I'm afraid. You two have something, if you'd like.'

'An espresso,' Anne-Marie said.

'Monsieur?'

I nodded.

'Et l'addition, s'il vous plaît,' Henry said. He waited for the waiter to leave. 'How is your mother?'

'Fine.' Anne-Marie sighed. 'She sends her regards. She's working on a new translation.'

Henry nodded, taking this in. He looked around for the waiter. 'Well, I really must go. Here, this should cover it.' He handed me a five-hundred-franc note. 'You two have a good couple of days.'

Anne-Marie said nothing.

I stood up and shook his hand. 'Thank you for the food, Henry. I hope your conference goes well.'

'Thank you. Goodbye, Anne-Marie.' He leant over and she offered him her cheek, reluctantly. 'See you Thursday,' he said, slinging the suit-carrier over his shoulder and picking up his holdall.

We watched him weave through the traffic towards the station. Anne-Marie didn't take her eyes off him until he had disappeared inside. The waiter came with the bill. Anne-Marie took the five-hundred-franc note from me and gave it to him without saying anything.

'Merci, Mademoiselle.'

'You okay?' I said.

Her face softened. She smiled. 'Yeah, I'm sorry.' She took my hand. 'Are *you* okay?'

'No sweat.'

The waiter came back with the change, and brought our coffee.

'Well, cheers!' I raised my cup. 'To Paris.'

'Yeah. To Paris.'

Over the next two days, Maguire, we worked to make the city ours.

Henry Parrot lived, as he does now, on the avenue de Lorraine, in a spacious five-room apartment on the top floor of a grey-bricked house, built in the 1800s and once owned, according to his housekeeper, by a government minister.

There were two bedrooms, a sizeable kitchen, a main living room, with a separate dining area, and another similar-sized room, which served both as a library and a study. Above the mantelpiece in the living room was a large print of Burne-Jones's *The Last Sleep of Arthur*, which Anne-Marie pointed out. There were more Arthurian pictures in the study, including pencil sketches of a knights' tournament, and a small painting in each bedroom. None of these was his daughter's.

Michelle, Henry's housekeeper, was on her way out as we arrived. She was a short French woman with frizzy jet-black hair and little time, it seemed. She spoke no English. She explained to Anne-Marie that she had prepared the spare room for us, and that there was salad and cold meat in the fridge.

We took our packs through to our room. Two single

wooden-slatted beds had been made up, which Anne-Marie made it her first priority to push together, while I left to explore the kitchen and put the kettle on. We stood on one of the two south-facing balconies, drinking coffee, looking out over the quai de Gesvre, between whose houses we could see tourists boat-tripping on the Seine.

The next morning we took one of these trips ourselves, cruising the river from the Palais de Chaillot to Notre Dame. I remember Anne-Marie's arms around me in the breeze, and how they'd only leave my waist for a second at a time, to point out things to see. We visited the Pompidou and the Louvre, and ate that evening at a floating restaurant called La Lis. The following day we spent shopping (I bought my mother her perfume) and locating the exhibition Gina had told us about. We found it on the rue du Mail, a small gallery that had once been a barber's shop. The whole trip I had never seen Anne-Marie so happy. She loved the exhibition and flitted from one picture to another like a roused schoolgirl. 'This is what I want to do with colour,' she explained. 'And look, look at *that* for simplicity!'

I followed her around like a proud relative, nodding at the right moments, observing her movements, at home among such beauty – for they *were* beautiful paintings, Maguire – and wondering at how much I was in love with her.

That night Henry phoned to say he would be back the following afternoon, a day early, and asked us to book somewhere in town to eat.

The next morning, we lay in. Anne-Marie had been sleeping with her back to me. I could tell she was anxious again. She turned to face me and I wrapped my arm round her. 'Why don't we just stay in bed this morning?'

She smiled. 'But don't you want to see the Tour Eiffel?'

'I've seen it before.'

So we snoozed the hours away, then lay awake and watched the sunlight journey across the ceiling and listened to a peal of bells far off somewhere.

'A funeral,' Anne-Marie said.

'Or a wedding.'

She kissed my chest, her ready pillow.

'We'd better book that restaurant,' I said, 'before it gets too late.'

'No.' She lifted her head, and sat up. 'I'd rather stay in tonight. I'm going to cook.'

In the afternoon she took me to an all-day market just off the quai du Louvre. Stall after crowded stall poured out precariously along the waterfront and into the side-streets. Tourists flanked the crafts and jewellery stands and gathered around loud Frenchmen demonstrating electrical kitchen applicances, while determined locals wove their prescribed routes for daily fruit and slices of meat.

'This is where Maman and I used to shop on Saturdays,' Anne-Marie said.

'How old were you?'

'I don't know – twelve, thirteen. Just before we left, I guess.'

I tried to picture a twelve-year-old Anne-Marie among the hive of stalls.

She stopped at a vegetable stand and chatted with the owner, more cheerfully, more animated than I'd seen her since we arrived in the city. When she spoke French for long periods, it was like listening to someone I didn't know. She laughed and joked and pointed and frowned, no, not that one, and smiled and nodded, yes, two of those, appearing to buy something of everything, and afterwards handing me two heavy bags to hold while she searched in her purse to pay. 'We're having roast vegetables,' she explained, taking one of the bags from me as we walked away.

'With what?'

She pointed towards the fish stalls lining the quay. 'Salmon. Papa loves salmon.'

Back in Henry's kitchen, she oiled a baking tray, then began salting the four pieces of fish.

'Can I do anything?'

'You can start chopping the vegetables, if you like.'

I tipped what Anne-Marie had bought onto one of Henry's giant chopping boards – onions, garlic, peppers, aubergine, mushrooms, carrots, courgettes.

'How big do you want them?'

'Big.' She laughed. 'Well, not that big. Here.' She took the knife. 'About like that.'

She returned to the fish, laying out the four pieces of salmon in the tray. Then she picked out a knife and joined me, splitting open a clove of garlic. I put the radio on and we rinsed and chopped and chatted as the afternoon wound on outside.

'What time did your dad – did Henry say he was coming back?'

'He said to book a table for seven. I expect he'll ring.'

At six we put the vegetables into the oven, poured ourselves some wine and sank into one of Henry's sofas.

At twenty to seven he still hadn't rung.

'Shall we put the fish in?'

Anne-Marie finished her last mouthful of wine. 'Yes,' she said. 'You do that. I think I'll phone him.'

In the kitchen the vegetables were well on their way. I slid the tray of salmon onto the top shelf.

'But I've been cooking, Papa,' Anne-Marie's voice sounded loud from the living room. 'Que veux-tu que je fasse? Tout arrêter comme ça simplement?'

I looked up and out of the window. It was growing dark outside. I heard Anne-Marie replace the receiver. She came into the kitchen, looking rather like she might burst into tears. She settled for anger. 'Forget that. Turn it off.'

'What?'

'We're going out to eat.'

'But you've cooked.'

She shrugged her shoulders, showed me her palms: she'd given up.

'He's booked a table at Lebédel's.'

'Where are you going?'

'To order a taxi.'

The kitchen smelt of garlic and vegetables roasting in their juices, fresh lemon and fish. I turned the dial on the oven to the off position.

'Five minutes,' Anne-Marie said flatly, when I joined her in the bedroom to change my shirt and fetch my jacket. She was stepping into a black dress, which she zipped up sharply. She snatched her bag off the bed and marched out into the living room where I found her a few minutes later – angry, defiant, standing by the door with her hand on the light switch. 'Ready?'

'Ready.'

Closing the door, without speaking, we made our way downstairs, leaving behind us our two days in Paris, alone with the cooked food to go cold in the kitchen.

Over the last decade Lebédel's reputation had soared.

'It's now one of *the* places to go in Paris,' Anne-Marie explained, as our taxi drove onto the bridge and up over the river. The Seine in darkness loomed bottomless and unfriendly. A few boats bobbed below us as we crossed the bridge, and the restaurants, bars, nightclubs and the living rooms of the rich lit each bank like two opposing strings of party lights.

When at last we reached the restaurant and I stepped out onto the kerb, I felt decidedly underdressed. I was wearing a pair of cords and the only decent shirt I'd brought. The two doormen sported top hat and tails.

Anne-Marie took my hand and stepped up. She looked as lovely as ever in the knee-length black dress she'd chosen twenty minutes earlier.

'Mademoiselle, Monsieur,' one of the doormen said, greeting us. Inside, an attendant took our coats.

'Monsieur Parrot?'

'Oui, Mademoiselle. Par ici, s'il vous plaît.'

Henry was sitting at a round table on the second floor by the window, with a view of the boulevard outside. He was wearing a different suit from the one I'd seen him in at the station, and drinking an aperitif. There were two other drinks on the table.

'There you are!' he said, as we approached. 'You look lovely, Anne-Marie.' He nodded towards me. 'Jack.'

'Henry.'

We sat down.

'Those are for you,' he said, indicating the drinks in front of us. 'Champagne.'

Anne-Marie drank half of hers and stared out of the window.

'So what do you think of Lebédel's?' Henry said. 'I had to call in a special favour to get us in.'

He looked across at his daughter, but she was still gazing down at the street outside, where people were opening umbrellas.

'This used to be a dancehall, Jack,' he said, 'built in the eighteen nineties. The main hall was downstairs, where you came in, and up here was the sort of balcony or dress circle. There were also two ballrooms, which were sold off in the thirties and turned into cinemas, but when the Boelle family acquired the place in the seventies, they bought the ballrooms back. They belong to Lebédel's now.'

The waiter brought Anne-Marie and me the menus.

'The fish is good here,' Henry said, 'or the special today is duck.'

I pretended to scan the menu. I was concerned about Anne-Marie. She was holding her menu so I couldn't see her face.

We survived an unbreachable silence until the waiter returned.

Henry clapped his hands. 'Well, what will it be, you two?'

'I'll go for the special, please,' I said.

'And you, Anne-Marie?'

She brought the menu down. Her face was pale and I could see she was on the verge of crying. 'The same.'

Henry turned to the waiter. 'Deux, s'il vous plaît, et moi je vais prendre le saumon.'

Salmon.

Anne-Marie let out a small helpless sound. Two tears rolled down her cheeks. She wiped them quickly away.

'What's the matter, Anne-Marie?' Henry said.

'I can't believe you. I just cannot believe you!'

Her father ignored her, and instead said something polite to the waiter, who left.

I just sat there, dumbfounded as to what to do.

Henry turned back to his daughter, who was wiping away each tear as it came. 'Anne-Marie, stop it! What's wrong?'

'You!'

She stood up.

I stood up.

'Pourquoi fais-tu ça? Pourquoi tu fais toujours ça?'

'Sit down,' Henry said.

But she didn't. Tears careered down her face. She was speaking quickly, words and words I didn't understand, and Henry just sat there, taking it all in with a bemused look on his face. Other people in the restaurant had stopped eating now and were looking over. The waiter had returned, and now stood like me – alert, uncertain.

Then Anne-Marie said something that made Henry leap to his feet. The woman at the nearest table gasped.

Henry shouted something fiercely at his daughter.

'Hey,' I said, raising a hand, open-palmed, in the air. 'That's enough.'

The waiter appeared at Henry's side and spoke quickly and steadily, but Henry wasn't listening. He was still staring open-mouthed at Anne-Marie, who suddenly lost her nerve. I watched as her confidence dropped away from her. She looked around the restaurant, from face to face, and at last found mine.

I took her hand. She clutched it and folded herself into me.

'I think we'd better leave,' I stated, uncertain whom I was addressing.

Henry exploded with something in French.

'We're leaving,' I said.

I led Anne-Marie around the opposite side of the table, towards the staircase. She buried her face in my side. Everyone was staring at us – customers, waiters. She clambered down the steps as, awkwardly, I failed to support her. Reaching the bottom, we headed for the door.

'Monsieur!'

It was our waiter.

Anne-Marie detached herself and swam through the revolving door.

I stopped and turned to face the waiter. He held up my jacket and Anne-Marie's handbag.

'Merci,' I said, taking them. I wasn't staying for anything else he had to say. I spun round and followed Anne-Marie out into the rain.

I found her at the bottom of the steps, crying for a taxi.

Henry didn't return to his apartment that night.

'Should we be worried?'

Anne-Marie was thrusting one item of clothing after another into her rucksack ready for the morning, when, she had declared, we would be leaving. 'No,' she said. She got up from where she'd been kneeling and came over. 'He'll stay somewhere else, or with someone else.'

I nodded. 'Are you all right?'

'No.' She smiled and hugged me. 'But I will be.'

In the morning we found two last-minute flights to Heathrow and, on our way out, posted Henry's keys back to him through his brass-studded door.

'We always seem to argue,' Anne-Marie said, as we rode the bus to the airport. 'Every time we try, I just come away thinking, What's the point?' She was silent for a moment, then turned to me. 'Aren't you curious about your father?'

I opened my wallet and took out the photograph of Matthew Saunders standing on the pier. We looked down at it together. 'No. I never knew him,' I said simply.

'Maybe it's easier that way.'

'Maybe.'

She took my face in her hands and kissed me deeply. 'I've had a wonderful time,' she said.

Then, staring at the photo of my father, still open in my hand, she sighed. 'Why do we do what we do?'

7

'Do we really want to know what the future holds?'

Anne-Marie asked this two months ago, before the stirrings of recent events, before I knw what I know now.

We had just returned from Sam's thirtieth birthday party. We've known Sam for years, from before we were married. Since we'd last seen him he'd lost some weight and also shaved off his beard (he looked so much younger without it), and for the first time in over a year he had a woman on his arm. They seemed good together, Anne-Marie and I judged from the apparent safety of marriage. Her name was Tania, and she was a fortune-teller from Sheffield, whose family, she claimed, had originally hailed from Georgia in northern Russia, her grandmother having toured with the State Circus.

The first thing Anne-Marie did when we returned home was to sweep my astrology book up off the coffee table and take it through to the bedroom. It was one a.m. She had the bedside light on and was giving me a look I knew well, one that demanded some kind of response from me, intellectually.

'Well?' she said. 'What do you think? After all, you're the one they're paying to do this.'

She was referring to the current Space and Time exhibition at the City Science and Industrial Museum, where for the past six weeks I'd been organising talks for the general public on the nature of the cosmos. And she sounded irritated.

'It says here,' she said, 'that the reason why astrology is so complicated is because it's a metaphysical subject. That makes sense. In metaphysics, everything is a symbol for something else.'

And for the first time in a long while I thought of my grandmother. She had died from pneumonia the year Anne-Marie graduated. At the time I'd considered moving back in with my mother, but she insisted Anne-Marie and I press forward with our plans for the flat on Hayworth Road. Anne-Marie came with us to the funeral and read a verse by Robert Browning. It seemed so long ago now.

Now I turned from where I lay, drunk, and looked up at my wife, sitting against the headboard of our bed, with her reading glasses on. Everything's a symbol for something else.

We had hardly seen one another at Sam's party, which was held in the coffee shop he owned on Friar Gate. I'd spent the first half of the evening standing nervously by a rubber plant, drinking beer, while Anne-Marie greeted the room, flitting from one person to the next (something she had begun to do more often when out at such events), and the second half engrossed in a conversation on the decaying orbits in atoms with a physicist from Leicester University. At one point I noticed Anne-Marie leaning slightly on the door-frame in the kitchen: she was wearing her green dress, her hair now down, and laughing at something Sam was saying, throwing back her head to finish off her wine. She poured herself another glass. I did not go over. As with most nights out this past year, we only gravitated back towards one another when other people drifted away. Anne-Marie had been deep in conversation with the fortune-teller, and for a good few minutes I'd stood, as though invisible, beside her. Occasionally the fortune-teller, Tania, took pity on me with her curious eyes, but Anne-Marie did not acknowledge my presence until Sam joined us and took away his new girlfriend in his arms. Had I done something wrong this evening? I racked my brains as Anne-Marie and I walked in silence through the town, but could think of nothing. It was the sort of question I was beginning to ask myself frequently, one I knew I should have been referring to Anne-Marie, but I no longer felt I wanted to, not these days, not any more. Her voice when talking to Sam and Tania was strong and keen and smacked of mischief, but not so much with me. I listened to her now as, sitting up in bed, in one flat tone, she read aloud about the hermetic philosophers – Cornelius Agrippa, Robert Fludd, the last people happily to mix science and religion.

'Astrology's redundant,' I said.

'Why is astrology redundant?'

I sighed. 'Because it's based on the egotistical assumption that the Earth is at the centre of everything, an idea that, although understandable in the past, was blown clean out of the heavens five hundred years ago by Nicholas Copernicus and ratified by every leading astronomer since – Kepler, Galileo, Newton.'

'But that doesn't matter.'

She had taken me by surprise. 'What do you mean, it doesn't matter?'

'Well, we may know now that the sun is the centre of the solar system, that the Earth revolves around it and not vice versa, but the relationship between the two remains the same. We still talk of the sun rising, don't we? Even though we know it is actually brought into view by the Earth's rotation. It's the relationship between the two that's important.'

I laughed. I was more drunk than I'd thought.

But surely, Maguire, in a way she was right. Surely the principles are the same today as they were a thousand years ago. A horoscope is a symbolic representation: no one ever claimed it was a photographic map. It's the symbolism itself that counts.

Anne-Marie was showing an unusual amount of interest in my talks. 'The key to synchronicity,' she went on, 'is precisely the idea that the relative position of the planets and the future personality of a newborn baby may be linked because both are aspects of the whole.'

She placed emphasis on these last words and nodded in agreement, as if it was Carl Jung who was sitting next to her in bed. She closed the book and laid it face down on the bedside table, ending the subject.

'Fortune-telling's just character analysis,' I said. 'Psychology.'

Yet, afterwards, I couldn't stop thinking about what she'd been saying. Were Anne-Marie and I out there in the stars somewhere? Had our lives been mapped out from the moment we were born, when Anne-Marie's parents were still living happily together in Paris on the rue de la Libération?

But it was late. Anne-Marie had removed her reading glasses and turned over; she lay with her back to me. Without saying anything, I reached for the bedside light, and dreamt I was living in the time of Cornelius Agrippa, before the split in art and science, when a well-educated man could still conceivably know everything there was to be known about the world.

Though there will be no dreams tonight, Maguire. Outside, Rennes is finding its groove for the night. There's a draught sweeping in from the balcony, but I don't want to close the door: the cold air keeps me alert. The food has helped, for my gendarme, my St Christopher, has been back in, bringing me my rucksack and a plate of food. It has obviously been some poor officer's task to stop off at the hotel in Paimpont to pick up our luggage. I wonder if they've been through it. Nothing to find in there, though. The food is a godsend. I haven't eaten since this afternoon, and now I have a plate of cold meat, along with some bread and a selection of cheese. But best of all I've got wine. I doubt very much whether officially I should be given alcohol, but that's the wonderful thing about the French. It's only a half-bottle, granted, but it's here all the same. Hospitality, you see. I could slit my throat, or go for the throat of the good saint outside. But I suppose he knows I'm not going to do this. I wonder where you are now, Maguire. Already on your way? It's pitch black out there. I still can't see any stars, just, faintly, now and then, the full, cold face of the moon.

My first job at the museum involved some pieces of the moon. Eight months after graduating, having worked an assortment of shifts for various outfits, including a month backstage at the theatre where Anne-Marie now works, I applied for the position of part-time administration assistant at the City Science and Industrial Museum. I got the job on the back of my physics degree, previous retail experience and a heavily trumped-up four-day stint in an accountant's office. Under Mr Wilmot, the head curator, one of the three people I'm employed to assist, my first task was to display six samples of moon rock, which had been procured from the London Science Museum as part of a new initiative to spread national 'treasure' around the country. 'Treasure' is what Mr Wilmot calls everything we exhibit, or in the case of those pieces of moon rock, 'little treasures' for they were tiny, Maguire, and unless you were told, you wouldn't have known whether they were from the moon or the banks of the Derwent.

'That's why you're labelling them, Prentis,' said Mr Wilmot, who, incidentally, is the only person besides my mother to call me Prentis. He mentioned my name during my interview – no doubt he thought it fit for a museum – and has applied it ever since. In fact, I'm sure my name alone served to save my job on more than one occasion during those first couple of years, when the council was cutting back relentlessly on part-time staff. But Mr Wilmot kept me on, and it is Mr Wilmot who is directly responsible for my current full-time position, helping to organise the Space and Time exhibition.

It involves various wall-mounted displays and glass-case cabinets containing letters, extracts from notebooks and photographs, charting the lives of the key physicists of the twentieth century. Primarily it is Mr Wilmot who is responsible for the project, which coincides with similar events taking place this autumn in Birmingham and Nottingham, but he has allowed me to get more involved than usual.

He knows theoretical physics is an area of special interest for me. He has even, on request, read a copy of my thesis – a naïve account of the possible benefits and limitations of string theory, which spilled too far into the realm of philosophy for a number of my tutors at university. Nevertheless, so far, many of those same tutors have been happy to come into the museum to lecture for a hundred pounds a session. These talks give a chronological account of the progress of physics in the twentieth century. We began with Albert Einstein's theory of general relativity, and in the first week debated the idea of scientific determinism. Can we really know what the future holds?

We can think of any event, Maguire – a touch, a kiss, a birth, a death – or, as a physicist might prefer, a single pulse of light – as something that happens at a particular point in space-time. (In general relativity, time isn't separate from space, as scientists had previously assumed, but combines with it to form an object Einstein called space-time. In Einstein's theory, instead of moving along curved paths in the three spacial dimensions we all observe, bodies follow straight lines in a four-dimensional space-time – three space dimensions and one time dimension – which is curved by the distribution of mass and energy in it. In other words, when space-time encounters a body like the sun, it bends around it. The planets, instead of moving on curved orbits by a force called gravity, as Newton believed, actually follow a straight path through a curved space-time.) In order to picture our pulse of light then – our event – we can use a concept known in general relativity as a light cone. A light cone is merely a way of picturing the history of a pulse of light emitted at a particular point in space-time. Rather like the way that, if I tap the wine in my glass here with the tip of my index finger, the ripples spread outwards towards the edges of the glass, so too, over time, does the light emitted from our event spread out in a sphere whose radius increases and increases. If we imagine a three-dimensional model of this – the two dimensions of the surface of my wine and the one dimension of time – the circle of ripples spreading out will plot out the shape of a cone, whose tip is the place and time my finger tapped the wine. We can call this the future light cone of our event: this contains all of the events that can be affected by our event. Events outside this light cone cannot be affected by our event because nothing can travel faster than the speed of light. In the same way we can draw the past light cone of our event, containing all of the events that are able to affect our event, that is those events from which signals travelling at or below the speed of light can reach our event. What all this means is, if we know everything that is happening at a particular time everywhere in the past light cone of an event, we can predict what will happen at that event.

Is the universe entirely deterministic? If so, then if we knew its complete state and history at any one time, we could predict its future.

8

Let us consider the past, then. Let me tell the story of Anne-Marie's parents, pieced together over the last eight years. A love story, of sorts. (But aren't all the best stories love stories? Aren't all our stories love stories?)

Paris, 1951, and Anne-Marie's mother, Gina, is born to Luc and Joséphine Dufeur. Luc Dufeur is a businessman who has achieved wealth and status for his family from the buying and selling of tobacco. During the war this was a lucrative enterprise if, like Luc Dufeur, you knew how to keep your wits about you. Joséphine, who at this point is still Joséphine Boyes (which will remain her stage name throughout her brief but well-documented career with the city opera) is attracted to Luc, first, because of his ability to maintain his position despite the Occupation, and second, because she likes his thick eyebrows. They are married in 1945, following the Liberation, and when Anne-Marie's mother is born they baptise her Georgina, after her English great-grandmother. That year the family live in an apartment on the rue de Bernaude.

Luc Dufeur soon gets himself on the board of a textile company, which goes on to manufacture clothes throughout the 1950s. At the same time he still has his finger in that now even greater post-war pie, tobacco. Thus, in 1954, when Gina is three, the Dufeurs are able to move into a house on the boulevard St-Mathieu. Gina's earliest memories are of this house, of waking in the morning and being able to see Notre Dame from her bedroom window. She doesn't question the city, with its absence of bomb-sites, its sprawling street cafés opening their shutters for business as usual, as if the war is already merely a memory. She sees only a cathedral, with a river running by.

As Gina grows up in the comfort and safety of the society of the boulevard St-Mathieu, so too does Paris resume its abundance around her, and her mother sees to it that she is paraded among the cream of the city. She has been sent to the best Catholic schools, where she performs averagely. But in her case such matters are irrelevant, for she is to be married to someone of importance, the right someone of importance and, as far as her parents are concerned, the sooner the better.

It naturally comes as a shock to them then (I picture a family scene, a row in a Parisian living room) when, in the summer of 1968, the seventeen-year-old Gina declares she is in love with an English undergraduate called Henry Parrot.

Such is the nature of young love: passionate, defiant. 'I swear it shall be Romeo . . .' etc., etc. Perhaps her parents give in. Perhaps an ultimatum is given. Here I don't have any facts to go on. I never got the chance to talk to Gina about any of this, leaving me like a detective, like you, Maguire, trying to piece it together, separating fact from fiction, if that's possible, picking out what's most significant.

Gina met him. That's what's important. Out of all the people, she met him.

When she first sees him, he is pacing up and down on the beach, with his hands in his pockets and his trousers rolled to just below the knee. This is Normandy, the

Calvados coast. I know this from Anne-Marie; she told me the year we were married of how her parents met on the beach at Arromanches-les-Bains where her grandfather, James Parrot, had died during the D-Day landings.

The beach, Gina has discovered, is one of the best places for crying. All she has wanted that summer is to go on a school field-trip to London, which her parents have ruined with their own last-minute holiday plans. Her mother has refused to let her go. This is not the first time Gina has walked alone along a beach in Normandy and found herself sobbing. She knows it is possible to walk for miles, undisturbed, and cry as loudly as you wish without being heard above the crashing of the waves. If someone stops you, the beach offers numerous excuses for your tears – it's sand in your eyes, salt from the sea. No one, not even her mother – that expert at staging tears for her Cassandras and Beatrices – can reprimand her for her puffy eyes if she's been walking on the beach. Which is why, this particular evening, Gina has left her parents at the restaurant finishing their coffee in order to stroll along the sea-front. She has promised to go only as far as the pier. Her parents can see her from where they sit by the restaurant window.

And when Gina gets to the pier she has every intention of turning back. Only it is then she catches her first glimpse of the man on the other side, walking back and forth on the wet sand with his hands in his pockets.

She stops short when she sees him. A wave folds over her foot: the tide is coming in fast. She retreats a small way up the beach, then ducks under the pier, wipes her eyes, and emerges the other side. What should she do? The man has turned again and is walking away from her. Then she notices his sandals. They are close to the pier; the tide has already claimed one, it's bobbing in the water, and the other is being systematically dragged backwards to join it. Gina takes a deep breath, removes her own sandals and makes a dash for his, splashing into the sea. A wave breaks on her ankle and ascends the side of her leg. Her dress is ruined. She thinks of her mother and laughs. Then she plucks the man's sandals from the water and hops back onto the sand again. And it's there, as she's bending to see if there's any way to dry her dress, she realises that he has turned back towards the pier and is now standing beside her.

At first she can't hear him, confusing his voice with the roll of the sea. Then she realises that he's talking to her. 'I believe those are mine.' He indicates the sandals. 'Thank you for rescuing them. I fear if it hadn't been for you they were sure to have drowned.'

His French is good, Parisian, clearly learnt in a class-room. He hasn't lived in France.

This is Gina's chance. I imagine her carefully selecting her words. His face doesn't falter once when she says her name is Dufeur, which she immediately takes as a good sign, for she's found it somewhat alarming, over the last week, just how far her father's name carries outside of Paris.

As he reaches out to her for his sandals, she takes in his wavy fair hair, his blue-grey eyes. His face is rugged, boyish. He's not much older than she is. They stand silently beside one another, holding their sandals, staring at the sea.

Then, as if he's been contemplating something and suddenly realises that she may be able to help him, he asks her, does she live here?

She says that she's here with her parents, just for a few

weeks. 'They're at the hotel.' She indicates the row of buildings out of sight beyond the pier.

He glances briefly in that direction. 'You come here often? This beach?'

'Maman likes Normandy. But I can't remember if we've been on this beach before. It's possible.'

'My father died here.' He shakes loose sand from his foot. 'I don't know where. Somewhere on this beach, they say.'

'The war?'

He nods.

It is that moment (I invent, I make believe) that Gina feels a sudden longing to know Henry Parrot, a desire to be intimate with him. The feeling has nothing to do with pity or sorrow, for she is old enough to understand that half of her generation has lost loved ones in the war; the whole of Europe is in mourning. What she feels is the urge to be closer to him than she has ever been to anyone. Of course, there must be something sexual in this, though perhaps Gina would have told you it has nothing to do with sex. It's a moment of 'connection,' that's what she'd call it. One day on the beach at Arromanches-les-Bains, off the coast of Normandy, Gina Dufeur 'connected' with a man she'd never met before, who was standing beside her as the tide came in, telling her about his father.

'Never found a body. There were so many, you see.'

They stand, clutching their sandals, unable to comprehend what had happened to the world in the final moments before they were born. It spits with rain; the sea forces them further back up the beach, but they can still make out the ghostly shapes of the old pontoons, bobbing in the distance, those great metal skeletons, now half eaten away by salt, built in the docks at Southampton, dragged across the Channel by the British navy.

'Mobile landing platforms,' Henry explains. 'They used them to deploy the launches.' His father on one of them, James Parrot, twenty-five years old, checking the weight of his rifle.

I picture Gina as she tries to imagine the ships massing along the horizon, the commencement of guns.

'Listen hard enough,' Henry says, 'and I can make myself hear them.'

But there is nothing except the empty sound of the pontoons in the rain.

'All those men,' he says, 'I can't imagine it. I don't think I'll stay long.'

Gina watches his face intently as, suddenly, he becomes aware of his surroundings again: the rain, with surprise; dusk seeping in; the sea pushing them back; the young woman standing beside him with no coat or umbrella, getting wet.

'It's late, Mademoiselle. Your parents will be worried. Are you very wet?'

'I'm fine.'

She feels her dress clinging to her legs; it's raining steadily now, the wind is up and the sea continues to encroach on them. The remnants of the pontoon loom large and menacing. She knows her parents will have long finished their coffee; they will not be able to see her from where they sit. So she puts her sandals back on her feet and, as gracefully as a girl in the rain can, she takes her leave of Henry Parrot – though not before he has offered to walk her back to the hotel and she has refused, and not before she has made him promise to meet her here at the same time the following day, when she knows her parents have pressing engagements in town.

How I imbue my mother-in-law with her daughter's qualities! Comparing Gina's deliberate rendezvous-making to Anne-Marie's own preparations for a model one March afternoon. Again I see Anne-Marie moving gently back and forth behind her easel. I see her mother, Gina, choosing her attire in a bedroom looking-glass, the right shoes, the right dress, ready to return to the coast and the beach where she will catch her man.

The scene, the atmosphere, the geography of the place. It's all in the book I have in front of me, purchased this morning from the Syndicat d'Initiative. *France Today: The North-west* by Pierre Bizet. I now know that, due to bureaucratic reasons, Normandy is divided into two: Haute Normandy to the north-east, centred on the city of Rouen, and Basse Normandy in the west. I know that it's possible to drive for miles in the open country and see nothing but farmland, for much of the region is crop fields and grasslands, although there are also forests – beech trees and oak trees and huddles of conifers. In spring, blossom appears to cover the apple trees in a white frost.

And if you ask Anne-Marie what she remembers most about the region, she'll tell you it's the apple orchards around Rouen, covered in white blossom, for as a child she connects them with some lines of the Tennyson her father was so fond of reading her. I first heard these lines the summer we travelled together as students, and it's strange how I, too, now have them by heart.

> And what is Avalon? Avalon is an isle
> All made of apple blossom in the west,
> And all the waves are fragrant and the winds
> About it and the fairies live upon it
> And there are those have seen it far away
> Shine like a rose upon the summer sea
> And thither goes the king and thence returns
> And reigns: some hold he cannot die.

As a child, in Anne-Marie's mind, the blossom on the apple trees of Avalon and the white frost on the apple orchards of Normandy are connected forever, later to merge with the trips her father will take her on to a forest in Brittany. And the notion of the forest as a place where answers can be found is something Anne-Marie will return to again and again, just as Henry journeyed to the Calvados coast in 1968, to find out what had happened to his father.

Later that year (this from Henry himself, today. I've lost all track of time!) in a restaurant in Caen, drinking cider brandy, Henry will explain to Gina about the apples, and he will recite Tennyson, at which point Gina will lean across the table, take Henry's hand and suggest that maybe, like King Arthur, Henry's own father is safe, too, on a tiny island covered with apple blossom. That is the moment Henry knows he loves her; that gesture, that taking of his hand in her own, that one act of kindness flurries something far down inside him. And when, as a child, Anne-Marie will ask him, when did you know you loved Maman? this is the story he will tell: the story of Normandy, of 1968, of the apple blossom.

Anne-Marie, too, in turn, would fall in love with the region, with its sights and sounds, its people and its food, with the sausages in Vire, the duck in Rouen, the fish at Caen and Dieppe.

Nowadays, when Anne-Marie visits her father – which has been only twice in the last four years – she finds Paris too stuffy, too cluttered, not the city she remembers looking out over as a child. But Normandy is different, with its industries still based on the old crafts – copper beating, weaving, lace-making, pottery – articles for sale everywhere, on market stalls, by the roadside, along the quayside. Yes, she could still easily live in Normandy, with its small houses and their sweeping slate roofs, great gables and elegant archways. Though she likes, too, the ruined barns she sees driving through the country, the patched-up sheds, corrugated iron replacing thatch, those old hand-painted adverts for Martini and Pernod still plastered on walls, untouched for decades. My wife says there is something about the domestic architecture of Normandy. It still has nobility.

And why shouldn't this region have nobility? Amazing what I can learn from my little five-euro book! All this history I've read about but not experienced serves to bestow on me a pseudo sense of proportion about things. Allows me to consider. I haven't forgotten your question, Maguire. True love. Self-control or Fate? A pair of star-crossed lovers? Star-crossed, or just another spate of adolescent *Angst*? These are big questions. Yet your question, to use your own phrase, is 'simple enough.'

But is it? How many times have I asked such questions

over the past week about my wife? Fate or Chance? How much were Anne-Marie's actions her own? Although that's idle speculation. I know what I believe: she did what she wanted to, deep down, and now I've got to live with it. Now, over the next few hours, I've got to decide what to do. For the best, as they say. For better or for worse. I must keep going back.

Let's go back further, then. Let us imagine that at the same time the six-year-old Gina is gazing at Notre Dame from her bedroom window, so the young Henry Parrot is looking out over what remains of central London. He has a splendid attic bedroom in the modest flat where he lives with his mother on Castle Road. From his own window, just as Gina can look out along the Seine, Henry can see the Thames, and on a clear day he can make out the Houses of Parliament and the top of Westminster Abbey.

When his father is killed at the end of war, Henry and his mother are forced to move to Trory Street, to a house by the railway, because, despite a war-widow's pension and his mother's teaching salary, they can no longer afford to live in their previous flat near St James's Park. His mother, Elizabeth Parrot, starts teaching at Hammersmith primary school. She does her son the courtesy of enrolling him at the Walcot School for Boys across the road, where, despite her kind efforts, for years Henry quietly suffers the taunts of the Hammersmith pupils.

Elizabeth Parrot is the daughter of Dorothy and Ian Barrow. A 'true London lass,' as she will tell Henry his father used to call her. She doesn't speak much about her parents for they died before Henry was born. But she doesn't mind talking about Henry's father, James Parrot; she will tell him anything he wants to know. They met at a harvest-festival dance in 1937. When war broke out they were immediately married, but had little more than a year together before he was called to fight. James's own father (Henry's grandfather) had been a conscientious objector during the First World War and had successfully instilled in his son all the horrors of the trenches. Therefore James Parrot knows what he is letting himself in for. He goes for mixed reasons: this war is different; Hitler is far madder than the Kaiser ever was, and this is more than a war for territory, it's a war against Fascism. So he sits, one among many, on a train to Portsmouth with a picture of his new wife and young son, perhaps understanding more than others what lies before him, and hoping he will come back in one piece.

But although Normandy escaped the fighting of the First World War, it becomes the scene of bitter combat during the second.

What's remarkable today is how some areas survive relatively unscathed. Between the two beaches that, during the Normandy landings, were code-named Omaha and Gold lies Port-en-Bassin. I stayed there with Anne-Marie that first summer when we were students and she took me to meet her father. A modest seaside resort. I remember the working port, the fish auctions, and the boats lining the quayside – masts, nets and rigging, winches left to rust in the rain.

At the commemorative museum of the Normandy landings, all that remains of the war is a single blockhouse on the north shore. At Colleville-Montgomery-Plage there is a statue of the British commander, for it was here in 1944 that Anglo-French commandos first landed on Sword beach to join airborne troops at Pegasus Bridge in advance of the British Third Division, while at Arromanches-les-Bains, four thousand ships and a thousand smaller craft landed the Allied armies within the shelter of a harbour area bigger than Dover, equipped with floating pontoons to enable troops to land at any state of the tide, whose corroding remains Henry and Gina would speculate on twenty-four years later. Here, Henry's father, James Parrot, died on 6 June 1944, some time in the afternoon.

Therefore, the day Henry Parrot first meets his wife-to-be, there on that same beach at Arromanches-les-Bains, there must have been a number of things spiralling through his mind. Perhaps he doesn't notice the young woman at first: he's too busy pacing up and down, taking in the deserted seascape, where he can find no impression of his father, nothing he can grasp, touch, rely on. He turns and begins walking back towards the pier.

Then he sees her – young, beautiful, standing in her pastel-coloured dress, holding his sandals, along with her own. Two pairs of sandals together. He walks up to her, taking in her dark hair, the shape of her bosom. Closer, and he sees her brown eyes, which are hesitant now. Perhaps it's this nervousness that makes her clasp the sandals to her chest when he reaches out for them. He pauses, with his hand in the air, unsure whether he should prise his shoes from her breasts.

Let us pan out for a moment. A deserted beach, stage of bitter fighting, unfathomable death. A young man and a young woman meet there for the first time. It's getting dark and spitting with rain. Barefoot, they are standing by the water facing one another, a private moment, for they're concealed from view by the shadow of the pier. Gina is clutching the sandals to her chest; Henry has just reached for them, when she pulls them away, and now his arm hangs in the air, uncertain. He has to question her clutching of the sandals, so his immediate reaction is to look into her eyes. Something passes between them. Only for a moment, but afterwards Henry feels he can proceed, and he plucks his shoes lightly free from her grasp. In order to accomplish this he has to touch her hands and his finger brushes the fabric of her dress. Taking the shoes, he says, 'I believe those are mine.' She blushes and releases them. He goes on for the sake of propriety, still thinking about his father. 'Thank you for rescuing them. I fear if it hadn't been for you, they were sure to have drowned.'

Unknowingly, subconsciously, they have hit on something: the relationship between sex and death. The moment they look at one another over the taking of the sandals. Let us recall that Henry is on the beach in order to contemplate the death of his father with thousands of other men. He and Gina have talked about death and suddenly she is clutching his sandals to her chest and he is reaching for them. No passionate kiss is required, no fornication under the pier. When Gina leaves Henry standing by the water and he watches her walking away from him, for the rest of the day he can't stop thinking about her, although he has already stopped thinking about his father. And Gina, too, when she gets back to the hotel, suddenly feels so tired that she has to make her excuses to her parents and fly straight to bed.

I remember that feeling well, Maguire, the first pitch and roll inside the stomach, where it's suddenly all hands on deck. That first physical collision of love.

It is not so different from loss.

Not so different from the nausea consuming me, as I sat, yesterday, on the banks of the Derwent, with my coat open to the breeze, alternating my gaze between the swans and the faint white band on the third finger of my left hand, where my wedding ring used to be.

A ring somewhere in your pocket, Maguire, on its way here. A ring on a table in a police interview room; you opposite me, waiting for an answer. I noticed your eyes were red and puffy, as though you hadn't slept in days. I wondered if that was to do with this case, or something in your personal life.

'Well?' you said, leaning forward, forcing me to look at you. 'It's a simple enough question. Do you love your wife?'

Can you hear that, Maguire? Rennes must be quite a happening place. Anne-Marie and I used to laugh like that, not so long ago. Coming back from a party at Sam's. On the beach in Barcelona. And then today as I sat on a stone slab among the trees and she lifted her head and gave me the look I've missed so much, the way she used to smile when she was still a student living on Belgrave Road. Here she was, after everything that's happened . . . and again I think of the moment I first saw her sitting quietly by the window doing her jigsaw. Perhaps now I can answer your question.

Yes, I'm still in love with my wife.

9

Not that you'd know it from the way things were between us two weeks ago, beginning the evening like any other, kissing on the lips, the best of intentions.

'Cup of tea?'

'Good idea.'

I sat down on the sofa in the front room. I could hear the kettle boiling. Outside the window, the sky was a washed-out grey. A headache sky, Anne-Marie would call it.

Anne-Marie moved in the kitchen, dunking the bags quickly, waiting just long enough for the tea to stew. Recently she'd been acting as if she had a strange feeling that at any moment I might disappear. The nights had already begun drawing in. Soon it would be Christmas; I thought of the endless list of things to do.

Anne-Marie returned, a mug in each hand. I just sat there, staring out of the window, my bag by my feet, my coat on my lap, as if I wasn't staying after all. She looked at me the way I imagined her considering a stranger who had called round to sell her something. Without speaking, she took my coat and bag and put them away in the closet under the stairs.

When she handed me my tea I said, 'Thank you,' too enthusiastically. She took the armchair opposite and perched on the edge of it, leaning forward, so that we seemed as close as possible. The clock ticked on the mantelpiece.

We sat in the dusk light, the room growing greyer and greyer. I knew she preferred it that way; natural light, that is, not the bright artificial living-room light pounding down on us as if we were on an examining table. Besides, she had a headache: I could see from the way she was squinting.

We finished the tea, but remained sitting there, empty mugs in hand, like we hadn't seen each other for weeks, though we shared the same bed, the same tube of tooth-paste, the marmalade, the coffee jar. How long could we go on being so intimate?

She asked me how my day was and I said fine. I said, Work is work. It struck me that this was the sort of thing you'd say to someone you didn't know. I asked her how her own day was. Then suddenly I couldn't bear to hear us any more.

'What shall we do tonight?' I said. 'It's just the two of us.'

She smiled then: a glimmer of her old self. It was the smile of a child who's been told the cancelled party is on again. Something passed between us, and we grinned at one another like two conspirators.

But then I got up, took her empty cup from her, and switched on the living-room light.

She sat there in the bright yellow while I went through to the kitchen and washed up, shirtsleeves rolled to my elbows. I called back to her: did she want to cook some-thing, or go out? 'We must eat, I suppose.'

'Yes, we must,' she agreed, appearing in the doorway.

It was decided and unspoken: we would make it work, this evening together. I couldn't recall the last evening we'd shared; it had been weeks.

'We'll go to the supermarket,' I said. 'We'll buy food and cook.'

'We'll get some wine.'

'Yes, we'll get some wine.'

I was in a much better mood now there was a plan. We would walk around the supermarket together and buy food. I placed the last of the washing-up on the draining board, where it dripped steadily. Then I touched her with my wet hands and kissed her. She liked that.

'We'll go now, before it shuts.'

She crossed the back room and disappeared into the closet to fetch the coats. I thought about following her in and tearing off her clothes. But there would be plenty of time for that later. There were things we needed to sort out first, things we had to talk about.

'Are we driving?' she asked, when we stepped outside into the fresh air.

'No. We'll walk.'

How she looked at me as we walked arm in arm along the road! I could smell woodsmoke. I looked up at the grey sky.

'It's a headache sky,' she said.

'Yes, it's a headache sky.'

She turned and kissed me suddenly, and I didn't know why.

The supermarket was one of those large supermarkets that try to sell everything you need all under one roof. On the way in we passed flowers, plants, plant pots, newspapers, racks of magazines, the top ten paperback books, CDs, DVDs.

She saw me looking at the flowers as if I was considering whether or not to buy her some.

Walking along the rows of produce, she didn't seem as excited as before, and she grew tired going from aisle to aisle. Afterwards, outside, I felt my own headache coming on, as if the evening itself was pressing in on me. The walk back didn't feel as relaxed as our journey there, and although we hadn't bought much, the bags of groceries weighed us down.

We walked in silence, and when she occasionally turned to look at me, I kept my gaze fixed ahead. She began to steal more looks at me. Perhaps, at moments, in the darkness, my face seemed foreign to her, lit as it must have been by the street-lamps we passed under and the lights from the traffic crawling by. I pictured my own jaw, harsh and angular in the fleeting red and amber, cheeks a little thinner than perhaps she remembered.

We continued in silence. Once, when she turned to look at me, I looked back at her. We stared at one another as though we were strangers. She blinked and turned away. Luckily, by then we were on Peach Street and there wasn't far to go. Otherwise I might have said something.

What I felt was embarrassment, an awkward, claustrophobic embarrassment. She must have felt it too, for the smile she gave me when we reached our house, was a shy, hesitant one. Then I realised that this embarrassment was the same kind of embarrassment I sometimes felt when flirting with other women, the same embarrassment I remembered at my first encounters with Anne-Marie when we were students. Could it be that we were going backwards? The thrill of the unknown? But it wasn't the same teenage thrill of expectation or of new experience. Or was it? How could that be?

In the end I decided I was embarrassed because the look had taken place at all. Such looks were not supposed to happen between married couples. The look said something was wrong: we were doing something wrong, our marriage was in jeopardy.

Yet there was also something exciting about that look. It said, So we don't know one another after all, and, yes, that's a frightening thing after all these years – but surely this, too, brought with it the thrill of expectation and new experience? If only we could somehow break out of this decaying orbit.

Something told me it would be impossible that night. We reached the house without having talked. I wondered if we could cook a meal in silence.

It turned out we didn't cook the meal at all. The argument came before we'd even finished putting away the groceries. We'd forgotten the wine. It was definitely in the basket; we'd spent a good ten minutes deciding on it. One of us must have left it at the check-out.

I said I'd go back for it.

'It's too late.'

'No. We'll go back for it. Drive back, I mean. There's still time.'

'They'll be closed.'

'It's still only ten to.'

'By the time you get there they'll be closed.'

'I'll ring them.' I strode into the front room and picked up the phone.

'Don't be ridiculous.'

'What's ridiculous? I'm sure they'll wait if I say I'm coming. One of them might have noticed we left it.'

'Forget it.'

I detected a splash of anger in her voice. 'So you don't want me to call them, then?' I noticed my own tone had changed, hardened, but I couldn't help it.

She continued slowly to unpack the food from the plastic carrier-bags. Glancing sideways, I was aware she could see me in the front room, striking a dramatic pose with the receiver in my hand. I saw myself standing that way in some film noir. Maybe she wondered if I was standing that way on purpose.

'Don't bother now,' she said. 'It's too late. We've left it. We'll just have to do without.'

'I could go to the off-licence.'

'Look, let's forget it. I'm sure we can eat one meal without alcohol.'

'I didn't mean that. I just thought . . .'

'What?'

'Doesn't matter.'

'Fine.'

She unpacked the groceries loudly, slamming the items we'd bought hard on the kitchen surface.

'What have I done?' I marched through to the back room and stood in the kitchen doorway. 'Have I done something wrong?'

'No, you haven't done anything wrong.'

'I'm sorry if I forgot the wine.'

'Forget the bloody wine!'

Her voice was very far away, and suddenly I was a camera panning the scene, zooming in on myself, watching Anne-Marie unpacking the groceries.

'This isn't just my fault, you know.'

Maybe she thought I was still talking about the wine.

'I didn't say it was,' she said slowly. Then, suddenly, 'Why does this always happen?'

I said I might go for a walk.

'Fine! You do that.'

I was going through the motions now, backing away, getting out. The words leaving my mouth were someone else's.

'Clear the air, that's all. Some space,' I said.

But then she said something unexpected, something not part of the usual routine. 'Maybe it will,' she said, 'Maybe that's what we need. Time apart.'

I paused at the door, something plummeting inside me. 'You mean real time apart?'

'Yes. Real time.'

I summoned the courage to meet her eyes. Perhaps she wanted me to stay, to take back what she'd said, for me to take her in my arms. Or maybe she meant what she said.

'If that's what you want,' I said.

And I left her.

For three hours.

Yes, from the way things were between us, it may seem incredible to believe that I'm in love with Anne-Marie. If you had asked me then, Maguire, if you had turned up at the scene of the crime, before a crime was even committed, and asked me did I love my wife, I might have said no.

The rest of that evening comes back to me so clearly. At half past eleven I returned to find Anne-Marie sitting on the floor in the front room, playing patience. It occurred to me, perhaps for the first time, that maybe I didn't know her as well as I thought.

She'd had a shower. She was kneeling on the carpet with a towel wrapped around her. Behind her, through the open door, I could see through the back room and into the kitchen. She'd finished unpacking the groceries. I didn't think she'd eaten, but I knew from the look on her face she'd guessed correctly that I'd been at the pub with Sam.

I stood unsteadily in front of her, waiting for her to look up.

She didn't look up, but went on turning over her cards: ten of diamonds, queen of hearts, jack of diamonds, nine of spades.

She seemed in another world, as if she was in one of her own jigsaws. Yet part of her must have been waiting for me to come back, the same way, all that time with Sam, part of me was waiting to go back. Did she want me to find her like this? Was all this card-playing on the floor staged? Maybe she wanted to find out if I really loved her. Another twist of the blade. For better or for worse.

But there was something else. She wouldn't look at me.

I knew that one of Anne-Marie's memories from her childhood was sitting in the hall at her convent school in Arcueil. Sister Agatha is watching her work out her arithmetic. No matter how hard Anne-Marie tries, she can't do the sum. The more Sister Agatha looks at her, the more she can't do the sum. That's how I remember feeling then, looking down at her, as if I was Sister Agatha.

She turned over another card, the six of clubs; it made a swiping sound as she picked it up off the carpet.

Without saying a word I swept past her, through the

back room and into the kitchen. I heard her sigh softly behind me. She stopped turning over the cards, perhaps conscious of the room again, her wet hair. I knew she could hear me rummaging for a glass. I found a bottle of Jameson's, marched back to her and declared that, yes, it would all be easier if people were clubs or hearts, diamonds or spades, jokers, even.

She didn't look up.

'Did you hear me?'

I caught her staring at the drink in my hand, but her look wasn't disapproving. It might have been jealousy.

'I said, did you hear me? All this playing of yours, these cards, those fucking jigsaws. It's amazing you—'

'I said I heard.'

Her tone startled me.

She smiled quickly. 'Could you fix me one of those?'

I looked at the drink in my hand as though I'd never seen it before.

'Sure.' I bounded back to the kitchen with a new burst of enthusiasm. 'What would you like? Ice? We've got orange somewhere.'

'The same as yours,' she called. 'I'm going to get dressed.'

She flashed through the back room in her towel and up the stairs. I returned to the front room and sat on the sofa, a glass in each hand. She'd put away the cards. When she came back downstairs she was wearing a pair of jeans and a thick burgundy jumper I knew was once her father's. She sat down next to me, tucked her feet underneath her and took the glass I offered. She sipped the neat whiskey. 'Did you go and see Sam?'

'At the coffee shop. Then we went to the Dolphin.'

'And what did Sam have to say?'

'He said we'd work it out somehow.'

She sipped her whiskey again. 'Why do you think friends always say things like that?'

'That's what I asked Sam. He said we'd work it out somehow because . . .' But I sensed my own smile dismantling. 'Well, because we always do.'

She nodded. 'What do you think we should do?'

I swallowed hard. 'I think we never used to fight like this.'

'I think you're right.'

She sipped again. She was sipping like nobody's business.

I wondered if this was what I'd expected – things happening so fast, our little universe unravelling.

Now it was Anne-Marie's turn to swallow hard. 'I spoke to Papa. He wants me to go and stay in Paris. For a week.'

'Maybe that's a good idea.'

'Maybe. Do you want another drink?' She'd finished hers.

I handed her the glass. Why couldn't I just take her in my arms? Why was I so weak? Why did the words *sorry, stay, love* seem to stick in my mouth?

She returned with the full glasses.

'Perhaps you're right,' I heard myself saying. 'Maybe we do need time apart. Perhaps we shouldn't see one another for a while. You could stay in Paris, maybe. For a while.'

(You see how we're both to blame? If I only . . . If she only . . . If only . . .)

'I can't leave the theatre,' she said. 'A week is one thing. This – this is . . . Is this breaking up? Do you mean separate?'

'No, I just mean . . . Well, this isn't working, is it? At the moment. With things as they are, like this. Is it?'

'No.'

That was it, then. But there was still time. I could tell her I loved her, that I didn't want her to go, that all this was a mistake. She could tell me she didn't want to go, that she wanted to stay here, work things out.

I see us as we were then, falling through some great hole opening up beneath us. How could we go back?

But there was no going back. I thought Paris wasn't such a bad idea, for a few days anyway. She couldn't say no now: pride wouldn't let her. I couldn't say, 'Don't go.' Has pride always been more important than love?

'So that's it, then?'

'No,' I said. 'Look, I didn't mean—'

'No, you're right. I'll go to Paris. After the new play opens. I'll book some time off. It will do me good. Do us both good. Then when I get back we'll take things one step at a time.'

'All right.'

I didn't know where this sudden power to take control came from, some hidden resource in her. One of us had to take charge of this thing, otherwise if we weren't careful it was going to founder. She managed to hold back her tears until we were lying back to back in bed and she was certain I was sleeping. I listened as she poured them, quietly as she could manage, into the pillow.

10

Anne-Marie has worked at the Theatre Royal for three years now. She started as a sales and promotions assistant, more interested in the promotional side of things, although for the first year she worked only in the box office, selling tickets over the counter and on the phones for productions ranging from Shakespeare to the seasonal pantomimes that would outsell the bard ten times over during Christmas and New Year. After a year and a half she was promoted to sales and promotions manager, the position she holds today, managing the box-office staff, the takings and ticket administration, and spending too much time, she says, attending various budgeting meetings with the accounts department and board of directors. This side of her job takes up most of her time and although at first it was the part she disliked most, over the past year or so she has seemed to slip firmly into the role, embracing invoices, taxes and gross margins the way she once revelled in capturing in paint a facial expression or the shape of a willow tree moping along a riverbank.

She pretends I like this new direction of hers, her gradual interest in numbers and mathematics, as if I've won her over somehow. The truth is I have lost a part of the old Anne-Marie to that box office. It is I who now attends more of the free plays we are entitled to; I who reads the new novels and sits of an evening, across the room from her, flicking through her discarded art books, like an addict craving a fix, one picture to make the day all right. Anne-Marie has none of her own paintings up in the house. She arranges exhibitions for other artists now. That's the second part of her job, which initially attracted her to the position. The promotional side of her role involves working with the marketing department to print posters and leaflets to advertise the plays, but also finding local artists to exhibit on the wall space above the stairs leading up to the auditorium. These are temporary exhibitions that usually coincide with the theme of a particular play that's running.

As you know, Maguire, the exhibition at the moment is of more importance than usual. On Saturday it got an official press night all of its own and is due to run for another two months. It comprises paintings and sketches by none other than the Spanish artist Sebastian Martinez, winner of the 2000 Joan Miró Prize.

According to Anne-Marie, the theatre just got lucky. Martinez's agent, Franz Kirker, approached them through his friend Ray Darmony, who wrote the play, and once the press got wind of Martinez, that was it. He hasn't exhibited publicly for three years. Needless to say Darmony's play, *Devil in the Detail*, is a sell-out. Therefore the day Anne-Marie met Martinez they were merely going through the formalities: everything had already been arranged through Kirker.

It's painful imagining that afternoon. That day – I work it out – was a week before Anne-Marie and I had the argument over the bottle of wine. I didn't go to the play because I had to work at the museum. Anger and jealousy are wily beasts. Why is it we do what we do?

I know about Sebastian Martinez because I spent a whole night last week logged on to the Internet, staring red-eyed at Sam's computer screen, making it my business to know. The photographs of Martinez depicted a thin-faced man with bushy eyebrows and a dark, clipped beard; his hair was slicked back and parted to a point. He didn't look Spanish. But according to an article I found he was born in Madrid in 1962, when Franco was still alive, and he spent his adolescence in the political aftermath of the dictator's death. The article said that he had lived with his father, a lawyer, and his younger sister, Elena, in an apartment on the Avenida de la Albufera. His mother had died from a brain tumour when he was three years old. He attended a local school and later won a scholarship to the city art college. In 2000 he was awarded the Joan Miró Prize for a painting called *Millennium*. One site had a photograph of this painting, taken from a newspaper article in *The Times*. It depicted a sculpture in an art gallery being viewed by various members of the public. From the picture the sculpture looks to be made of white marble: a naked woman, in the process of leaving a room, wearing only a pair of black sunglasses.

I wasn't impressed, Maguire. In retrospect, I think I prefer his new direction: the landscapes now hanging above the stairs at the theatre. Yet what was so special about any of these pictures? About this man? Didn't I always support Anne-Marie's painting? Haven't Sam and I tried for years now, slowly, subtly, to persuade her to return to her art?

I remember a day when a combination of those slow, subtle persuasions ended in a full-blown argument. The details are gone but Anne-Marie's face remains, red and tear-stained. We were in the back room in Peach Street, so it must have been after we were married, in the last three years, and I was sitting at the table by the window filling in an application for something. I don't remember what. Anne-Marie was standing in the middle of the room in her light grey suit with a white blouse, which means she must have just returned from work, some important meeting or other – looking, now I think about it, not unlike her mother – but also as if she was lost, as if she had suddenly found herself in someone else's house and didn't know whether it was appropriate to sit down or remain standing. We'd been shouting at one another.

'All right, so you tell me, what's the point?'

'Fuck you.'

Now I can't even recall what started that argument, who said what to whom exactly, or how things got resolved. We'd make love mostly, then afterwards pretend the disagreement had never taken place. Perhaps all the disagreements we've ever had are actually about the same thing, one grand argument, only that we don't know what the problem is. Why make any attempt to find out when in the end it might damage us? And why did I want Anne-Marie to paint again, really?

Because it was a part of her I had fallen in love with, because she had changed, because, over time, we'd all changed, including me, and I didn't like it. I wanted us to be as we always were because I thought that was love, and that if we changed the parameters, if we changed, what would happen then? Because there is a point in a relationship where we choose the one we love quite consciously: we stand back and surmise, and then say, yes, yes, all right.

When we were married, as a wedding present, Anne-Marie's father had given her a silver mantel clock; it has a faceted crystal-effect finish and a rotating pendulum, and sits on the mantelpiece now in the front room. At the time, Anne-Marie had said that she and I were like the two hands on that clock, from that moment to move always together, as one, through time. And over the years, Maguire, at first, we really seemed to do just that. Until, almost without our noticing, it was as if the clockface slowly turned transparent: as though the mechanism behind us was starting to show itself. Now we were conscious one day it could stop.

True love? Is there such a thing as true love? A question as old as civilisation. The Holy Grail. The quest of the Western world. A bounty as boundless as the sea? True love? Or springes to catch woodcocks?

Sebastian Martinez said of my wife, my Anne-Marie: 'Up until this moment I think perhaps I've never been in love my whole life.'

11

'I spoke to Papa. He wants me to go and stay in Paris.'

But I already knew this. Because on arriving home the previous day, opening the back door, I heard Anne-Marie's voice in the front room. She was saying, 'I'm fine, fine, under the circumstances.'

At first I thought someone was with her. Then I realised she was on the phone. She had her back to me and was looking out of the window into the street. She was wearing her long purple skirt and a black top. Her hair was up; a wisp kept getting tangled in the receiver and she continued tucking it back behind her ear. As she talked, she sighed and took her free hand on and off her hip. She appeared impatient to sit down.

Pausing in the back room, I slipped off my shoes and went upstairs to the bedroom, where I selected a fresh shirt, a pair of jeans. *'I'm fine, fine, under the circumstances.'*

I'm not a man who spies on his wife.

Sitting on the bed, I picked up the receiver and for a second my pulse ran high. A number of scenarios, plausible and wild, whorled through my mind. Then I heard her father's voice. Often they speak in French, but not today. I wondered if it was Anne-Marie who insisted on English. They were both still adjusting themselves to a new kind of relationship.

'How are Peter and Louis?' Anne-Marie was asking.

Peter and Louis are her father's dogs, which he's had for three years now.

'Peter has a stomach cramp. I took him to the vet and they gave him some drugs. Louis shit all over the carpet this morning. How's Jack?'

Henry remained as conciliatory towards me as ever.

I was about to replace the receiver, hopefully without too much sound, when I heard Anne-Marie's answer, heard her telling her father that I was fine, although I was working hard; we didn't spend much time together. I wondered how many phone calls of this kind she'd been having with her father. I kept the receiver pressed to my ear.

'That's what you get for marrying an Englishman!' her father said.

'Maman married one.'

There was a strained pause. They rarely talk about Gina. Henry and Anne-Marie haven't seen one another in over a year. Yet here was Anne-Marie discussing our marriage.

'I don't know,' she was saying, 'Sometimes Jack and I are so distant from one another. I don't know what he's thinking. What he thinks about me any more.'

'Why don't you come to Paris?'

'Papa, I'm not coming to Paris. It's just that he's either working or I am. The time we do get together, it's for something at the museum, or a new play. We parade around like the perfect couple. We know each other so well, perhaps too well, yet we're changing all the time. And it's like we're trying not to show it, trying to show one another we're just the same after all. The same as when we met. Do you understand what I mean?'

No, he didn't understand.

The conversation turned to her visit to Paris again. Anne-Marie's words rang in my ear. *'We never see one another.'*

I was on the verge of replacing the receiver for the second time, when he said it. Her father's voice was unrecognisable to me.

'You know what you need, don't you?'

'What?' Anne-Marie asked.

'What you need is a lover.'

'Papa, that's not funny.'

'No, I'm sorry,' he said, 'I don't suppose it is.'

But then again he always had that wry sense of humour.

It was these words of her father's that were to lodge themselves so destructively in my mind. It was these words I repeated to myself two weeks later – yesterday – the day after Anne-Marie had left for Paris. I pictured her at her father's house, the two of them together, dissecting our relationship, discussing Anne-Marie's 'needs.'

I was forcing myself to return to the theatre. My emotions were starting to subside and settle, the pain to dull. And I couldn't have that. That would necessitate a return to normality, an acceptance that things were all right after all. I wanted to twist the knife before the wound began to close; I wanted the pain to last, like a bright sign branding me. I was the victim here. Everyone should see.

But when I reached the Theatre Royal, the silence in the foyer threw me. The immediacy of the place – the walls, the carpet, the staircase, the box office with its plaque, *Anne-Marie Stone: Sales and Promotions Manager* – hit me unexpectedly, physically, like a punch straight to the stomach. I felt like keeling over. I felt sick. Saturday night replayed itself rapidly, the chatter and raucous laughter, and then the silence diluting everything, the pointing and the staring, Anne-Marie screaming.

It was too much.

As I turned to leave, Anita Felts appeared from the door behind the box office. A sudden image of her walking towards me in a strapless red dress, a glass of champagne in her hand, flashed through my mind. Now she was wearing purple, paint-stained dungarees, her blonde hair was bobbed, and she was carrying a packet of pre-packed sandwiches.

'Jack! What are you doing here? How—'

'Unexpected?'

'Yes, how . . . unexpected.'

She smiled at me. There was an edge of panic in her voice. Now she was standing without moving, as if she was participating in a game of musical statues.

'I'm here to see the paintings,' I said, hoping this might prompt her back to life.

'Anne-Marie isn't here. Why, she's in Paris.'

I avoided glancing at the plaque above the box office. When we were married, Anne-Marie's father wanted her to keep her maiden name professionally. He's never got over his daughter's decision to remain in England. 'I'm not here to see Anne-Marie,' I said, removing my coat. 'I'm just going to take a look round.'

Anita smiled nervously. She was still staring at me, as if I was a known felon and she was debating the best way to call Security.

Before she could say anything, I stepped round her and

started up the stairs. Briefly I thought of Martinez at the bottom of them. I needed to be alone. I couldn't deal with any questions. The staircase curved upwards in a slow spiral. I reached the half-way landing, and glanced down at the foyer. Anita was still standing there, holding her sandwiches, staring up at me.

What I felt was guilt, shame, but I pushed these thoughts aside. I had business to attend to. I was in the business of making myself feel worse. I turned, forcing myself to face Martinez's paintings. There were only six, though they were large canvases, positioned neatly by my wife, displayed to make the best use of the space. I let them strike their sharp blows one by one. The man himself seemed to rise before me. I should not have come. Still, I made myself look. There hadn't been time to study them on Saturday.

What confused me at first was what Anne-Marie saw in these paintings. They were quite different from his earlier *Millennium*. I know my wife's taste in art better than anyone, or I thought I did, and this certainly wasn't it. These paintings seemed too abstract. They were landscapes mostly: *Apples in the Night, Storm Damage*. Next to that there was a small postcard-size print of Burne-Jones's *The Sirens*, the mariners on Odysseus's boat gazing wide-eyed across the water, transfixed by the women. I knew there was a famous quotation, but I couldn't remember it. It made me think of the print above Henry's mantelpiece in Paris. But surely that wasn't the connection.

To one side of the paintings there was a photograph of Martinez with a brief biography, which was what I had already gleaned from the Internet at Sam's. The photograph, however, was in colour, and this was much more like the man in life – his brown beard, his hair parted to that point, those dark, Spanish eyes. He was forty-two. Fifteen years older.

That pain again. I inhaled through my teeth, then breathed out steadily.

Beside the biography, there was a display of various sketches and drawings for compositions. Now I saw what had attracted Anne-Marie. Among the pictures was a set of five charcoal sketches, a series called *The Garden*, each as small as the Burne-Jones postcard. The first two were a view through a forest, close-ups of the bases of tree trunks. Along the ground a white mist coils around the roots like a will-o'-the-wisp. There are no animals in Martinez's forest, no humans, just the trees and the mist, the black and the white, the shadow and the light. This was more like the Anne-Marie I knew. A landscape of pure fantasy.

My life was so caught up in the very being of Anne-Marie that, looking at them, I felt like a man being slowly but steadily undone. And I felt ashamed to be there, snooping over these paintings, as if I was spying on her, as if I was rooting through her handbag, or listening in to a telephone call.

It was stuffy in the theatre. On the wall, Martinez's paintings stared at me like an accusing jury. They seemed to blur. Unable to bear the closeness of them any more, I turned and made my way down the all too familiar steps to the foyer.

It was then, as I descended the staircase, that I first saw you, Maguire, standing in that ridiculous cord jacket of yours, talking to Anita.

I remembered expecting your accent to be American. You reminded me of all the American police chiefs I'd seen on TV, and I imagined you munching ring doughnuts or sucking sunflower seeds. Up close I took in your grey-black hair, that one tuft that won't stay down, no matter how often you stop and use that tiny comb of yours, and your frantic moustache: a caterpillar treading water when you speak; your permanent half-frown and thick eyebrows. The heavy bags under your sharp blue eyes, like Jouette's, had 'police' written all over them.

As I approached, you were trying to quote *Macbeth* to impress Anita, who looked like she wanted to be anywhere else.

'I'll see you soon, Anita,' I said, catching her eye as I left.

'This is Inspector Stephen Maguire.'

I stopped, feeling obliged, intrigued why Anita seemed so nervous. So I took your hand. 'Pleased to meet you, Inspector. I hope everything's all right.'

'Fine, fine,' you said.

And hearing your voice properly for the first time, I knew you were English through and through. Do you know you sound like a sergeant in the British army? One from years ago, like you see in films, tuned in, as they say, a man in the know, a man with his head screwed on the right way.

'Just making enquiries, that's all. Another missing person, I'm afraid.' You turned to Anita. 'I'll be in touch, Miss Felts. Remember to call me.'

Anita nodded.

'It was nice to meet you . . . I'm sorry, what was your name?'

'Jack.'

'It was nice to meet you, Jack. Good evening.'

After you had gone, Anita bade me a hasty farewell, leaving me alone in the foyer, thinking about Anne-Marie, who was by that time safe in Paris, thinking that I should go home, that I couldn't avoid it for ever.

But I didn't go home. I sat at dusk by the river, staring at my wedding ring in the middle of my open palm. Which was one of two silver bands purchased by Anne-Marie and me from a Frenchman with his stall on La Rambla, four years ago on a trip to Barcelona, the day I proposed to her.

The rings have an inscription (the police all love the inscription, the Latin letters like a secret code they have to decipher). It says 'carpe diem.' Maybe that's what all this is about: seizing the day. That's what Anne-Marie did, after all.

Right now, a ring of a similar description (you see the phrases I use under questioning) is waiting in a plastic forensics' bag. I imagine you have it with you now, Maguire, in your cord-jacket pocket. Surely you're alone. Surely the department can't afford to send two of you to France. If only you would get up quietly from your seat – the carriage is almost empty, the couple opposite asleep – and standing on the boards above the coupling, open the window and cast that ring far from the tracks, up and away and down along the nettled bank, for an intrepid child to find some day. Save two lives. Save a broken marriage. Enough is enough.

But that's pointless. You won't be on any train. They'll fly you out directly. Anyway, you're not the type. You've wanted me from the word go.

There was a moment on Sunday, after I watched Anne-Marie force one of the suitcases – the medium size of the three we'd bought to take to Spain – into the taxi she'd booked to take her away, when the house no longer felt my own. But I can't pinpoint it. Was it when I looked at the state she'd left the bedroom in, haphazardly packing? Or when I looked out of the window, along the taxi-less street, to find her truly missing? Or was it before? But I can't think about that yet. I couldn't think about it then, not at the house; it was too soon. The city was too depressing.

Which was why, the next day, after meeting you at the theatre, I had gone to the river, to try to think around it, to theorise it out, the way equations balance, the way time bends around planets. So I sat by the water, watching the swans glide under the Lombes bridge and the curve of the Derwent slowly making its journey towards the North Sea. Symbol of my childhood that river, bisecting the county from north to south, from peak to lowland, for sixty miles, until its confluence with the Trent. You see, Maguire, I know my facts, a by-product of working for the city council.

As it was a Monday, the museum, not far off, was closed. Fishermen flanked the opposite bank, their silver one-man tents pitched like space pods in the dusk-light. Traffic passed over the bridge, the Lombes bridge, which has been standing since 1836, lined then by inns trading off the new stagecoaches running to Nottingham and Manchester, for although the Derwent is a completely rural river, except in its short stretch through the city, it never leaves a roadway for more than a mile. Road-makers have never been able to improve on its perfect penetration of terrain, the route also brokered by the railways. It's hard now to think how much has happened in that time, how many things have been thrown into that river and fished out again; what trophies it has brought to its surface or covered for ever; what secrets have sunk to its depths.

12

Now I remember the Burne-Jones quotation – Odysseus and his mariners standing on deck as their ship slowly winds its way through the canyon, while all around them the sirens lie waiting on the rocks. 'The men shall look at the women and the women at the men, but what happens afterwards is more than I care to tell.'

I'm coming to the part I don't want to talk about, don't want to go back to. But I must tell, I must. I want some more wine. It's good stuff this. I might be on holiday here in this hotel room. Anne-Marie might be in the bathroom, freshening up.

But she isn't. And I know I must go back to last Saturday night in Derby, the opening of Martinez's exhibition.

Saturday night, then. I'd been at the Ten Bells on the whiskey. When the barman suggested irrefutably that I'd had enough, I staggered outside onto Sadler Gate. It had stopped raining, but moisture still hung heavy in the air; drops pattered from the roofs, and rainwater swashed in the gaps between the cobbles. This was one of the most fashionable places to be seen on a Saturday night, but I didn't feel very fashionable. I was finding the cobbles awkward to walk on. It wasn't until I got to the end of the street, the cathedral end, that I realised I must have left my jacket. I stood in my shirtsleeves. Across the road, the cathedral was lit spectacularly from beneath, which gave it a sinister appearance against the night sky.

I decided to forget about my jacket and set out for the theatre. I imagined the people milling around, getting drunk on cheap wine. And, of course, Anne-Marie would be there, comparing it all; the last few days would not show on her face. Maybe she was pleased to be away from me. I had this horrible feeling, a feeling I'd been carrying around with me recently, that she might leave me. It was the most frightening feeling I'd ever had.

I reckoned I was the last person she would expect to see that night.

Not wanting to enter the foyer through the main entrance and risk being taken off-guard, when I reached the theatre I made my way round to the stage door. It was open. In the semi-darkness, I could make out the figure of the front-of-house manager half dozing behind his desk. A portable television had the football on. A newspaper was open on his lap, although he couldn't possibly be reading it in such poor light.

As I approached, he started and sprang to his feet, sizing me up, categorising me: drunk. Then he recognised me.

I got in first. 'Anne-Marie. I'm here to see Anne-Marie. Is she still here?'

'She's at the opening. It's press night.'

'Yes, I know. Can I go through this way?'

I tried to think of the man's name, but couldn't remember it. He looked me up and down. I hoped he wanted to be rid of me.

'Go on through,' he said.

'Thanks.' I sauntered past the desk.

'Mr Stone?'

'Yes?'

'You know you really shouldn't come in this way, don't you?'

'Yes. I appreciate it.'

Before he could change his mind, I stepped up into the passageway.

The exhibition had opened an hour and a half ago. I tried to remember the order of events. I thought there were refreshments and a viewing of Martinez's paintings at seven, followed by Darmony's play, which was due to start at eight. I could hear voices backstage. It must have been the interval.

The walls of the passageway were lined with photographs of various productions – *Anna Karenina*, *Death of a Salesman*, *King Lear*. I paused at each, trying to think what I would say to her.

When I opened the door at the end of the passageway, I found myself behind the box office. Anita Felts was already walking towards me in her red dress, strapless, I noted, and unexpectedly becoming. In the foyer people were busy talking and raising wine glasses. There was the sound of voices all at once, loud laughter. I couldn't see Anne-Marie anywhere; couldn't decide if that was good or bad.

'Jack!'

Anita looked anxious and flustered. Her concern seemed to multiply the closer she got. 'Why, it's good to see you again. We're very busy, as you can see.' Her eyes widened as I helped myself to a free glass of wine. 'I only hope it lasts. It's been going so well.'

'You're quite right, Anita,' I said, pleasantly surprised

by the volume of my own voice. I patted her bare shoulder and returned my empty glass to the table. 'In fact you've spoken so well of everything, I must go and see these paintings for myself. The artist is Spanish, I believe.'

'Jack!' She clutched my arm. 'Do you think . . . I mean, do you really think that's wise?'

'Why not?'

She leant closer. I could smell her perfume; her breath was on my ear. 'Jack, you're drunk.'

Whereupon I informed her, along with the woman standing nearby and anyone else who happened to be in the vicinity, that I certainly *was* drunk. I should think so. And where was my wife?

I gave Anita my sharpest look, and thought about overturning a table or two.

'I'll go and fetch her,' she said, 'On condition you wait here.'

'I shall be viewing the paintings!'

Pushing her aside, I headed for the stairs, which was a harder task than I'd surmised, the foyer pitching from left to right as I negotiated it. I smiled, congratulating myself, when I reached the steps. But then I saw Anne-Marie on the landing above me, talking to the artistic director.

At first, she was laughing: the perfect hostess. I felt an old sense of pride for her. But when she saw me, she looked rather like she might burst into tears. I wished I hadn't come. 'Jack, you remember Richard,' she said automatically, when I reached the landing.

The director nodded politely to me, then excused himself quickly.

I wasn't prepared for this. It was as if in one moment I

knew unquestionably that I loved her, and at the same time that I'd lost her. It was as if we had been plucked out of our lives together and now stood looking from the outside in. I wanted her to put her arms round me in front of everybody. I hated her, Maguire.

Anita caught up with me and we stood, the three of us, beneath Martinez's paintings. Luckily everyone else was too busy getting on with their own business to take any notice. For a while no one said anything. Anita was at a loss. She had positioned herself between us, like a referee determined to see fair play.

Anne-Marie had on her black dress; her hair was tied up and she was wearing a red neckerchief. Then I noticed she had mascara on, a touch of lipstick. She never wore makeup.

I watched her turn to her friend. 'Thanks, Anita. I'll be okay.'

Anita looked from me to Anne-Marie and back again, obviously unconvinced. Eventually she made her way back down the stairs to the foyer, glancing repeatedly over her shoulder.

'You look tired,' Anne-Marie said.

I told her that I was tired, that for some reason I wasn't sleeping, but that she on the other hand looked fine.

'I am.' Her voice faltered.

We were standing a whole arm's length away from one another. We'd never stood like that before, except at the beginning, that day in her room on Belgrave Road. Now here I was, eight years later, standing once more in front of her, my hands useless at my sides.

Anne-Marie twisted her own in front of her, a habit of hers. 'This is ridiculous,' she said at last. 'It's awful. I don't want us to be like this.'

I felt myself about to cave in, sweep her up. I could see tears brewing in her eyes, which wobbled, as if they were about to spill.

'What do you want me to do?' she said.

'Nothing. I don't expect you to do anything. I've never asked you to do anything.'

'I know.'

'I never expected this.'

'I'm sorry.'

'So that's it, then?'

'What?'

I waited.

'I don't know what to say,' she said.

'Then that says everything.'

But by then I couldn't remember what I'd come for. The room was beginning to feel too bright. It was too hot. Looking around, I saw myself playing a character in a play. I wanted all the best lines, so she'd remember me saying them later on. Right now I wanted to say, 'Well, goodbye, Anne-Marie,' turn once on my heel and march out of her life, leaving her to ponder the loss of me for ever. But I just stood there, aware the whole room was looking up now, as if indeed it was the two of us on stage. People had stopped talking, glasses no longer clinked; they were waiting for me to say something, to deliver my line.

I said, 'You could have told me.'

Anne-Marie looked up. Tears collected on her cheeks; her mascara smudged.

'Anne-Marie!'

A man's voice, with an accent, somewhere in the foyer.

Below, Sebastian Martinez strolled across the room, the crowd parting before him like the Red Sea. He breezed up the stairs. He was wearing tuxedo trousers, a white shirt and black bow-tie.

As soon as he was in range I punched him so hard he knocked two people over on his fall back down the stairs. He tried to get up, but his legs buckled. He tried to say something, but no sound came. His nose was bleeding.

I turned to Anne-Marie, whose mouth hung open. She closed it. Her eyes narrowed. 'Get out!' she screamed. 'Get out! Get out!'

My hands were shaking. My heart beat so fast as I descended the steps and edged around the bleeding Spaniard that I thought my chest would burst. I couldn't look back at him. I had to get out. I stumbled across the foyer, the crowd dividing again. They all knew who I was, knew how drunk I was.

As I left through the revolving door, my head spinning, the girl on the PA, oblivious to what was going on down there, announced for people to retake their seats.

In the street, it continued to rain. I sat down hard on the kerb, confused and sobering rapidly. Whatever I had planned was in pieces. I was also harbouring a small hope that Anne-Marie might follow me out, but she didn't come. No one did. I was getting wet again. Where was my jacket? No matter. I would walk in the rain. I would walk by the river. And I didn't care what anyone thought: he'd deserved it.

I headed back through town towards the bus station. Couples, hip to hip, holding coats above their heads, dashed between pubs. Strangers crowded together under the bus-station roof. I passed them by, taking the path to the river as the rain eased into a lighter drizzle. By the time I reached the riverbank, it had stopped altogether. I stood looking out across the water, which seemed to stretch endlessly in the darkness. I imagined Anne-Marie back in her role at the theatre, distilling the situation, making a joke of our lives. She might have been in a toilet somewhere, crying. I wondered if Martinez's nose had stopped bleeding, if she'd sat next to him at the play.

I began pacing the riverbank, only stopping when I reached the grassed area outside the museum. I stood at the top of the stone steps leading down to the water. Through the rain I could see the headlights of passing cars trailing along Meadow Road on the opposite bank.

I thought of the terrible look on Anne-Marie's face. I said her name aloud in the cold night air.

But she just screamed, 'Get out! Get out!'

13

The only time I'd seen Anne-Marie wear such an expression was when her mother died, four years ago.

Gina Dufeur had been driving back to her home in Nottingham, having attended a dinner party thrown by friends to celebrate the publication of a textbook she had helped to translate. She'd left David and Margaret Collis's house around one thirty, despite an invitation to stay the night. At two her Renault Laguna collided with a removals lorry on the A52. It seemed she had pulled out to overtake a car in front and mistimed the manoeuvre. She died on impact. The driver of the lorry, Jonathon Hobbs, died in the City Hospital an hour later from first-degree burns. Both he and Anne-Marie's mother tested positive for alcohol, but neither were found to be over the limit. An inquiry would later declare a verdict of accidental death.

I'll never forget that first frantic hour, Maguire. Anne-Marie and I had been in bed, curled up in our separate worlds of sleep, when the three a.m. call from the Nottingham police woke us into a new reality.

In the early hours of that merciless November night I took Anne-Marie to identify her mother's body.

She sat silent and pale beside me as I drove us through the darkness, her gaze fastened on the road in the head-lamps ahead, sprawling towards then under us.

Our way into Nottingham was on the A52. I didn't realise the implication of this until up ahead we could see the lights and cones cornering off the scene of her mother's accident. The traffic had slowed to a crawl: we approached car length by car length. The removals lorry lay fuming on its side, with what was left of Gina's Laguna embedded in the front of it. Police were clearing the road of shards of furniture. There was a fire engine behind the two police cars. Small flames still flickered from inside the wreckage.

'Stop the car!'

I slowed down.

'Anne-Marie, I can't stop here.' A policeman was waving me on into a green light ahead.

Anne-Marie fumbled for the handle of her door. I braked and cut the engine. She was out. Smoke spilled in from outside. She ran away through it.

I opened my door. The van behind me sounded its horn. A policeman in a bright yellow jacket was jogging over.

'Anne-Marie!'

I caught her up. It was a cold night, but warm where the wreckage smouldered and heat still rose steadily.

What little remained of Gina's car was now part of the removal lorry: the dashboard was folded like a piece of card; the passenger seat lay on its end in the burnt-out shell of the cab.

'Hey!' The policeman caught us up. 'You can't be here, I'm afraid. Sir, is that your vehicle? I said—'

'Yes, that's my car.'

Anne-Marie stepped towards the cab. The policeman took her by the arm. She tried to shake him off.

'My mother's in there! Maman!'

'It's okay, Miss. Let's step back, shall we? Then I'll let you go.'

Another policeman joined us. He also touched my arm, when he saw me step forward to intervene.

'Was that—'

'Yes,' I said. 'Her mother. Gina Dufeur. We got the call from a Sergeant Billingham. We're on our way to the morgue.'

He nodded.

His companion released Anne-Marie, who seemed suddenly to become aware of what was going on again, and that her mother was not, after all, among the flames. She collapsed silently into me and I held her. She was shivering.

'Look, you're going to have to move your car,' the first officer said. 'Do you want to travel to the morgue with us, Miss?'

Anne-Marie looked up at me. Her eyes were wide and wild: she looked terrified.

'Her name's Anne-Marie,' I said. 'I'm Jack. We'll follow you, if that's all right.'

I tried to coax Anne-Marie back to the car, but for a moment she wouldn't turn. She was staring into what was left of the flames, as if everything she'd ever known was perishing there. As if this was already the crematorium where, four days later, behind blue curtains, the fire she would not see would lick and curl across the lacquer on her mother's coffin. In fact, from the moment she received the news of Gina's death until long after we had scattered her mother's ashes in the Trent, Anne-Marie's face was a permanent crucible of anger, fear, pain.

The next year was certainly the hardest for us – for our relationship, I mean. Anne-Marie and I were renting a flat on Hayworth Road at the time. I was working at the museum, but still only part-time, and she was rushing from one bar job to the next, picking up occasional work with the council's literature office or organising the odd arts event with Sam. We didn't have much money coming in and Anne-Marie's shifts made it practically impossible for her to meet her mother's lawyer, liaise with her father, who'd returned to Paris, and sort out Gina's will and the sale of her house. I helped as much as I could, taking care of our own financial worries, while trying my best to be physically around for her. Anne-Marie bore it all with a fortitude and grace I found admirable, worthy of her mother, and I loved her more than ever.

Grief, as I'm sure you are aware, Maguire, is a peculiar phenomenon. In many ways Gina's death brought Anne-Marie and me closer. It may even have played a role in her marrying me. At any rate, after her mother died Anne-Marie took another step into my world. And during this time my own mother was a godsend. She would casually drop in on Anne-Marie and me as if she was just passing by Hayworth Road, and she would talk to Annie-Marie about the loss of my grandmother.

I feel for my mother. Old now, Maguire, she has been in the city hospital for the past week undergoing treatment for bronchitis. I can't imagine my life without her. I can't imagine what it must have felt like for Anne-Marie the day of Gina's cremation, when, for a brief time anyway, death served to bring us all together, at first attracting us like moths too late to the flames – the phone call, the morgue, Henry's arrival from Paris – then afterwards, in the cold certainty of absence and ashes, to each other.

At the service, Henry and I sat on either side of Anne-Marie. My mother sat the other side of me. Sam was there, too, along with some of Anne-Marie's friends who had known Gina. Most who attended were strangers to us: they were people Gina had known from Nottingham, her own parents having been dead for years and no one from her family left to come. Henry had arrived that morning, a last-minute decision, after a bitter row with his daughter and his ex-wife's lawyer over the funeral plans. He only stayed for three days, my mother putting him up at Woolrych Street to keep him out of Anne-Marie's way. He was adamant that Gina had wanted to be buried in Paris even though, when drawing up her will, she'd informed her lawyer of her wish to be cremated in England and her ashes left in the city where she had lived for the past twelve years.

It was strange seeing Henry again. Although Anne-Marie had been to Paris to visit him – only twice, I think, in four years – this was the first time I'd seen him since our trip that first summer. After his objections to the funeral plans, I'd expected an even more defiant man than I'd met in France, but when he arrived he was different: something about him had changed. He was older certainly: his hair actually ran white in places. For the duration of his stay he looked like a man who had had the wind utterly knocked out of him. I'm sure the reason he didn't read at the service was not because he refused to but because he was unable to. Gina's death, I believe, affected him more profoundly than perhaps even he would have expected it to. Afterwards, I think Anne-Marie had also picked up on this, for over the next few years, especially after she and I were married, she really did try to reconnect with her father, though admittedly with little success. Yet on the day of Gina's funeral, at any rate, they were father and daughter – pale-faced, dry-eyed, inconsolable.

During the service, all I could think of was my incapacity to know the right thing to do by Anne-Marie. And of my grandmother. I remembered sitting with my mother just like this when I was eighteen, in New Normanton church, with my grandmother's coffin raised on a platform at the end of the nave. I remember stepping up to it, how there was a single chip in the recent finish of the wood. Flowers from her stall had been laid around her and every petal bloomed bright with life. Though she was gone from us for ever.

As Gina now was.

My mother squeezed my hand, no doubt sensing my concern for Anne-Marie, who sat up straight, twisting her own hands in her lap, clutching the order of service in front of her. Or perhaps my mother was also thinking of my grandmother, and holding my hand for her own comfort. I guess we all come to fear what death serves up and offers us: those faces that look so like the ones we loved.

It was a brief service. Gina's pine coffin concealed the severity of her burns. Those who loved her would be spared that sight.

Except for Anne-Marie, who at the morgue saw everything. There, the policeman we had tailed into town, a PC Phillips, introduced us to a tired but kind-looking man with a grey moustache and silver-framed spectacles. 'I'm George Temple, the head mortician here.'

He directed us to a room at the end of a white corridor.

Two silver autopsy tables were bolted down in the centre of this room, and they glistened as though recently cleaned.

'This way.'

We were led though a swing door into a smaller room. This was also empty, except for a bed on wheels in the corner, which had something laid out upon it, covered with a green sheet.

Anne-Marie, dressed in the jeans, sweatshirt and cord jacket she'd frantically thrown on, clung to me.

'You are Anne-Marie Parrot?' the mortician asked. His voice was soft but steady, trained for this sort of thing, I thought. He looked about forty. He was wearing dark suit trousers and a light pink shirt beneath his three-quarter-length white coat.

Anne-Marie nodded. Yes, she was Anne-Marie Parrot.

'Gina Dufeur's daughter?'

I noticed he was referring to the form on his clipboard: this must have been part of some kind of script.

Anne-Marie nodded again.

George Temple smiled politely. He walked over to the table and pulled back the sheet, revealing the head and shoulders of what was now clearly a body. From where I stood, Maguire, it looked as black as ash.

'In your own time, Anne-Marie.'

She breathed in deeply, then slowly disengaged herself from my arm. She stood for a moment a little away from me, then walked over to the bed, where I heard a harsher intake of breath. Her hand went to her mouth. She made a single sobbing sound.

'I'm afraid I have to ask,' George Temple said, 'for the record.'

'Yes.' She said this loudly, too loud. Then she choked, and the rest was a whisper. 'Yes, it's her.'

'Thank you, Anne-Marie.'

The mortician steered her back to me, but she was already somewhere far beyond my reach. When our eyes met, she looked through mine. She seemed to disassemble in my arms, her nails digging into my chest. Then the first tears came, hot and strong. She was shaking violently. I held her and told her I loved her. But I was aware, Maguire, that I could have been anybody: I had paled into insignificance for her. Even though we would be married eight months later, at that moment in the morgue I was no more than a coincidence; I was a crutch, a wall to lean on, a man who happened to be there. I was nothing.

14

These couples I can hear now, laughing and swearing in the street, kissing and embracing, all those I know back home – married, unmarried – whose houses I visit, the old men and women I see walking arm in arm by the river; would all of these people have been equally happy with someone else? How much different might their lives have been?

There was a woman outside the commissariat de police, when Jouette put me in the car to drive me here. It was dark, and she was pushing a pram along the pavement; a large man with a bald head wobbled behind her. There must have been a point somewhere in her life when that woman made the decision, however unconsciously, to stay with that man. What if circumstances had been different? If she had said no to that first drink? If her bus had been early instead of late that day? If she hadn't dropped that pile of paperwork and he'd stopped to pick it up? She might be pushing that pram with someone else's child in it. She might not even be pushing a pram.

Are we to believe that the decisions we make in life are all chance? That we may be in charge of, say, the relatively small ones, but the main ones, the ones that affect everything, the way our entire direction in life goes and with whom we share that life, are we to believe that these are merely down to pure, indifferent luck?

But then there's fate. There's a question, Maguire. Are our actions controlled? Are our destinies – as my grandmother so earnestly believed – pre-ordained? Does God or Nature or Fate or whatever allow us a reasonable amount of flexibility, of free thinking, but then, if we wander too far from the path, are we nudged gently back on track again?

Fate or chance? Chance or fate?

What made Anne-Marie do what she did?

Her answer today, in the woods: 'I don't know why. I just did it. Suddenly I did it.'

Perhaps it's not that Anne-Marie was in love with Sebastian Martinez, or that she was out of love with me, necessarily. Perhaps, indeed, she doesn't quite know what it was that made her catch a taxi across town (at least twice, from her account) to where he rented a flat on Wilson Street. Perhaps it hasn't occurred to Anne-Marie that her real infidelity to me, what in the end hurts most, isn't necessarily the sex but the intimacy of her visits to his flat. Although, as far as I know, they did nothing more there than drink coffee.

I wish I had another bottle of wine.

According to my wife, what surprised her the day she at last consented, or rather chose to make love to Martinez, was how 'unremarkable' the event seemed afterwards. Here I console myself. Unremarkable! The word she used today in the woods. Though surely that was for my sake. She enjoyed it, of course. It was exciting, after all, with a stranger. What she meant was, it was unremarkable in comparison to how important, how monumental she had set up this sin to be. I conjure a film of her, lying back, or clambering on top, held down or forcing him down, whatever's desired, but always oddly conscious of herself: here she is with another man after three years of marriage and, yes, he's intriguing and, yes, she loves him in a way (surely that's only natural once you've allowed so much intimacy) and, yes, the sex is good, but is it worth locking her up for?

But then she got what she wanted. She was alone and intimate with another man. Perhaps the sex was just the finishing touch, the last act. She must have expected it. After all, it was why Martinez had initiated all this (let's not kid anyone). Then again, maybe the sex is everything. Maybe it's the whole point. I don't know. I don't care any more.

She wanted me to find out.

I wonder if she thought I'd leave her, whether she wanted rid of me. Was that the reason? To make me jealous? The gist of her story in the woods: the more she made love with Martinez that day, the more she knew she was in love with me. Ah, the old deceptions. I think of the first time she and I made love. She seduced me that afternoon; it was clear the moment I turned that easel round. She laughed it off, of course; it was a joke, a story to be told many times at many parties, the story of how we met. 'Well,' she'd say, and I see her now placing her hair behind her ear, rolling her eyes, 'I had to check him out. You know, beforehand.'

Yet that blank canvas has darker implications. For almost three hours she'd been pretending to paint me, as I stood naked by the window. Three hours is a long time. What young man could resist a woman who'd do such a thing? And it was this that attracted me to her. Attracts me to her still. Although maybe now I'm beginning to understand it.

She stood to lose everything then. Perhaps, indeed, there was something that lured Anne-Marie to that idea – losing me, her job, too, maybe, certain shared friends, no doubt, even Martinez – to be an empty body walking the streets. She could go shopping. She could buy books and read them. Maybe, after all, she could take up painting again.

She said to me today, 'You're the only one who ever believed in my painting.'

As if that makes everything all right.

Perhaps she thought of it as an action, rather than a solution. Perhaps she knew it wouldn't solve anything.

All last Wednesday she sits in the box office, selling tickets for *Twelfth Night*, thinking about what she's going to do that evening, when I've already told her I have to work at the museum. Perhaps she hasn't considered Martinez; perhaps he is merely a fleeting thought at first, a flicker of vague possibility as she cashes up at the end of her shift. She pictures herself walking into town, buying flowers from the shop opposite the bus station, returning home, setting them on the mantelpiece. She thinks of herself as an actress acting out a part. Her childhood in Paris has a filmy residue over it. She can't recall her student days, our days together in England, like she used to.

Outside it's a bright September afternoon. The sun is out and the grey sky shot through with blue. Walking across the Tarmac she feels the sunlight settle on her face and perhaps she thinks about giving the whole thing up. She presses on. At the phone-box on the corner of Cromwell Street, she calls Martinez. 'Six o'clock,' she says.

It's arranged then, though quite what she has arranged

she won't allow herself to consider as, smiling now, she struts to the flower shop and buys a bunch of white lilies. Then she weaves her way home via Merrick Park, the autumn sun still strong for another hour or so, reviving everything – the greens of the grass, the leaves, already falling, piled beside the goalposts. Turning on to Peach Street, she is herself.

A feeling immediately undone by the familiar objects waiting for her in the silence of our empty home.

In the kitchen, she switches on the radio and fills her blue vase for the flowers. She takes it into the front room and sets it on the mantelpiece beside the clock her father gave her. She has just less than thirty minutes, time enough for a shower, which she indulges in, turning the water up hot, pleased after all to be alone this evening. Though not for long, she thinks. But she forces that thought away, stepping dripping from the cubicle to select a lemon-fresh towel. She dries her hair, considers which style to tie it up in, then leaves it down; in the mirror it falls to just below her breasts. She throws her hair behind her and looks at herself. She selects a matching black lace bra and thong, then sits on the bed to think. She puts her skirt and blouse back on. She has just returned from work, that is all. She leaves the towel strewn across the chair, the hairdryer on the dressing-table, for she won't be coming back in here so soon, she decides suddenly, as she skips downstairs to answer the ringing doorbell.

When she sees Martinez standing awkwardly below her, she puts her arms round his neck and kisses him openly and deeply on the doorstep. He does not embrace her back, however, for he has a bottle of wine in one hand and a bunch of roses in the other. She laughs when she sees the roses. She ushers him in, rolling her eyes, as she looks both ways, up and down Peach Street, then closes the door, which locks automatically behind them.

In the front room she mixes the roses and the lilies in the vase, while Martinez finds two glasses in the kitchen. She does not go to join him but stands in the sunlight, peering through the net curtains at the empty street. She starts when she hears him come in. He hands her her drink. 'To us?' he says. A question loaded with all that been left unsaid, and so far undone.

Anne-Marie considers this question carefully, or not at all. 'To us,' she says at last, and raises her glass. She swallows the wine. Martinez glances around the room, then back at her and moves as if to speak. But she stops him, shaking her head a little, a length of her hair falling across her cheek. She tucks it behind her ear and, taking a breath, steps closer, brushing the fingers of her free hand through his hair. When she goes to stroke his face, he lifts his own hand quickly and holds hers there, pushing her fingertips into his beard, and tilting his head to kiss her clean wrist. She glimpses the pavement glistening outside the window, then closes her eyes, hears him place his glass on the mantelpiece. A child squeals loudly in another street somewhere. Then he's kissing her. She keeps her eyes shut. The fact she's still holding her own glass behind his back persuades her that there's nothing she can do about the fact he is now unbuttoning the blouse she has worn all day. She doesn't open her eyes until he has removed the bra she has chosen especially and she can feel the draught in the room on her nipples.

Moving against him she gropes for the mantelpiece and puts her own glass down. Then she steps back.

'This way,' she says.

She takes him by the hand, leads him through the back room, and up the stairs. The bedroom still harbours a touch of moisture from her shower. Her towel speaks of nakedness from where she has abandoned it upon the chair. She walks to the window, draws the curtains – the room fills with an artificial darkness – and removes her blouse completely. She turns to face him across the bed. He approaches her and touches her. She pulls him round her and kisses him – fuller, harder. Perhaps she's thinking only of herself, or him. Perhaps she realises she doesn't want this after all. But it's too late to go back: he's behind her; they're on the bed and she is pushing her skirt off her ankles. When he enters her, she stretches forwards and clasps the headboard, just having enough time to turn her head and see that the clock on the bedside table reads twenty-five minutes to seven. Back and forth they go.

It's possible she has planned it so they will be lying in bed together afterwards, if she's planned it at all. Either way she doesn't hear my key turn in the door, an hour early, and it isn't until Martinez comes inside her and she eases herself slowly down upon the creased sheets, that she realises I am standing inside the room.

15

I burst out into the dying sunlight. A girl riding a bike. A
man walking a dog. I couldn't look back. I crossed the
road, one foot in front of the other. Anne-Marie on her
knees, legs parted. The dog barked at the girl on the bike.
Martinez behind her. I stopped when I reached the inter-
section. I was surprised cars existed at all. The sound she
was making.

Like a man who cannot wake from a bad dream, no
matter how hard he hurts himself, I sleepwalked into town.
The sun was setting like a bloody yolk around me – over
the blocks of the student halls, through the gap between
the newsagent and Bubbles Launderette. Beneath its lens,
knowing there was nothing I could do, no place I could
run to in the city to escape the images replaying relentlessly in my mind, I floated down Ellison Lane and out
onto the main drag of Friar Gate. If only I could keep
walking, I half convinced myself, maybe everything would
be all right.

Soon I passed The Cob Shop, closed for the day. Even
the library was locking its doors. Stay, I wanted to say to
the shops, stay open just a little while and leave your lights
on. But it was too late. One foot in front of the other –
the shops, the park, and then out along the wide curve of
the slithering river. I thought I could walk forever. They
might have been doing it again, the minute I was out the

door. They would hear a dog barking, somewhere in the distance, spurring them on. She'd apologise for me. My interruption. My existence.

How many tears does it take to flood the Derwent?

I turned back into town, and crossed the cobbles of St Peter's Square to where one green fluorescent sign switched on and winked, promising oblivion. Safe in the snug at the Crossroads, one by one the glasses came, as if by their own free will. And with their exact percentages of numbness and release flowed images of Anne-Marie rising and falling in the ocean of our bed, while above, behind and under her, Martinez flailed and gasped and grinned like the last man in the flood. I decided I must smash my empty pint glass.

'Hey!' The barmaid with the pierced belly-button and red hair, looked up from where she was emptying the ashtrays. 'You be careful, Joe, you hear?'

I'd told her my name was Jack, but she'd misheard me. A taller, younger man, with his white shirtsleeves rolled to his elbows, waded over and squared up. 'Now, Joe. Is that your name? Was that a mistake or was it deliberate?'

I looked up at him. My having drunk the Crossroads into a tidy profit that slow Wednesday evening, I was aware that he really wanted me to leave politely, or just quieten down and order another. But I didn't like this man, who appeared to be the owner – he was too young to run a pub, I decided – and now he had made the mistake of talking to me. I'd been waiting for someone to talk to all night.

I tried to stand, but instead collided with the table, condemning two more glasses to a bitter end.

'Right. That's it,' the young man said.

The red-haired barmaid rushed over. I was flattered.

'Is he hurt? Are you hurt, Joe?'

'Hurt?' I looked up through the enclosing room to see her sweet face spinning there. 'Hurt?'

'He'll be all right.' A new voice, which, slowly, I recognised. The room blurred. 'Look, I'm really sorry,' the voice was saying. 'We'll pay for any damage. He'll come with me.' I was pulled roughly to my feet, which failed me, and I fell a second time. But Sam caught and saved me.

Later, stretched out on the sofa in Sam's two-room flat above the coffee shop, I finally found unconsciousness for five hours. I woke, and my dream was real.

The next morning I couldn't eat anything. Sam offered alcohol but I refused.

'You must want to kill him.'

'Yes.'

But I didn't, not then. It was Anne-Marie who I wanted to squeeze until she got smaller and smaller and didn't exist any more.

I cried into the marmalade. Sam, unsure whether a hug was appropriate, settled for a light slap on the back and a refill of the coffee cups.

'There's orange juice too, if you want it.'

'Thanks, Sam. Thank you.'

'What you going to do?'

'I'm going to see her. Now.'

Sam dropped me off on his way to the supermarket. He stopped the car opposite the house and we both looked over. The curtains were open upstairs. I imagined Anne-Marie moving about, preparing breakfast, Martinez lying comfortably in bed. 'Stay as long as you want,' she'd say.

'Come here.' 'You'll have to let yourself out.' 'I said come here.'

'Jack? You okay?'

Sam's voice found me from very far away. When I looked at him, it was as if I was taking in his face for the first time. He still looked strange without his beard. I nodded. Yes, I was all right.

'Take this,' he said. 'It's a spare front-door key. Come round after. Or, you know, whenever you need. It's just in case.'

'Thanks, Sam.'

'I'll see you later.'

I got out of the car, and Sam drove off. I waited until he had turned on to Wright Street, then retrieved my own key from my pocket, crossed over and let myself in.

The front room was cool and dark.

'Anne-Marie?'

I felt as if I was returning home after a very long time away. It seemed entirely strange to be calling her name like this.

'Anne-Marie? It's me.'

I tried to keep my voice calm but steady. She might still have him here. They might be at it again, right now. That was why they hadn't heard me. I was going to walk in on them all over again.

I pressed forward into the back room, and called up the stairs. 'Hello?'

The house was empty. I knew this instinctively. Even so, the mere thought of them together was making me feel faint. This was our home, Anne-Marie's and mine; we had built three years of marriage here, between these, at times, too familiar walls. I returned to the front room, opened the curtains and sat down carefully on the edge of the sofa, keeping my coat on. I noticed that the carpet we'd had for three years was a blue and grey colour. My notepad loomed at me from the coffee-table, as if from a millennium ago. I'd forgotten about the lecture for the museum; it was less than a week away. What I kept picturing was Anne-Marie and Martinez at the theatre, post-coital, joking and laughing, organising Martinez's exhibition.

Then I saw the two glasses on the mantelpiece, one of them half full of red wine. There was lipstick on it. She'd worn lipstick then. She didn't even finish her drink before they . . . She wasn't even drunk.

I dashed upstairs to the bathroom and threw up in the white toilet bowl. Again and again. And then nothing.

I marched through to the bedroom. I was sweating now, but still I kept my coat on: I wasn't staying, I continued to convince myself. Up here, sunlight poured in through the open curtains. The bed was stripped: no evidence. I looked around the room, not knowing what I was looking for. No cereal bowls or coffee cups, no discarded clothing, just our room as it had always been: a towel drying on the radiator; Anne-Marie's hairdryer on the dressing-table; her white blouse and black skirt from yesterday folded over the back of a chair. I picked up her blouse. It smelt of perfume, sweat. How many times had she unbuttoned this for me? And now he . . . this man . . . and she'd wanted him to.

I replaced the blouse exactly as she'd left it and retreated out of the house, feeling frustrated, cheated of the confrontation I'd come for. I'd wanted her to be there, expected it, ready to explain or defend herself. I didn't believe the woman yesterday was her. Hanging on to the headboard like that, oblivious to everything, offering her back to him. How could it be? How could she?

But the ordinariness of our still and unassuming house had emptied me of all the words I'd prepared to hurt her with. She had gone to work, business as usual. It was only me, I realised, with a sudden sickness and disgust, for whom the world had shifted orbit.

The next morning, at Sam's, I received an email from her.

Jack,

I don't know how to describe what I'm feeling, or to begin to tell you how sorry I am. I'm so sorry for causing you pain. I didn't mean this to happen, certainly not the way it has. I don't know who I am at the moment, or what's become of me, or you, or us. But I love you. And I'm sorry. I know you may not be able to forgive me. I know you may not believe me.

I've decided I am going to go and visit Papa after all. I'll go on Sunday, once the opening is out of the way. You have his number (there's a copy along with his Paris address by the phone). Please ring if you want to talk. Sam called to say you're staying with him. If you want to come home this weekend, I'll be there. Though I'll be at the theatre mostly. I don't know what else I can say to you. Perhaps time apart will do us good. Jack, please forgive me. Forgive my moment of madness, my stupidity. I love you. Contact me, if you want to, or I'll see you when I get back.

A.M.

I went out walking, retracing my route from the previous evening, along the banks of the Derwent, back through St Peter's Square and along Friar Gate. I carried a printout of her email in my pocket. I'd read it by the river; I read it sitting under the cathedral; I read it outside Superdrug. Over and over. It was the banality of it that got to me. But, then, what did I expect? The world to end? To turn on its head? Yes, that was the least it could do. The least the world could do was oblige. Couples shouldn't be holding hands. Children shouldn't be laughing. They shouldn't be selling jacket potatoes. Anne-Marie shouldn't be able to use phrases in brackets, like 'there's a copy along with his Paris address by the phone.' That showed just how little she regretted it, how little she was 'sorry.'

16

Perhaps we want to believe that things happen for a reason – some grand scheme – precisely *because* we attach such significance to extraordinary events in our seemingly ordinary lives. Is an accidental meeting merely happenstance? Is a coincidence really a coincidence?

Such thoughts strayed through my mind while I marooned myself on Thursday night and all day on Friday on Sam's sofa, questions that served only to re-emerge significantly, suggestive and malign, on Saturday night, an hour or so after my escapade at the theatre, the storming of Martinez's exhibition, when walking by the river I first saw Rachel Seaga standing on her own beneath the Lombes bridge.

As you now know, Maguire, Rachel works as an assistant for the Derby City art gallery, and as such she is employed by the same department of the council as I am, the art gallery and industrial museum currently strolling under one cultural umbrella. This week she's been at the museum helping Wilmot with a new project that will overlap with the Space and Time exhibition and then succeed it: a series of paintings about the birth and development of science.

And now there she was, alone on the moonlit path, a stone's throw from work.

As I walked towards her, I saw she was wearing a black

dress not unlike Anne-Marie's, and holding a red-sequined handbag. She took a step backwards when she noticed me – a lone silhouette of a man approaching in a crooked line.

'Hello, Rachel.'

'Jack? What are you doing here?'

She smiled and stepped back into the light, which caught the sequins on her handbag and set the fibres of her short blonde hair alight like filaments. Her blue-green eyes appeared to shine older and younger than her twenty-three years. In my drunkenness, I allowed myself to stare at the silver locket resting on the skin, still slightly tanned, below her throat, just above the cleavage conjured by her dress.

'It's a Pisces,' she said.

She held it out in her thin fingers, leaning forward flirtatiously so I could look down. She seemed to have had a drink or two herself.

'Do you believe in the stars, Rachel?'

She straightened, letting the Pisces fall back into place. 'I do.' She smiled her smile again. 'Well, I like to think I do.'

We listened to the river for a while. The usual small-talk was not forthcoming, and the more we were silent the more our silence seemed complicit.

'You didn't answer my question,' she said.

'I was just walking. I've been to the opening of a new play at the theatre.'

'Where your wife works?'

'Yes. She's still there.'

'Ah.'

'And what about you? Surely you haven't been at work?' I nodded in the direction of the museum.

She tapped her handbag. 'Forgot my phone yesterday.

Thought I could live without it for two days, but it turns out I'm as bad as everyone else.' She didn't take her eyes off the dark swill of the Derwent. 'I was out with a friend, who turned out not to be so friendly.' She looked up. 'I was going to call a proper one. But now you're here, so . . .'

'So,' I concurred.

We stared into the river again, until at last she shivered. 'Do you fancy another drink, Jack?'

'Another?'

She linked her arm in mine (she smelt of some kind of perfume) and we began strolling back along the path. 'Call it a hunch.'

Although the air remained mild, it had started to rain again. We sat in a new bar called the Thirst as the shower drummed upon the windowpanes like an impatient hand. I'd not been there before. Rachel explained it was licensed until two a.m., and she promptly caught me up, drinking three glasses of white wine, while I sat opposite her, staring at a pint of bitter, having had my fill of alcohol; it was starting to taste bad for me.

'So what would your wife, Anne-Marie . . .'

'Anne-Marie and I are finished,' I stated flatly.

'I see.'

I sipped my beer, then looked up at her. Her eyes did all the questioning. She drank some more wine.

I didn't ask her what her own story was that evening, the 'friend' she'd been to dinner with, why all the wine and flirtation in this plastic pub, her hand on my knee, why me. What was the point? It wasn't as if I wanted to know. Which was unfair, I thought, looking at her across the dim-lit table at last orders, enjoying her exploring eyes, landing on and off me, lightly, like two blue-green butterflies. I was way beyond fairness, Maguire. The hand I placed on her rain-wet thigh in the taxi, as we time-travelled in a haze of half-familiar streets, still ached from where it had come into contact with Martinez's face.

'Kiss me.'

Her hair and cheeks were wet with rain, her mouth warm. She tasted of alcohol. I thought of Anne-Marie and Martinez, and kissed her harder.

The taxi stopped and clipped the kerb.

'Blackstock Avenue,' the driver said. He turned and gave me that look men sometimes hurl, jealous and congratulatory. 'That will be seven pounds fifty.'

I gave him the money – the least I could do – while Rachel opened the door into another warm shower and stepped down on to the splattered kerb. I followed her dash to the door, as the cab veered away into the slanting rain. Waiting patiently while she fumbled for her key in her red-sequined bag, I began to feel sober. I buried the thought of Anne-Marie as I mock-carried her over the threshold of our new house on Peach Street – a memory that seemed to arise from the weather.

'Come in,' Rachel said, leading me through into the living room of her ground-floor flat. The floor was wooden, most of it covered with a multi-patterned rug of reds and yellows. There was a sofa, a TV set by the window and a bookcase and desk at the far end of the room.

'Do you live alone?'

'Yes.'

She pulled me towards her. 'But not all the time.'

Her dress was soaked and clinging. I unzipped the back, then steered a hand inside and cupped her breast. She began unbuttoning my shirt. 'Jack.'

But it was no use.

I pushed her away. I sat down hard on the edge of the off-white sofa.

'I'm sorry,' I said, tasting whiskey.

She lifted her stray strap back on to her shoulder and zipped up her dress.

I looked up. 'I love her.'

'I see.'

In the semi-darkness, Rachel's eyes appeared the same green as the clock on her video player that blinked 02.45. She took three steps towards me and stopped, her abdomen level with my chin. Her wet blonde hair was plastered down on her forehead.

'You sure?'

At six Sam awoke to the sound of me banging on the coffee-shop window, where eventually a light came on, illuminating the chairs that were perched like acrobats upside down on the tables. Sam, the ringmaster, appeared among them and came to open the door. 'You're like a bloody homing pigeon, you are.'

'Sam, you won't believe what I've done.'

'I don't want to know. Come on, come up.'

Sam's kitchen sliding into view. A mug in my hand. Sam sat opposite me in his tartan dressing-gown. A clock ticking.

I thought of the first time I'd met him, at the city's annual literature festival, for which Anne-Marie had painted some stage sets, years ago now, before we were married, when he still had his unruly red beard and considerable paunch. He looked so different now.

He stifled a yawn. 'What did you do?'

'What time is it?'

'What happened, Jack?'

I felt my hangover kick in suddenly, like an alarm.

Later on that Sunday morning I got the impression that my friend might have been pleased I was leaving. Once more he drove me home.

'Talk to her,' was all he said.

Again I found the house empty. I checked for post but there was nothing of interest, no note from Anne-Marie. In the front room I collapsed on the sofa, exhausted. I felt like I hadn't done a thing for days. I saw Martinez falling away from me backwards down the theatre stairs.

The two wine glasses were no longer on the mantelpiece, but the flowers were there, lilies and roses, shaped like two torsos entwined. In the centre of the mantelpiece was the silver clock Anne-Marie's father had given her. It read ten forty-five.

I went upstairs to check the bedroom. Clean sheets had been fitted on the bed, which had clearly been slept in. Anne-Marie's clothes were all over the place, the wardrobe door open, but no note anywhere. Nothing. Where was she?

I returned downstairs and sat in the front room with my head in my hands. Anne-Marie's jigsaw stared at me from above the fireplace. It was the one I had seen on her desk at Belgrave Road, eight years ago when we were students, the day she asked to paint me. Finished now, the jigsaw depicted a lake. Behind the lake there were trees, the beginnings of a dark wood. The trees were close together and so tall they stretched right up out of the painting, so you couldn't see where the trunks ended.

At first I'd found these jigsaws of Anne-Marie's endearing. She buys them, as she did when she was a student, from charity shops, because she enjoys the excitement of not knowing whether all the pieces will be there. Sometimes she might do a whole jigsaw and it won't be right until the end that she'll find a piece is missing; she can do nothing but leave the picture as it is, incomplete, and buy another jigsaw. Remarkable, I used to think, this strange fetish of hers. Often I've awoken in the night to find her sitting by the window, slotting the pieces in, bent over the dressing-table, as still as the moon. Usually she'll be oblivious of me, her skin a bright white, her hair all those different browns reaching for her waist. The only sound will be when she lifts a piece up and slots it in somewhere, or when she makes a mistake, sighs, yawns, pulls out a piece and starts again. Sometimes she'll sit for an hour, unaware of me watching her, and eventually I'll fall asleep, only to wake in the morning, either to have forgotten about the whole episode or unsure whether I've dreamt it. Other times, sensing her tiring, I'll rise from the bed, go silently over to her and we'll make love. But usually I'll sleep right through, unaware she's been up all night, until I wake to find a whole picture complete in the sunlight.

The bottom line, of course, is that my wife is not a good sleeper, and when she has bad dreams, or when we argue, she retreats into the world of her jigsaws and her playing-cards.

The doorbell rang.

I wondered if it was Anne-Marie. I thought it might be Sam.

It was Anne-Marie.

'Where have you been?' It was the first thing that came to mind.

She rushed in with carrier-bags. 'To the shop. I needed some paracetamol. I saw Sam. He told me he'd just dropped you off.' She was flustered.

'Why didn't you use your key?' I asked.

'I don't know. I didn't want to disturb you. I guess I thought I might not be welcome.'

'For Christ's sake, Anne-Marie, you live here.'

'Do I?'

She pushed past me into the back room and put the carrier-bags down on the table. She was wearing blue jeans and her brown suede jacket. 'I'm going to get a taxi,' she said.

'What? Anne-Marie, what's wrong?'

She looked distracted.

'I'm going to Paris. Now.'

'I see. How's Martinez?'

Her eyes filled. She stepped into me and I put my arms round her. Everything was so familiar, her warmth, her smell, the shape of her body. She was crying. She was shaking.

At last she pulled herself away. 'Oh, God, Jack. I've got to pack. It's at one o'clock.'

'Don't go.'

'I have to.' She wiped her eyes. 'I need time to think. I think we both do. For a while. I don't know. Did you get my email?'

'No.'

I followed her up the stairs and watched from the

doorway as she scurried around the bedroom, darting from one side to another, from wardrobe to drawers, making her choices quickly, the suitcase in the middle of the bed, doing everything as smooth and light as a bird.

She filled the suitcase with clothes. I noticed the carrier-bag she'd brought contained some fruit, the packet of paracetamol, a book for the plane. I picked it up and put the items on the bed for her. She met my eyes, briefly, and smiled. Her own eyes wide and red: she'd been crying. When she retrieved her passport and plane ticket from the top drawer of the dressing-table, I considered how long they'd been there. She pulled another carrier-bag out from underneath the bed and put it into the suitcase, which I carried down for her. She overtook me at the bottom of the stairs, but this time she didn't smile. I didn't know what to say. Perhaps I wanted her gone. It was all arranged and paid for, after all: her father was expecting her.

From the front room, I could hear her in the kitchen.

'Look, what time did you say your flight was?'

'One o'clock.'

It was eleven-ten. 'Anne-Marie, you need to go now.'

'I know, I know.'

I picked up the phone. There was a taxi number on the pad. I dialled it. But when the woman's voice answered I couldn't speak because I was crying.

Anne-Marie came out of the kitchen and walked through.

'I can't,' I said. I held out the receiver, watching the tears well in her eyes to mirror my own. I wiped mine away. 'Come on.'

She took the receiver. 'From thirty-five Peach Street,

please. The bus station. That's fine.' She looked up at me. 'Five minutes.'

She returned to the kitchen, where I heard her filling a bottle of water. I opened the front door. Another bright day outside. No sign of further rain.

The taxi arrived on time. Anne-Marie clutched me in the doorway and wouldn't let go. Tears spilled down her cheeks and made dark brown patches on her jacket.

'I'm so sorry. Oh, Jack, I'm sorry. I love you.'

'Come on.'

She struggled outside with the case. I took her knapsack and carrier-bag, opened the taxi door and put them on the seat. 'The bus station,' I told the driver.

For a moment, we stood facing one another.

'Do you have enough money?'

'I've just been to the bank. I don't want to go.'

'You must. Ring me from your dad's.'

She calmed herself. 'Okay.'

She climbed in and sat on the back seat, twisting her hands in her lap. The taxi seemed far too big for her. She looked lost in it. I didn't want her to go. Anne-Marie. I leaned forward and kissed her cheek. Her face collapsed; the tears returned.

'I'm sorry.'

'It will be okay,' I said, without thinking.

'I love you.'

I moved to close the door. 'Take care. I did get your email.'

The taxi pulled away and immediately other cars turned onto the street and followed it, so all I could see was a black roof slipping away, getting smaller and smaller.

Back in the house, I had the sensation of time slowing down. I stood in the bedroom, Anne-Marie's clothes all over the bed, where she'd held on to the headboard.

When my own tears returned, I couldn't touch the bed but sank down where I was standing.

17

Monday, after meeting you at the theatre, Maguire, having fretted away the afternoon beside the river, I sat up late, trying to prepare my concluding lecture for the Space and Time exhibition. It took me longer than I'd planned. I leafed fruitlessly through the notes I'd written; the events of the previous days spiralled before me, and later kept me awake long after I lay listening to the city settling into sleep.

My lecture wasn't until two o'clock the next day, and I had already booked the morning off work to visit my mother at the city hospital. At ten o'clock that morning, though, I still lay, as if anaesthetised, beneath two blankets on the front-room sofa, where I had spent a second uncomfortable night, unable to bring myself to sleep upstairs in our bed. Even as I lay there, watching the hands on her father's clock spin into the early hours, I was tormented by the red roses and white lilies embracing in the blue cubicle of Anne-Marie's vase.

I gazed wide-eyed at the walls, unable to move; it was as if, after all that had happened, my body had finally folded. Eventually I fell asleep, but only for Anne-Marie to scream at me through my morning dream, 'Get out! Get out!' I got up, showered and forced myself to eat.

Outside, the day was fresh and clear. I was glad Anne-Marie had not taken the car. It was now covered in a thin layer of frost, already dissolving in the sunlight. I dumped a folder containing the notes for my lecture on the passenger seat and fumbled in the glove compartment for the de-icer. I walked around spraying the windows and windscreen, and stood back watching the chemicals get stuck in. For the first time in days, for the moment anyway, I felt okay.

The sun was warm. We seemed to be having a good few days of it for autumn, despite the frost, which all through the city was melting now as I drove the not-so-busy streets towards the edge of town.

It is the second year running my mother has suffered from bronchitis. I remember when I first saw her in a hospital ward, the previous year: she had been lying in her nightgown in one of the beds, hooked up to an oxygen cylinder, holding a mask against her face with a wrist too frail and thin to be my mother's. She had been in the middle of one of her prescribed 'ten minutes on the tank,' as she called it, and had waved me in with her free hand, rolling her eyes as if to say, 'See? See what I put up with?' And I had to sit in silence watching this sixty-two-year-old woman summon all her concentration just to breathe. Deprived of the capacity to speak, she seemed so unlike my mother it was as if, for the first time, I was seeing her as others must do – an old woman, a widow with flowing shoulder-length white hair.

Now, a year later, she had been admitted again, although this time, apparently, the illness was not as severe. She had phoned to say she would be out by the weekend. 'So there's no need to come, darling. I'm not dying,' she had joked. The breaking in her voice worked hard to contradict her.

'I'm coming,' I said, 'I've booked the time off work.'

I don't think my mother likes me visiting her in hospital, witnessing her at the mercy of others. I don't like seeing her in there either. I was glad she had been given the all-clear; at least that was one good thing in my world.

I was late. It was already eleven fifteen, but all the same I made my way into the main outpatients' building, where there was a pharmacist and a newsagent's that sold flowers.

The selection was small, tulips, roses and hyacinths, but I liked choosing all the same: it reminded me of the Saturdays when I would select a bunch from my grand-mother's stall to take for her. I bought some tulips, and proceeded back outside and along the path that, if I remembered correctly, would take me to B block.

I've never had much to do with hospitals – just last year, visiting my mother and that horrific night at the morgue to identify Gina's body. I always feel ashamed, as if I'm not supposed to be there, and disoriented – too many paths and roads with markings weaving in and out of unreal-looking buildings, yet each with a map and arrow declaring, 'You are here.'

My mother is in a new building, separated from the others across an expanse of grass; it has a small cobbled courtyard and a fountain, which always makes me think of Anne-Marie's halls on Belgrave Road. In fact, the whole place reminds me of being on campus.

'Can I help you?'

The man on Reception had blond wavy hair, parted in the centre; he was wearing a tie depicting a cartoon char-acter I didn't recognise.

'I'm here to see someone in Ward Thirty-six,' I said. 'Catherine Stone.'

'I'll get you a pass. Have you been before?'

'Yes.'

He rummaged in a drawer I couldn't see beneath the desk, and took out a plastic credit-card-sized wallet. 'What's your name, please?'

'Jack Stone.'

'And that's for Ward Thirty-six?'

'Yes.'

'Do you have a vehicle on the premises?'

I gave him the registration number.

'Okay, Mr Stone. This is your pass.' He finished filling in the form, tore off a section, slipped it into the plastic wallet and handed it to me. 'Go down the corridor there, right to the end, turn left, and keep going straight. Ward Thirty-six is at the end. You'll have to go up some stairs, I think. It's all signposted.'

'Thank you.'

I proceeded to follow his instructions. The corridor reminded me of a hotel (but not like this one, Maguire, something more monotonous and modern); it had beige walls, intersected by pine doors, and dark brown carpet tiles. There was nothing on the walls – no noticeboards or watercolours – just the signs hanging overhead, which eventually signposted Ward 36 up a flight of stairs, like the man had said.

On opening the door at the top of the stairwell I found myself in a smaller foyer, also with a reception desk. The whole thing was like a miniature replica of the set-up downstairs, only behind this desk sat a nurse, in uniform, with a name badge that read Sandra Cook pinned to her considerable bosom.

'I'm here to see Catherine Stone.'

She looked up. 'That's fine. Kate's around somewhere. She's been having some tests this morning.'

'What tests?'

'I suggest you ask her.' Nurse Cook smiled. 'If I was you I'd try the smoking room.'

'Right.'

'It's down there on the left. Remember, it's twelve o'clock for lunch.'

Another carpeted corridor, another pine door. Then suddenly I saw my mother emerging from one of the rooms ahead. She fell in line in front of me and began walking in the same direction. She hadn't seen me.

'Mum.'

'Prentis!'

I caught her up: she looked okay to me. She was holding a plastic cup of coffee in one hand, which I could feel her waving dangerously close to my back as she hugged me.

'Thanks so much for coming.'

I doubted her sincerity, but she did look pleased to see me.

'I hear you had some tests this morning.'

She rolled her eyes, and suddenly, not for the first time, I was struck by how well she had aged. She looked entirely different from the frail woman I'd come to visit the previous year. Her face was slightly flushed, her white hair down as usual. She was wearing a black skirt and a red polo-neck, and looked a little as she did at Christmas, except that she had the plastic cup in her hand and not a glass. 'I was up at seven,' she said. 'Seven! And you know me, I need at least two hours to put my face on. I told them if they were going to test me for anything at that time in the morning they'd have to have an ambulance on standby and the oxygen on tap just in case I had a cardiac arrest or a lung collapsed. Speaking of which, we must go to the cafeteria, darling. I must be able to smoke. I haven't been allowed to have one all day. It's so good to see you.'

She coughed, then smiled and took my arm. We continued along the corridor. 'We won't go to the smoking room,' she said. 'I know you don't like it. They're going to do away with it soon. Can you believe that? Anyway, earlier, there was a woman in there with the most haggard, haunted face you've ever seen.'

We turned left into the cafeteria. There was a pool table and a table-tennis table, which made me think of school youth-club nights. Clutching her coffee, my mother hurried me across the room and out into a small adjoining conservatory with more chairs and some potted plants. It looked out over the grass with a view of the fountain. 'Now, you're not supposed to smoke in here,' she was saying, 'but otherwise you have to sit outside and it's freezing.' It was actually quite pleasant out there, but I wasn't going to argue.

'I say balls to it,' she said, 'I say we open this door here and perch ourselves right up close.'

She said 'we' as if I, too, was implicated in her smoking. She was already dragging one of the chairs to the conservatory door, which opened onto the grass, glittering with melted frost. She propped the door open with one of the plants and placed her chair next to it, indicating that I should get myself one and do the same.

Her smoking continued to sadden me, especially now that she was in hospital for the second time. And for bronchitis, of all things. When she'd been admitted last winter I'd lectured her severely, which had resulted in the harshest row we'd had in years. It made me more conciliatory now, but no less concerned.

'In case you hadn't guessed,' I said, 'these are for you.' I handed her the tulips I'd been carrying.

'Oh, thank you, darling. They're lovely.'

I leaned over. She kissed my cheek, half-way though lighting her Red Band.

'Though I'm not convinced you deserve them,' I added, securing myself a chair.

She sighed, exhaling smoke. 'Don't start, Prentis. It's bad enough as it is in here. I'm being good. This *is* my first today.' She turned the tulips in her hand. 'You *are* a sweetheart. You see, there are some advantages of being the grandson of a flower-seller. That's how your grandmother and grandfather met. Did you know that? God, there was love there.' She pointed her streaming cigarette at me. 'I mean *there was love.*'

I wondered why she was talking about my grandparents. But I wasn't going to push her, so I sat back and listened to the story of how my grandparents met, a tale I must have heard a dozen times from my grandmother although, as far as I can recall, this was the first time I'd heard it from my mother.

'He was going to meet this girl at the pictures,' she was saying, 'and on the way he decides he's going to stop off to get some flowers. I can't remember her name. Your gran used to know.'

I couldn't remember either.

'So he stops by the market – which was in St Peter's Square in those days, before they moved it indoors – and who's behind the flower stall but your grandmother. Seventeen she was then. "Beautiful!" your grandfather used to say. So beautiful he nearly forgot to buy the flowers. He'd say it seemed wrong to be buying flowers for anyone else when the girl behind the stall was so pretty. Anyway, he did buy them. Geraniums, your gran said they were. She'd say he looked tall and handsome, like a character in a book, which always made him laugh and suck his stomach in. Your gran said she'd half forgotten about him by the end of the day, but then, just as they were packing up the stall for the night, he appeared at the top of the street, still holding the flowers he'd bought earlier. The other girl never got them. He gave them to your grandmother instead.'

'Love, then.'

'Love.'

'So, what tests?'

My mother looked up at me. She sighed. 'Cancer. Can you believe that? I mean, Je-sus.' She tried to roll her eyes and fob off her fear like a piece of ash.

'Mum, what did they say?' I took her hand. It was cold. I became aware of the draught from the open conservatory door.

She patted my hand. 'Oh, it's okay. I've been given the all-clear. They were concerned because of the bronchitis again and apparently I've got this ulcer in my throat.'

'But that's it? That's not cancer, though, right?' My stomach was pitching.

'No, no.' She squeezed my hand. Now she was in control,

which was how she preferred it. 'I'm clean. It was just a bit scary, that's all. Your grandfather died of cancer, you know.' She stubbed out her cigarette on the grass.

'I never knew that. Gran just said he was ill.'

'People didn't talk about that sort of thing then. It was a dirty word.'

My heartbeat was steadying again. I was wondering how much more I could take at the moment.

'Right, that's me done,' my mother said, relieved. 'I'm going to get another coffee from that machine over there. You want one?'

'Yes, all right. Here.'

'I've got money!' She shooed me away. 'I'm going to the coffee machine,' she repeated, 'and in a minute, when I get back, you're going to tell me all about what's going on with Anne-Marie.'

So I did, Maguire, although I hadn't meant to. It had been dammed up inside me for so long that when I opened up a chink it all came out: Anne-Marie, Martinez, Saturday night, Anne-Marie's email (though I left out the episode with Rachel Seaga). I'd spoken to Sam about it all, of course, but this was different: I couldn't remember the last time I'd been so open with my mother. She sat there, smoking, listening and, unusually, not interrupting. Her eyes didn't leave mine for a second. I felt a failure. I felt shame. But being my mother she seemed able to brush away these concerns, without words, banishing them with a flick of her wrist.

'Go and see her,' she said simply, when I'd finished.

'To Paris?'

'You must. You need to sort this out.'

'Are you saying I should forgive and forget?'

'I'm saying that Anne-Marie's confused.'

'Mum, I tell you, I'm confused.' I turned away from her and looked out through the glass walls of the conservatory. A lone blackbird was pecking at the wet grass. 'I don't know what to do,' I said.

'She loves you, you know.'

I gave my mother a stern look: that was beneath her.

'That email is all the proof you need,' she said.

'That's guilt.'

'Why feel guilty if she doesn't have feelings for you?'

'She doesn't know what she's feeling.'

'And you do?'

My mother coughed, her breath caught short, but before I could say anything she held up her hand. Her voice was gravel. 'Tell me that things between you and Anne-Marie were perfect up until you found out about this man. I know what I'm talking about. Tell me you weren't already having doubts.'

But I couldn't, could I? Because I was.

She cleared her throat. 'Do you love her?'

'I don't know.'

'Then you'd better find out.' She looked me in the eye; her gaze softened. 'Go to Paris.'

'Am I supposed to just forgive her?'

'If you love her, yes.'

'Like you forgave my dad?'

Now it was her turn to look outside. 'I threw my life away,' she said, quietly. She lit another cigarette and choked on it: her voice became a steady wheeze. She cleared her throat again, which started another coughing fit.

'No, you didn't, Mum. Don't say that. What are you talking about?'

My mother was looking at me in a way I hadn't seen before, and yet there was something in that look. Then I realised I had seen it before: it was the look she had given me twenty years ago, sitting on the stairs in our home on Woolrych Street when she first spoke of my father. She tried to speak now, but her throat was dry. She coughed harshly, and when I went to speak, she shook her head. She raised her voice in an effort to keep it steady.

'That was my life,' she said, finally meeting my eyes, 'and now this is yours. Believe me, darling, if you love her, I mean really love her, everything else comes second. Doesn't it?' She stared at me. 'You know. I know you do. If you love her, go to her.'

I smiled. I leaned forward and took her hand. 'I'm glad you're all right, Mum.' It was all I could think of to say: my mind was reeling.

'Kate, how many times do I have to tell you?' Nurse Sandra Cook loomed suddenly in the doorway. Her face had twisted itself out of its former pleasantness.

My mother glared at her, yet relishing, I think, the intrusion: she and I had come to the end of our little mother-son confessional, and it was time to assume our places again. 'I'll just finish this, and then we'll be gone.'

'Put it out, please. It's the rules; you know that. You can smoke in the smoking room, if you have to.' Nurse Cook turned to me. 'You know she shouldn't really be smoking at all, don't you?'

As if it was my doing, as if I could stop my mother doing anything.

'Anyway,' she continued, 'it's lunch-time. Twelve 'til one. You'll have to come back to see your mother later, or you can wait in the lounge in C Block.'

Without waiting for my answer, she turned and marched back into the cafeteria.

'She likes me really,' my mother joked, when the nurse had gone.

I didn't doubt it. Concern for my mother surged through me. 'You know, you're going to have to stop this,' I said. 'Mum, are you listening to me?'

'All right, all right. It's out. See?'

18

An hour later I was entering the City Science and Industrial Museum, clutching the manila folder that contained my lecture notes, and a packet of prawn-mayonnaise sandwiches, which were all that was left in the hospital vending machine I'd accosted after leaving my mother. My mind was full to overflowing and couldn't settle on one thought at a time: I felt as if my brain had swelled and was pushing against the edges of my skull. What had plagued me most, far more than it did when I was with her, was the sudden knowledge that my mother would die; maybe not now, maybe not for a good few years, but one day, like my grandmother, she would be gone from me, the way Gina was gone from Anne-Marie. Images of cancerous cells multiplied through my imagination. I was angry with myself for having talked only of my own problems. But I was relieved the tests had given her the all-clear, just as I was relieved, as always, by her advice. She was right. If I loved Anne-Marie, what else was there? At last I saw a faint flash of hope for Anne-Marie and me, a soft pulse from some quasar floating in the far reaches of our darkened universe.

'Mr Stone, are you all right?'

I realised I was standing in the foyer. In front of me Mrs Hughes perched behind the information desk, a touch of worry on her kind face. She has a way of saying my name that is quiet and unobtrusive. Mrs Hughes, or June, as she always insists I call her, is in her early fifties; not so much younger than Mum, then, I reminded myself. Like my mother, that afternoon June was wearing a polo-neck, but hers was black, and as usual her bifocals hung round her neck on the multi-coloured cord woven for her by her granddaughter two Christmases ago.

'I wasn't sure you were coming in today,' she said. 'Well, with everything . . .'

'She phoned you?'

'Who? Anne-Marie? No. A friend of yours called this morning. Samuel Pike. He said you were ill. Are you okay?' She looked me over. 'Is he a friend of yours?'

'Yes. A good one.'

'Well, Mr Wilmot says we can reschedule the talk if you're unwell.'

'No, that won't be necessary. I'm fine.'

'Are you sure? It won't be a problem, you know.'

'I'm sure. Thanks, June.'

I signed in and made my way into the main exhibition hall, which was filled with the Space and Time exhibits and where later I would give the project's final lecture.

The exhibition hall, rectangular in shape, is about the size of an average swimming-pool; it has a dark wooden floor, polished twice a week by the janitor, and at one end a raised platform erected from grey stage blocks, on which usually stands a lectern. Although the blocks are temporary and can be dismantled and moved at any time, this platform has been here the entire five years I've worked for the museum, perhaps longer (it wouldn't surprise me) than some of the permanent exhibits upstairs. Empty, the exhibition hall reminds me of school assembly.

It had a little of that air about it now, set up as it was for this series of weekly lectures. Indeed, someone had already put out ten rows of chairs facing the platform, which saved me a job. I walked over to one and put my sandwiches and folder on the seat. There was no member of the public in the hall, just the security guard, Henderson, sitting on a chair in the far corner. He tipped me a small salute. I could hear high heels clicking in the adjoining room.

This smaller room had once been used as a kind of ante-room, when the building was first converted into a private residence during the nineteenth century, before it became a museum. It no longer has an outside door, and we now use it to house less sizeable exhibitions. It was here I found Rachel Seaga, standing alone, considering one of the paintings on the wall, which I took to be a new addition. The room is round, which always makes for a strange effect when hanging pictures; it reminds me of an aquarium. All the paintings that were up so far were Joseph Wright's, procured from the city gallery – *A Philosopher Lecturing on the Orrery*, *The Alchymist*, *Landscape with a Rainbow*. And now here was another.

'Early Christmas present?'

Rachel turned.

'From London,' she said. She didn't smile.

'Another Joseph Wright?'

'Yes. *An Experiment on a Bird in the Air Pump*.'

We both looked up at it for some time, not really looking at it at all.

'Are you all right?' I said, finally.

'Fine.'

I pictured her on Saturday night, standing beneath the

Lombes bridge in her black dress. I thought of our kiss and the softness of her breast, now safely tucked away, unattainable beneath pink wool. How pathetic I'd been. She'd said, 'Don't worry about it, really.' She'd made coffee. It had gone three thirty a.m. when I left. Yet now it was Tuesday morning and here we were at work again. She could say something. I could say something. I didn't want her to think I was avoiding her.

I didn't say anything.

Rachel's short hair, dry today, had a tousled look. It twinkled in the light above us. 'Don't let's be like this,' she said, looking at her watch.

'All right.'

'Are you?'

'I'm fine.'

'Look, I have to go. I'm meeting someone for lunch.'

I wondered if it was a man, her 'friend' from Saturday. She met my eyes and this time she smiled. She took a last look at her new acquisition and turned to go, pausing to hand me a set of keys. 'Lock the door when you're done, will you?'

Then she was off for her lunch. I listened to her heels tap-tapping on the hall floor, until they faded away and the silence resumed.

When Sam did his stint at Alcoholics Anonymous, they told him that FINE meant 'fucked-up, insecure, neurotic and emotional.'

I stared at the new painting on the wall, as if at this moment it would reveal some profound meaning to me. The two children depicted certainly affected me. Sisters most likely, I thought. One turns away in horror from a white cockatoo trapped inside an evacuated glass dome, but the other child stares straight into the glass, where the natural philosopher – our scientist – is about to suffocate the bird. It was this girl who interested me: the look on her face, that frightened yet open expression, was similar to the look Anne-Marie had flung at me on Saturday night, the one I'd seen her wearing at her mother's funeral.

I checked out the other Joseph Wright paintings with which I was familiar from the city gallery. I was struck again by his incredible use of light, his ability to capture the wonder surrounding science in those first moments as it exploded into being. This new exhibition would chart the rise of the discipline to which I had so far dedicated my life, and yet, I thought, ironically I was about to deliver a lecture discussing the possibilities of its demise.

I closed and locked the door on Rachel's paintings with the peculiar sinking feeling of a man who has glimpsed what will succeed him. Next week the Space and Time exhibits – the glass cabinets and wall displays, the orrery, the papier-mâché atom with its circling electron, currently suspended like a freeze-framed beach ball – would be carefully dismantled.

The thought made me sad. I returned the keys Rachel had given me to June Hughes, then sat in one of the empty rows of chairs, eating my sandwiches and trying to collect my thoughts. Still one final debate to go, I consoled myself. That afternoon I had to bring these talks I'd organised to a satisfactory conclusion; forms were waiting to be filled, boxes to be ticked.

Eventually a few members of the public drifted in and

took seats. At two o'clock I mounted the raised platform and took my place at the lectern. I surveyed my small congregation – twenty or so members of the Women's Institute, the usual train fanatics (here, really, for the model railway, the Rolls-Royce engines), an enthusiastic student or two – most of whom looked wet, shaking out overcoats and umbrellas, letting me know I was the best alternative to the rain.

I took a deep breath. 'Ladies and gentlemen.' I leaned forward on the lectern, and tried to find a serious expression. 'What I want to talk to you about today is the End of Science.'

Granted, a somewhat dated phrase now, coined by the bigwig physicists, but still a dramatic phrase, with the ability always to make those nodding off in the back rows buck up and take notice. I could see already a murmur of excitement stretch across the faces of my meagre audience.

But then, just as I was about to make good on my opening gambit, just as I was about to launch into the lecture I had spent two weeks preparing, I became aware of a commotion bubbling at the back of the room. I heard June's familiar voice far away somewhere, as though under water. Then the double doors opened inwards, and there you were, Maguire, centre stage in your faded suit and brown cord jacket, flanked by two constables. Your comb-over tuft of grey-black hair had stuck to your forehead with the rain. In fact, compared to the constables, who were wearing their standard-issue weatherproof jackets, you looked soaked.

I faltered, noticing you. But only once. It was more your uniformed companions who unnerved me, as the three of you just stood there on the periphery of my vision, dripping patiently. How could I have known then that, in many ways, this was indeed the beginning of the end?

But the End of Science? How ridiculous such a concept would have seemed in Joseph Wright's time; or to the men who first erected the building we were in, back in 1717, when it was a silk mill; to George Sorocold, whose job was to fit together thousands of toothed wheels and bobbins, spindles and star wheels, so that in the end he had ninety-four thousand moving parts all motivated from a single source of water-power, until the paddles he had himself designed caught in his clothing and took him up and down and into the Derwent. Fortunately for him, the same paddle on its way back round scooped him out on to dry land again. A merciful river, then? An ungrateful river? A river not so happy to be exploited after all?

I think of a ring sinking slowly through its swirling sediment, driven this way and that way by the currents, until finally it lodges in a soft bed of clay, somewhere in that unreal underwater world. Carpe diem. It is here Martinez and I meet, our common, shifting, silty ground. For he, too, was on a quest for love.

Yet the more I think about him and Anne-Marie together, the more I can't stomach it. It's like trying to come to terms with some merciless equation. Like that day Anne-Marie and I argued about her painting and she stood in the middle of the room looking as if she didn't know me, or the incident over the wine bottle, when she stared at me as if she thought I might disappear at any moment.

Is this love then? A kind of paint-stripper? A thinning

down of someone until you can almost see through them, until you are holding a ghost in your arms?

I imagine my father somewhere across the Atlantic and my mother alone in hospital undergoing tests for throat cancer. I think of Henry and Gina at Arromanches-les-Bains, with the old pontoons strung out in the sea, and I think of Anne-Marie, twenty years old, hovering back and forth behind her easel, painting her phantom strokes.

Perhaps what we are looking for is any kind of company. Something to get us through. Who needs religion or ambition when you have found 'true love'? When you have found some rock on which to anchor a sense of self? Someone to revolve around, a bright light at the centre of existence. So that finally you can say, *My world starts from here: everything else finds its purpose here.*

My life without Anne-Marie?

'I'm sorry,' she said.

But who am I to forgive?

Whatever Anne-Marie may be she is not stupid. Perhaps she doesn't just want her life to be one long museum of me. Perhaps she doesn't love me. No one means nothing to anyone. She wanted him. Knelt on the bed, gripping the headboard. Back and forth they go. Standing in the doorway, I can almost reach out and touch his shoulder. But they've finished. She's sinking down slowly, turning her head and spotting me. The clock ticks indifferently. A hundred billion stars, a hundred thousand million, and I can't live without her. I won't. Because I love her. And that's part of the whole problem, isn't it? You can't stop someone loving someone. I can't stop my mother loving the ghost of my father. I can't stop Martinez loving Anne-

Marie, any more than I can stop myself loving her. Or her loving me. Will you ask her, Maguire? Don't you see?

Or are you only interested in the facts – the who, the where, the when and the how? Do you think that if you knew all these facts you would understand? That if we knew enough, we could predict – Are these what you were after, Maguire, are these all you wanted from me, as you stood waiting at the back of the hall? Weren't you listening to my little speech?

We cannot predict with a hundred per cent certainty a single thing in this awesome universe of ours. Physics is on a knife-edge. While advances in science this century have given us nuclear energy and the microelectronics revolution, the same theories that govern the transistors and circuits in our televisions and computers, as well as forming the basis of modern chemistry and biology, have also shaken theoretical physics to its foundations.

In 1926 the German physicist Werner Heisenberg discovered that the more accurately you try to measure the position of a single particle, the less accurately you can measure its speed (or velocity), and that the more accurately you try to measure the velocity of a particle the less accurately you can measure its position. This is known as the Uncertainty Principle, and, like the fixed speed of light, it is a fundamental property of the universe. It was this discovery that led Heisenberg, Paul Dirac and Erwin Schrödinger (our infamous cat lover) in the 1920s to reformulate classical mechanics into what they called quantum mechanics. In the science of quantum mechanics no definite result for an observation is predicted; instead, what's predicted is a number of different possible outcomes, and a likelihood for each one given. The Uncertainty Principle is immutable: at its most fundamental level the universe is governed by chance.

And isn't that, after all, Maguire, what our own insignificant lives on this tiny planet orbiting this tiny star (one of a hundred thousand million, in a galaxy that is one of a hundred thousand million others) are all about? Tearing around like the particles we're made of, colliding with one another, coming together, then rushing apart, here one moment, gone the next, appearing and disappearing in random flashes?

The Uncertainty Principle brings to the end the hope for an entirely deterministic universe. How can we possibly predict the past or future, how can we predict anything, when we can't even measure the present state of a single particle?

19

My first time in a police station. An analogue clock hung on one wall of the interview room like a white dinner plate. It read three twenty-five p.m. I'd been left alone for fifteen minutes. You'd said something about going to fetch some evidence, Maguire, and I wasn't sure, but I thought you were taking your time on purpose.

Do you realise how different such rooms are in France? When you get here, you should compare them with that box you had me in in Derby – the walls windowless, a dull metallic grey, that off-white lino. Can it really be only yesterday we sat there together?

I watched the hands on the clock as I waited. The single plastic table was the foldaway type I remembered sitting at for school lunches. There was nothing on it, except your coffee, which steamed slowly in a Styrofoam cup. It would be cold by the time you got back, and I was regretting not having one when asked, but I wasn't going to let you know that.

Eventually you opened the door and came in with an armful of paperwork. You had another officer with you, a younger woman, in police black and white. She wore her brunette hair clipped back in a bun and had on a little too much makeup.

'This is PC Helena Quinn,' you said. 'She'll be sitting in with us.'

'Am I under arrest?'

'No. We'd just like to ask you some questions. But you are entitled to have a lawyer present.'

You were studying me closely as you said this. You tried your coffee. It must have been stone cold, but your face didn't flinch. That's when I decided I liked you, Maguire, when I saw you drinking your cold coffee.

'Ask me anything you like,' I said.

'You understand this conversation is going to be recorded?'

'I do.'

Quinn produced the tape-recorder, placing it in the middle of the table and pressing a button. A red light blinked on. She also had a plastic bag in front of her, but I couldn't see what was in it.

I watched you read the necessaries into the recorder: 'Tuesday the fifth of October, three thirty-two p.m.' etc., smiling that wry smile of yours.

Then, suddenly, it was as if the three of us had launched ourselves into some terrible pastiche of all the crime thrillers I'd ever seen. It didn't seem real, Maguire, our time in that interview room. It was certainly not as it is on TV, and yet at the same time it was: I felt as though I already possessed a kind of pseudo-script for this. Like the classic suspect, I was rapidly deciding I would say as little as possible. Like the main lead DI, you were relishing your silence and leaning back in your plastic chair. That peculiar green Jackson Pollock–splattered tie was very you, Maguire, but the too white shirt, fresh out of the packet, was causing you problems. I could see the stiff collar was bothering you because you kept jamming your fingers into it and rolling your neck when you asked a question.

'We'll start with some simple ones,' you said. 'You are Prentis Stone, also known as Jack Stone. Is that correct?'

'Yes.'

'Why Jack Stone?' Quinn asked.

'My mother named me after Jack Prentis, a submarine commander.'

'She named you after a submarine commander?'

'Jack Prentis is the main character in Jane Adcock's *On Wings of Love*. Are you acquainted with romance, PC Quinn?'

'Okay. Enough.'

You have a clever way with situations, Maguire, your tone soft yet persuasive. I can see why you have such a knack for this job. You changed tack. 'Would it be fair to say that most people know you as Jack Stone?'

'My wife calls me Jack. I'm not fussy either way. You can call me what you like, Inspector.'

'Where is your wife?' Quinn asked.

I wondered if the two of you had scripted this. I glanced across at Quinn, hoping to discomfort her, but she held my eyes. Her own were a deep brown, like Anne-Marie's, but narrower and somehow less engaging, despite the eyeliner – and the uniform.

'She's in Paris,' I said.

'And when did your wife . . . Anne-Marie?'

'Yes.'

'When did Anne-Marie go to Paris?'

'On Sunday.'

'That's a shame. We'd very much like to talk to her.'

I noticed how her voice had a kind of inbuilt sarcasm. I got the feeling that, so far, Helena Quinn had had a bad day. You, on the other hand, Maguire, kept your tone patient, for now.

'What is Anne-Marie's business in Paris?' you asked.

'She's visiting her father.'

'I see. And when was this arranged?'

'The week before last.'

'The week before last?'

'Yes.'

'And she left on Sunday. The day before you and I met at the theatre?'

'Yes.'

'Where your wife works?'

'That's right.'

I thought of you standing in your cord jacket, trying to quote Shakespeare to impress Anita Felts. Another missing person, you were afraid.

Quinn consulted her notebook. 'Your address is thirty-five Peach Street?'

'It is.'

'And you have lived there how long?'

'About three years. Since we were married.'

'You and Anne-Marie, you have a good marriage?'

'We have our problems.'

'Such as?'

'Such as it's none of your business.'

'I'm afraid it is, Mr Stone,' you cut in. Then you altered your tone for the machine: 'Suspect is being shown photographs of the victim.'

You placed the photographs face up on the table. One showed the steel arm of a winch pulling a body out of the Derwent, the section of the river where it runs by the

Council House, just beyond the weir. Police were standing on the bank. One diver was in the water. The other photos showed the body of Sebastian Martinez, lying on a silver table. He was naked; his skin was bright white, blue in places, and shrunken. Blood had dried on his face and chest. In the photographs, it looked black.

'Do you know this man? Mr Stone?'

I felt the planet turn beneath me. 'No. I know of him. I don't know him.'

'But your wife did. Anne-Marie knew him, didn't she?'

My confusion fused with sudden concern. 'Who've you been talking to? Is Anne-Marie all right? Where is she?'

Slowly, you smiled. Had you expected this reaction? I could see Quinn, beside you, asking herself what it meant.

'As far as I'm aware, Mr Stone, your wife is in Paris. Like you said.' You chewed each word carefully. You were in your element now, Maguire, I could tell. This was the bit that did it for you: your voice had acquired a certain cavalier delivery.

'Can you tell us who he is, Mr Stone? He's quite dead by the way, in case you can't make it out. I know these photos can be a little hazy. His throat's been cut by something, you see? Mr Stone?'

I glanced at the photographs again. It didn't look like him. I wouldn't let it look like him. An image of Gina's body flashed in front of me, Anne-Marie lifting the sheet at the morgue.

'His name's Sebastian Martinez,' I said. 'He's an artist. He's famous. My wife was organising an exhibition of his at the theatre.'

'The one on Saturday night?'

'Yes.' I tried to control my voice. 'When did this happen?'

'We fished him out this morning. We're still searching the area. Didn't you see on your way in? We've taped off part of the riverbank.'

'No, I . . . I came in the front entrance. The way we left.'

'Unfortunate. For you, perhaps.'

I tried to think. Why hadn't June or Rachel said anything? One of them must have come in that way. Surely you hadn't got to them already, Maguire.

But you had questions of your own.

'Tell me about your wife's relationship with Martinez.'

'What do you mean?'

'Was it professional?'

'I don't know what you mean.'

'They weren't friends?'

I felt Quinn's eyes latch on to me. I attempted to calm myself, to speak slowly. 'As far as I know she met him for the first time three weeks ago, when they had a meeting about the exhibition.'

'I see.'

'You never met Sebastian Martinez?' Quinn asked.

'I met him once, the night of the exhibition.'

'You didn't meet him before then?'

'No.'

She put down her notebook, whatever that meant. 'Did you like Sebastian Martinez?'

'Like him?'

'Did you get on well with him at the exhibition?'

'I had nothing against him, if that's what you mean.'

'We have eleven witnesses who say you threw him down the stairs.'

'Only eleven? I'd have thought more would have come forward than that.'

She waited until I met her eye. I now knew where this was going.

'I didn't throw him down the stairs. I hit him. He fell down the stairs.'

Quinn almost smiled. I'd wondered what that would be like. But you appeared more interested in your notes, Maguire, than anything the constable and I were saying.

Eventually you looked up. 'Well?'

'Well what?' I was becoming irritated.

'Why did you hit him?'

'I was drunk.'

Now it was your turn to put your papers down. 'You hit most people when you're drunk?'

'No.'

'Then why Martinez?'

'I don't know. I was drunk. I wasn't thinking straight.'

Quinn glanced at you, but you kept your eyes fixed firmly on mine.

'According to witnesses, he called Anne-Marie's name and went up the stairs to meet you both. Is that right?'

'Yes.'

'I assume, then, he knew who you were. Knew you were Anne-Marie's husband.'

'I guess so.'

'So then what happened?'

'I hit him.'

But you weren't going to let it lie, Maguire.

'That's what our witnesses say, too. Martinez came up to you and you hit him.'

'Yes.'

'Bit strange. You'd never met him before. He comes up to you and you just hit him. Don't you think that's strange, Mr Stone?'

'I told you. I was drunk. Anne-Marie and I were having a disagreement. He just came up to us, you know, all smiles. I lost it and punched him.'

'A disagreement?'

'Yes, a disagreement, like you have when you're married. I'm sure you and your wife have your fair share, Inspector.'

'I think my wife and I have more than our fair share. But, then, I don't go assaulting complete strangers because of it, do I?'

'I don't know.'

The tension in the room had turned almost palpable. As if sensing this, as if some far-off training session suddenly kicked in, you paused, Maguire, took a deep breath and leaned back in your chair. Over to your colleague.

Quinn picked up her notebook. She seemed more comfortable when she had it in her hand. 'What happened after you hit him?' she said. 'Tell us, what happened next?'

'Nothing happened. Anne-Marie told me to get out. I walked out.'

'Where did you go?'

'I just walked. I was drunk.'

'Where did you walk?'

'By the river.'

She scrutinised me, letting the word 'river' hang in the air.

'And then what?'

'I went home.'

'Home?'

At last, something you found interesting, Maguire.

'You mean Peach Street? That's odd. That's very odd indeed. According to our information, you didn't return home at all that night.'

'Who says that? Anne-Marie?'

I realised I was sounding on the verge of panic. I could feel my blood being pumped around me, as if an executive decision had been made, somewhere in my body, that I might need it soon. I unfastened my cuffs, rolled up my right sleeve, and reminded myself to breathe.

'As far as I'm aware Anne-Marie's in Paris,' you repeated.

'Then why ask me?' My palms were sweating. I rolled up my left sleeve; it slid back down.

'Because I wanted to see if you knew where she was.'

You were observing me extremely carefully, Maguire. Your coffee-stained caterpillar moustache twitched as you spoke, and there was now a faint twinkle in your eye. You leafed through your notes again.

'We have a witness. Miss Anita Felts. Do you know Anita Felts?'

'She works at the theatre. She's one of the director's PAs.'

'That's right. Her and Anne-Marie, do they know each other well?'

'I don't know. I should think so. Yes, she talks about her. They've been out before.'

I rolled up my left sleeve again; this time it stayed.

We have had Anita over for dinner on numerous occasions, Maguire, and before she broke up with her husband, we had been to her place for New Year. But I wasn't going to offer you that; I didn't like the way this interview was going. Luckily, I seemed to get away with it.

'That's what we thought,' you said. 'Miss Felts says she rang Anne-Marie early on Sunday morning, and that Anne-Marie told her you hadn't been home all night.'

An immense hatred for Anita Felts swelled in me. She materialised before me in her strapless red dress; then in her purple paint-smeared dungarees, from when we'd met yesterday afternoon and you'd given her your card, Maguire. What had Anne-Marie told her? Did Anita ring you this morning, or did you contact her?

I noticed you were waiting for me to look up. I checked my anger and tried to keep my voice as calm as yours. 'I stayed at a friend's.'

'What friend's?'

'Sam Pike's.'

But you'd already pre-empted me. 'Ah, yes. Samuel Pike.' You checked your notes. 'Mr Pike says he found you – I like this – banging on his restaurant window at six a.m. on Sunday morning. Still drunk, were we?'

'Yes.'

'How long did you stay at Sam's?'

'I didn't. I went home later that morning.'

'Did you see Anne-Marie before she went to Paris?'

'She'd already gone.'

'I see. And Saturday night? Between the hours of ten o'clock on Saturday night, when you left the theatre, and six o'clock on Sunday when your friend found you, if you weren't at home, where were you, then?'

'Drunk, I guess. I don't know. Walking.'

I needed a drink then, Maguire. I needed to get out of that room.

'Now, come on, Mr Stone. Walking? For nine hours?'

'I don't remember.'

Perhaps this was the best line of defence: amnesia.

'Well, I suggest you'd better start remembering, Mr Stone.'

I'd had enough. I remember looking you straight in the eye, Maguire. 'What are you saying? Are you accusing me of something?'

'Do you wear a ring, Mr Stone?'

I could tell you'd been waiting for this.

'A wedding ring. You know, third finger of the left hand? Where that white mark is.'

'I lost it.'

'When did you lose it?'

'Yesterday.'

'Do you know where you lost it?'

I sighed, deciding to save you the long drawn-out trouble. 'I threw it into the river.'

Quinn shot you another of those looks, and almost smiled again. 'Why did you throw your wedding ring into the river, Mr Stone?' she said.

'I was upset. Like I told you, Anne-Marie and I had had an argument.'

'That was on Saturday.'

'Like I said, I was upset. I thought my marriage was over. I was angry. I threw it into the river.'

'At what time on Monday did you do this?'

'I don't know exactly. Later on in the afternoon. Five, five thirty. After I saw you at the theatre, Inspector.'

You put your fingers in your collar and turned your neck. I tried to decide if you were buying any of this. Then you gave in and undid your top button. 'The ring,' you said, 'describe it to me.'

'It's silver. Medium band. Quite plain.'

'And does it have anything written on it? A name, perhaps?'

'No.'

You nodded at Quinn, who produced her evidence bag on cue. I pictured the two of you rehearsing moments like these over and over.

Quinn took out the ring. 'Suspect is shown silver ring with inscription "carpe diem" on it,' she said, for the tape-recorder.

'Well, Mr Stone,' you said, 'do you recognise this ring?'

'No.'

'Do you know where it was found? It was found on the body of Sebastian Martinez. Do you have any idea how it might have got there?'

'No. I've never seen it before. Mine's much wider than that.'

'Oh, I know this isn't your ring, Mr Stone. It's too small. This is a woman's ring. Does your wife wear a wedding ring?'

'Of course. That's not it, Inspector.'

You met my gaze and held it.

'Pity we don't have your ring to compare it with, isn't it? Clear all this up once and for all.'

'I didn't think I would be needing it, Inspector. Otherwise I would have kept it, especially for you.'

'Quite. And yours is a plain band, like you said.'

'That's right.'

You pushed the photograph of Martinez's body back towards me.

'Well, *this* ring was found in Sebastian Martinez's jacket pocket. The coroner says he died between midnight and six on Sunday morning. If I were you, Mr Stone, I suggest you start telling us where you were during that time.'

My mind spun frantically, replaying the past few days. 'I was with someone,' I said at last. 'Not Sam.'

'Who?'

'A woman.'

'What was her name?'

I caught Quinn out of the corner of my eye, pen poised. 'I'd rather not say. My wife.'

'This is a murder inquiry, Mr Stone. A name, if you please.'

'Murder? I thought you said he drowned? That doesn't necessarily mean murder.'

'He did drown. But he also had a sharp instrument inserted into the base of his throat. It could have been while he was in the river. We're waiting for a full forensics report to show whether the wound was inflicted before or after water started collecting in his lungs. Meanwhile, yes, I'm treating this as a murder inquiry. So, her name, if you please.'

I sighed. 'Rachel Seaga. She's been working with me at the museum.'

'The lady with blonde hair? The one who was there just now, at the lecture?' You sounded surprised. 'And how long has this been going on?'

'It hasn't. Saturday night was a one-off, that's all.'

Quinn glared at me.

'And you were with her all night?' you continued.

'Yes.'

'I don't suppose you have her telephone number?'

'I don't.'

'She'll still be there now, at the museum, no doubt. We're going to need to talk to her. And your wife, she knows nothing of this?'

'I told you, it was a one-off.' I was beginning to think I needed that lawyer pretty desperately now. 'Am I under arrest?'

'No, Mr Stone, but I don't like people who lie to me.'

Well, that was something, I thought. Perhaps you didn't have so much to go on after all. 'Is it a crime to protect your wife?'

'We'll be in touch,' you said, ignoring my question. 'This is your mobile number?'

'Yes.' I rose to leave. 'Good luck, Inspector.'

'Yes, yes. I wish you luck too, Mr Stone. Oh, Mr Stone?'

Here it was.

'Yes?'

'Do sit down. Before you go, let me see if I've got this right for my notes.'

I resettled myself into my plastic chair again.

'Anne-Marie arranges the exhibition of Martinez's work. The exhibition on Saturday. You and Anne-Marie have a disagreement. You're drunk and hit Martinez. Then you leave, meet up with Rachel Seaga and stay the night. What time did you leave Rachel Seaga's house?'

'About a quarter to six. She had family coming round early. We thought it for the best.'

'So you go to Mr Pike's coffee shop.'

'Sam lives above it. Yes.'

'Where he finds you just after six.'

'Yes.'

'So then you go home late Sunday morning, by which time Anne-Marie had already left for Paris.'

'Yes.'

'Right. Then on Monday afternoon you go walking, and in a fit of depression you throw your wedding ring into the river.'

'No. In the afternoon I went to the theatre. I met you.'

'Ah, yes.'

I didn't like the new sarcasm in your voice, Maguire. You were sounding too much like Quinn.

'Then you went to the river.'

'Yes.'

'And then what? After you'd thrown your ring away, what did you do then?'

'Then, Inspector, I went home. I prepared my lecture for today. I slept.'

'I see. And what about this morning? Where were you this morning?'

'I'd booked this morning off, over a week ago. I went to visit my mother. She's in hospital.'

'That explains it. We were trying to locate you. What did you and Anne-Marie argue about?'

'What?'

'You said you had an argument at the theatre. Before you hit Martinez. What was the argument about?'

'I don't remember.'

'You don't remember? An argument that was so bad you slept with another woman, and threw your wedding ring into the river?'

'I was drunk. He was flirting with her.'

I figured I had to give you something, Maguire, otherwise, as you said, this was beginning to sound incredible.

'Martinez was flirting with your wife,' you said, rephrasing my statement for the tape-recorder.

'Yes.'

'Women are so fickle, aren't they? Like monkeys. Always one hand on the next branch.'

'Yes.'

You picked up a piece of notepaper, torn from a spiral pad. 'Apartment five, eleven avenue de Lorraine. This is the address Anne-Marie left with colleagues at the theatre for her father in Paris, with this telephone number.'

You slid the piece of paper over. Anne-Marie's handwriting was like a blow to the stomach. I glanced at it briefly. 'Yes, avenue de Lorraine, that's right. I'd have to check the phone number.'

'And she's there for how long?'

'She said a week. But you can phone her.'

'We will, Mr Stone. And we'll be talking to Miss Seaga, as I said.'

'I understand.'

'And you understand also that I must ask you, by law, not to leave the country.'

'Of course.'

I stood up a second time. 'Goodbye, Inspector.'

'Goodbye, Mr Stone.'

20

I leaned wholeheartedly on the wall outside the police station, frightened I might faint. It couldn't be possible Sebastian Martinez was dead. In fact, my brain was rapidly assuring me that none of this was happening. But already my heart was sprinting like a man on the run. Soon I was seeing Martinez everywhere – among the crowd of shoppers opposite, approaching along the pavement, climbing into a nearby car; face up and bloodless, like a black-and-white playing card, on the gleaming autopsy table. Dead. Deceased. No longer capable of drawing breath, ever. And now I knew how difficult that might feel, as I stood contemplating the fact of the man's extinction, with one hand hard against the red-brick wall, gasping to gulp down air. Dead. Deceased. 'You must want to kill him,' Sam had said. 'Yes.'

My hands were shaking when I paid for the taxi I had taken straight home. They shook when I fumbled with my key at the door, then blundered into the front room. Without pausing to remove my coat, I rummaged through the papers on the coffee-table until, at last, I found the folded printout of Anne-Marie's email. 'You have his number (there's a copy along with his Paris address by the phone).' I searched frantically and found it on a Post-it note. I dialled Henry's number. I needed to hear her voice. The police had already been talking to Sam, and I couldn't go to my mother with this, not in her condition, not in any condition: it would break her. I knew, despite everything that had happened, there was only Anne-Marie: only Anne-Marie could soothe and save me. But what *had* happened?

I got her father's answer-machine. I listened to Henry's suddenly familiar tones rising and falling in a foreign tongue. There followed a long bleep. But I couldn't bring myself to leave a message. What was I supposed to say? Now my legs were shaking. I sat down on the sofa, deliberately leaned forwards and bowed my head between them. I felt dizzy. If I was going to get through any of this I needed to get a grip on myself. I breathed deeply. I knew I had to get away, that somehow I had to buy myself some time. And I wanted my wife. I would go to her, that's what I would do. Like my mother said, I would go to her.

I rose carefully and went upstairs. In the bedroom, I selected clothes from the wardrobe, but it was as if my actions couldn't keep pace with my thoughts: my mind continued to race and reel, and soon I was tearing around the bedroom, flinging garments on to the bed, just as Anne-Marie had done the previous day. I pulled one of the suitcases down from on top of the wardrobe, then discarded it, opting instead for the rucksack I hadn't used in years. It still had luggage tags for Nantes looped round one of its straps. I filled it with some clothes and made up a small toilet bag – toothbrush, razor, shampoo; in the side pocket I secured my passport, phone, wallet and all of my credit cards. Then I carried it downstairs to the front room, where Martinez's flowers were wilting in Anne-Marie's blue vase. The dead Spaniard rose in black and white before me, his dripping body hauled up out of the Derwent. His body. How in the world, in my world, mine and Anne-Marie's, could he be dead? I sat down again. Closing my eyes, I saw him in his white dress shirt, falling away from me down the theatre steps; then his body curled up on the foyer floor, his hands to his face. The blood. What had I done? What on earth was going on?

I opened my eyes and concentrated on the pine bookcase, until I was breathing regularly again. Then I got up, plucked down a copy of Tennyson and scanned the other spines until I found *In Search of Arthur* by Henry Parrot. I packed these into my rucksack and went to the window to look out along the street, where the sun was setting. I needed a plan of action, something I could focus on. I thought about the airport, but decided it was too obvious. I wasn't sure how much power an inspector like you had, Maguire, or how much trouble I was in. Surely someone like Martinez, with his international standing, would have a number of enemies. Had you talked to his agent? I wasn't taking any chances. My paranoia, fuelled by television drama, had me leaping to all sorts of conclusions. I thought you might be having me tailed, though I could see no one outside; there was no car with two silhouetted figures in the front seats. Even so, I decided I would leave via the back door. And I wouldn't wait until morning. By then you might have too much information to go on.

I returned upstairs, to what, inadvertently, has come to be called the 'computer room.' Our terrace has two identical rooms upstairs: one is our bedroom, and the other I'd always hoped would one day be Anne-Marie's painting room. But that hadn't happened. She had never taken her equipment down from the attic, where she stored it, along with all her canvases, without a word, the weekend we moved in. The room has become a haven for all the things we don't know what to do with – boxes of old clothes, a broken exercise machine, my piles of science magazines, Anne-Marie's unfinished jigsaws. It is also where we keep our second-hand computer. I sat down before it, on the uncomfortable wooden chair. (When we'd first acquired the Internet, Anne-Marie had joked that the uncomfortable chair was necessary because we couldn't afford to be on line for long.) I logged on now and searched through Google for Eurostar, the quickest way to Paris, I surmised. It would mean getting to London and picking up a direct train from Waterloo, but I could make that journey tonight and stay over somewhere. It would be better than waiting here until morning and risk being picked up again. So I booked the 06.34 train to Paris Gare du Nord and arranged to pick up my tickets in London. I would travel there by rail, too. I wanted the car on the drive so it looked as if I was still in Derby. Even if it bought me a day it would be worth it.

I checked my email, but there was nothing from Anne-Marie, so I shut the computer down and drew the curtains. I went through to the bedroom and did the same there. Downstairs, waiting for it to get dark, I made myself some beans on toast. My mind was spiralling again, and I had constantly to keep my thoughts in check, reminding myself to be patient. And to eat.

By seven twenty it was pitch black outside. I left out of the back door, through our small concrete yard, with my bird-table and Anne-Marie's tiny herb garden, struggling at this time of year. I locked the back gate behind me and didn't turn out onto Peach Street but set off in the opposite direction, up the alley, bunking the wall at the far end and emerging quietly onto the pavement in front of the Methodist chapel. For a moment the manoeuvre made me feel like a teenager. Then I remembered. The truth rushed back and almost scuttled me, there on the already windy London Road, where once again my brain crashed through its processes, out along the highways and down the blind alleys of memory. And I recalled everything. Except those hours my conscience most required.

Derby railway station was relatively empty although, as usual, a number of people were waiting for the London train. But no police, I assured myself, no personnel approaching me, packing my picture. Still, I was relieved when the eight o'clock train arrived on time and I was able to board and settle into my window-seat for the journey south, where, a little more relaxed, I drank black coffee from the buffet car, going over all that had happened in the last three weeks. Factories and scrapyards rushed by – large angular shapes and flashes of metal – then trees and open fields. Once out in the country I could see more stars in the sky. I considered whether I should call June in the morning and make up some reason why I wouldn't be at work. I wondered whether you had talked to Rachel yet, Maguire. You might have even been on your way after me, I thought, but consoled myself that I'd be out of the country soon. Anyway, June wasn't going to call the police if I simply didn't show up for work. Unless you'd asked her to.

Maybe I should have risked the airport. I began to feel

vulnerable on the train. At every stop I thought the doors were going to open, and there you'd be, Maguire, stepping on. At each station I scanned the passengers through the window, watching their faces slip away.

At the museum, as part of the Space and Time exhibition, there's a board with a diagram explaining Einstein's relativity theory; it has a cartoon picture of a boy at a station and a girl on a train. It's the old 'if you throw a tennis ball at 50 m.p.h. on a train travelling at 50 m.p.h.' story, explaining that all time is relative: the ball will be seen as travelling at a different speed by the boy standing at the station than by the girl throwing the ball on the train, but that if you make the speed the same for both (i.e., the speed of light, which is fixed) then it is time and space that have to vary.

As the train jolted and shuddered out of Loughborough, that was what I was thinking about, the speed of light, the one constant in the universe. That was what I longed for. I wanted something to cling to, something absolute and fixed in my world, which abruptly appeared at all points to be unravelling. How must it have felt to be a physicist in the 1920s, to have to deal, after a lifetime of classical physics, with the impact of quantum mechanics, suddenly to have Heisenberg's thorn of doubt and unpredictability lodged permanently in the side of science and the universe?

The more our technology increased, the faster we collided particles and the further our telescopes saw, the more the uncertainty rang true.

According to general relativity, the gravitational field of a body, such as a star, causes the paths of light rays in space-time to bend round it. This was helping. I forced myself to think the theory through. A star is formed when a large amount of hydrogen gas begins to collapse in on itself due to gravitational attraction, causing the hydrogen atoms to collide ever faster and more frequently, until at last the gas becomes so hot from these collisions that instead of bouncing off one another the atoms fuse to form helium. This reaction is like a hydrogen bomb explosion; the heat released from it is what makes the star shine, and the increased pressure from this extra heat is what balances the gravitational attraction. Eventually, however, the hydrogen will run out and the star will no longer be able to balance itself against its own gravity. When this happens, it will start to contract again. If the star's mass is less than a certain amount – what is known as the Chandrasekhar limit (after the Indian graduate Subrahmanyan Chandrasekhar who calculated it) – then it will eventually stop contracting and settle down to a final state as either a white dwarf or a neutron star. However, if the star's mass is greater than the Chandrasekhar limit, the star will continue to contract, the gravitational field will get stronger and stronger, the light cones bending inwards even more, making it difficult for even light to escape. As nothing can travel faster than light, nothing can escape: everything is dragged back into the gravitational field of what has now become a black hole – a point of infinite mass and density contained within a region of space – an example of what mathematicians call a true singularity. At this point the curvature of space-time is infinite, so here all our theories of science (including the theory of general relativity itself), which are based on a space-time that is smooth and almost flat, break down.

That's how I felt, Maguire, as I fled the Midlands for France, as if I could actually feel the curvature of space-time bending further and further back on itself towards a point where everything at once would come to a head. At any moment, I thought, things were just going to stop: the train would scream to a halt on the tracks, then there would be shouts, doors opening and police.

But there weren't. Passing through Bedford, it began to rain. We seemed to be going faster and I could no longer see what was outside because of the wall of water beating the window.

It was almost ten o'clock when I emerged from St Pancras station onto Euston Road. I remembered it was somewhere along here that I first met Gina, when she took Anne-Marie and me to Bellini's. I wondered where Castle Road was, where Henry had grown up and gone to school. And suddenly I found myself having to fall back on the laws of probability from my own schooldays to fight off a strange sense of concurrence – my grandmother's influence. It was a big city, I reminded myself; Bellini's was eight years ago now, and a lot further up Euston Road. This was the King's Cross end.

I wove my way between the crawling traffic, and after only a five-minute walk I found myself a room at a Travel Light for seventy pounds. It was literally just a room with a bed and a table with a kettle, a cup and some coffee sachets (as bare and simple as this room, Maguire, but without the history). No doubt they were used to people turning up for one night, paying cash. I noticed later, going out for a takeaway, that by night King's Cross remained as commercial as ever, continuing to flaunt its own forms of attraction. That night, Martinez and Anne-Marie writhed and groaned above me as, exhausted, I drifted to sleep in my single bed. I woke to see Martinez's dead body stretched out on the sheet beside me. Then woke again.

By morning King's Cross had undergone a transformation. Although too early for the main tube rush, a few fresh-suited men and women, sporting briefcases, umbrellas and newspapers, trickled down Euston Road into the Underground. I joined them, unapologetic with my pack, and took the Northern Line south to Waterloo, where my tickets, as promised, were waiting for me at the international terminal. The departure board showed two trains: the 06.29 to Brussels and the 06.34 to Paris. I took the escalator down to the concourse where a young woman from Eurostar took my ticket and put it into the automatic gate.

Then she asked for my passport.

A billow of adrenaline folded through me. I'd half expected this, but secretly hoped it wouldn't be necessary. She glanced, first at the photograph, then up at my face, and met my eyes. I held my breath.

'Have a pleasant journey, sir,' she said, in a French accent. She smiled.

'I will.' I breathed, then cleared my throat. 'Thank you.'

With thirty minutes to go, I ate breakfast at a cafe in the departure lounge and bought myself five hundred euros at the bureau de change. I knew you'd probably be talking to Rachel that morning. It was just as well I'd be in France soon, I reasoned, returning to the departure board, where the 06.34 was now shown as 'boarding.'

The terminal had become busy. Through its glass walls,

outside, a faint rainbow arched then dissolved as I queued at the gate for platform twenty-four, where all eighteen coaches of my train stood waiting.

My seat was forward-facing, thankfully. An announcement was made, in English, then in French, but it wasn't until we were on our way – Brixton, Herne Hill, Bromley South – that I began to relax. I took out Henry's *In Search of Arthur*, based, according to the blurb, on French legends surrounding a forest in Brittany. Which reminded me of something Anne-Marie had once said, though I couldn't remember what. Had she and I been there on our trip that first summer? I didn't think so. For the first time, the thought of seeing my wife terrified me. What would she think of me? Consider me capable of? What if she already knew?

An hour later we passed Westenhanger, the last station before the Channel Tunnel. Above us, overhead wires appeared, flanked by danger signs warning of the 25,000 volts careering through them. Another announcement, again in English, then French: we should advance our watches by an hour. The train was increasing speed, faster and faster, until finally we flashed into the tunnel. I felt like an atom in a particle accelerator. Outside the window: darkness, broken only by the glare of fluorescent lamps every few seconds, which flared from the cross-passage doors that connected to the service tunnel running alongside us. The driver announced that in four seconds we had attained a steady speed of 98 m.p.h. Soon I could see a large waterpipe on the tunnel wall. We were under the sea, which seemed itself to cast an eerie silence: the wheels were making little more than a swishing noise on the tracks. Beyond the windowpane, in the dark, Martinez and Anne-Marie flailed in one another's arms, then sank slowly away from me. I closed my eyes. I felt as if I was passing through an event horizon and entering the throat of a black hole, where all our certainties break down, where all our laws become null and void.

21

Emerging from our passage beneath the ocean was like the conscious continuation of a dream. As we were afforded our first views of France, the train's speed increased even further, until finally our driver, now adhering to the metric system, announced we had reached a maximum speed of 300 k.p.h. That was 186 m.p.h., I worked out. Light travels at 186,000 miles per second. Once more I had to resist the pull of some strange synchronicity at work. At Arras we came up alongside a motorway. We were travelling twice as fast as the cars; the overhead bridges were mere flashes, and the lorries and tankers appeared almost stationary.

As I'm sure you're aware in your line of work, Maguire, the human mind is a curious thing, able when necessary to take emotion – panic, fear, confusion – and compress it into cool, calculated action. The train penetrated the world like a bullet fired through water: everything around me seemed to struggle in a slow and liquid motion. Gradually, I began to feel more focused than I had been in days. And I knew what I had to do. I had to get to Anne-Marie before you rang, Maguire, before she heard of her lover's demise, his *murder* (I could hardly bring myself to think the word) from some official, and of her missing husband, presumed on the run and wanted for questioning. I didn't know how, ultimately, my wife would take Martinez's death, but I knew news of it had to come from me: if there was to be any way forward for us, she had to hear confession from me. But confession to what?

The train's speed decreased for the approach into Paris, where it came to a stop, on time, at ten twenty-three. Coming out of the Gare du Nord onto rue de Dunkerque was like stepping back onto the kerb of the world. I walked a little way along the street, unused to the weight of my pack, and flagged down a taxi. I presented the driver with the note containing Henry's address, the one Anne-Marie had left so diligently by the phone.

Considering my wife is half French, my French is unforgivable. Anne-Marie's never been too concerned about my learning. 'If you want to learn a foreign language,' she'd say, 'why don't we learn one together? Italian or Spanish. I'd love to speak Spanish.'

I had no idea where we were going. One moment we were driving south along the rue du Faubourg St-Denis and the next we had joined the boulevard Strasbourg, where we quickly became pinned down in heavy traffic. After a while we managed to turn off and soon we were ducking and diving through small streets with no names, alleys with high walls and few windows. It must have been raining earlier, for the cobbles were wet. Then we were back on one of the main boulevards, the buildings bigger now and more tourist-like, safe public places sweeping into view – squares with statues, parks. There were tourist signs for the Seine, with small symbols for Notre Dame and the Tour Eiffel. Eventually we turned onto the avenue de Lorraine.

I was almost with her now, and still I could remember nothing of those early hours of Sunday morning, only, faintly, a sense of scenery passing and a heaviness aching in my feet, as though I'd been walking. I knew from my earlier forages into biology, Maguire, all those years ago, before I settled on physics as my raison d'être, that one of the many skills of the human brain is to bury painful memories; there are neurons working ceaselessly, suppressing anything deemed too painful for the body to relive – any memory too much for our fragile beings to bear or cope with. Was that what my mind thought it was doing – protecting me? If only it could understand my need to know. Why could I not recall those hours, and yet recall, as I walked once more down Henry's street, its features so distinctly after eight years?

For all along the avenue de Lorraine, déjà vu lay waiting for me, lurking between its large grey-bricked houses, withdrawing suddenly from second-floor wrought-iron balconies. And at once I was twenty-one again, here with Anne-Marie in the first freefalls of love. So little appeared to have changed.

I spotted Henry's building from half the street away. When I reached it, number eleven, I pushed open the black iron gate and climbed the front steps to the green-painted door. That had changed: I was sure it was black before. I pressed the buzzer for apartment five.

I had no idea what I would say to her. What if she appeared at the door now and spoke my name in a way I found unfamiliar? Perhaps I should have tried phoning her again. I pressed the buzzer a second time, uncertain whether I'd be relieved or annoyed if no one was in.

'Oui, qui c'est?' The man's booming voice caused the intercom to crackle.

'Henry, it's Jack.'

Nothing.

'I'm here to see Anne-Marie.'

'C'est la police?'

'What?'

'You're not with the police?' He relented into English. He knew who I was now all right.

'No. Why? Where's Anne-Marie?'

'You'd better come up.'

The door clicked open.

I took the lift, suddenly familiar, to the fifth floor. The game was up, I thought. She knows. Did she fancy her husband a murderer? I was sweating. I was out of breath.

I realised I had never seen Henry himself here. He answered the door in corduroys and a pale blue shirt. He wore sandals. A cigarette burned in his right hand. His hair was now all grey, but he'd allowed it to grow a little so that it fell in two waves. His eyes were still that steady blue. They swivelled and sharpened on me. His face seemed to draw back into itself, and for a moment he looked frightened, as though he was recalling my existence from somewhere far away, but couldn't quite place it. Then he understood, and he drew himself up a second time with a look, partly of the old contempt, partly of nervousness, and also with a brief expression of what might have been relief. But I couldn't believe that.

He led me into the living area, through the short tiled hallway I recognised from before, although now a thin shelf obscured the top of the radiator, which had some ornaments and figurines on it.

'Michelle's out taking the dogs for a walk,' he said matter-of-factly.

I struggled to keep up with my own heartbeat. Not much

had changed in Henry's apartment: the same open-plan living room and dining area, with the giant Burne-Jones print framed above the fireplace.

He went over to the window and opened the curtains to let in more light. There was a model of a ship on the window-sill. Particles of dust stirred in the air, and I watched Henry's eyes fix on them, as if he was daring them to land on the clean carpet.

She wasn't here.

'Where's Anne-Marie? Has she been here?'

My father-in-law turned round to face me. 'Yes, Jack, she has.'

When he spoke, it was the English imbued in him by his mother, widow and primary-school teacher. Yet hearing him say 'Jack,' there was a hint of an accent that betrayed his years in Paris, pronouncing my name softly, the way the French pronounce J like the sound of the sea.

It occurred to me that Henry Parrot and I were more alike than perhaps I cared to admit: both brought up by our mothers, the absence of a father. When he looked at me now, his eyes were kinder: they seemed to be eyes that were lost or asking something of me.

'A policeman telephoned this morning,' he said, 'The English police, I mean. A detective inspector.'

'Maguire.'

'Apparently Anne-Marie left my number with colleagues at the theatre, in case they needed to get hold of her. It was the last thing I was expecting, you understand.'

'What did he ask you?'

'He wanted to talk to Anne-Marie. Well, she wasn't here. She barely stayed 'til lunchtime yesterday. Anne-Marie and

I, you see, our relationship . . . you have to understand, it's not for me to question. But I knew something was wrong. So I said she was staying with me like we'd planned, but that she'd gone out for the day. Visiting friends, I said.'

'And what did Maguire say?'

'That someone Anne-Marie was working with had died. They wanted to confirm her whereabouts. He also wanted to know if I'd heard from you. Well, I hadn't. I said I'd tell her he'd called, and that he was welcome to ring back later. He said the man who had died was Sebastian Martinez. I take it that's not *the* Sebastian Martinez, the Spanish artist?'

'It is.'

Henry stared at me. 'Is she in trouble?'

'She might be.'

But I didn't share his concern, not then; what I felt was relief seeping through every pore of me like a balm. You hadn't reached her after all, Maguire. There was still time, if indeed there was time, for her to hear everything from me. I breathed more freely and felt my palms grow cold as the sweat evaporated into Henry's centrally heated air. Meeting his gaze, I tried to make my own eyes as soft as his. He looked relieved and nodded his consent to whatever pact was passing between us. He stubbed out his cigarette in the ashtray on the coffee-table. He didn't ask me what kind of trouble. His hand was trembling.

'Would you like a cup of coffee?' he asked.

I decided it was pointless to persist for the moment, so I smiled back at my father-in-law, having told him his only daughter might be in trouble, and accepted his offer of coffee. The routine of making it would give him something to focus on, something to stabilise him while we talked.

He left the room. Presently I heard him in the kitchen – the clink of the best china, the filling of the kettle. How quiet it must be living here, I thought, living on your own. Whatever slim hope I might have been harbouring, the silence assured me now that Anne-Marie was definitely not in the house. It was only then that the loneliness of Henry's life became apparent to me. In a way Anne-Marie, I thought, was all he had left.

There were now two smaller paintings on the wall opposite the fireplace. One was of a sweeping grey-glass lake with the turrets of a palace just visible below the water's surface. The other was of a forest that became denser and denser towards the centre of the picture. It reminded me of the jigsaw Anne-Marie had above the fireplace at home. I walked over to look at the Burne-Jones again. *The Last Sleep of Arthur.* Propped on the mantelpiece below it there was a postcard print of another painting. In this picture Arthur is only present as a statue on his own tomb, over which Lancelot leans to steal a kiss from the grieving Guinevere, who is putting her hand to his lips, probably to stop him, but it isn't certain.

'Dante Gabriel Rossetti,' Henry said, 'completed some time between 1855 and 1860.' He was carrying a silver tray that had two china coffee cups on it, a sugar bowl, a milk jug and a small cafetière. 'Before his wife's suicide.' He placed the tray on the highly polished coffee-table, and came and stood beside me. 'It was William Morris's wife, Jane Burden, who posed for it, which was fitting, since at the time Rossetti was having an affair with her.'

How acutely Henry's words cut home. I turned to him, but he had moved to sit down. We sat opposite each other, with the coffee-table between us.

'Love. Jealousy. Betrayal. The oldest story there is,' he said, indicating the postcard and the painting. 'Anne-Marie grew up on that stuff.' He paused. 'I brought her up on it.'

Did he know?

'Sucre?'

I shook my head. Henry sat back and drank. I noticed the cups we were using were Crown Derby. The morning sun struggled in. It looked like it might rain again. 'Anne-Marie was seeing Martinez,' I confessed.

Carefully, my father-in-law put his cup down on the saucer: he hadn't known.

'Seeing?'

'Fucking. I don't know, Henry, whatever you call it.'

'I'm sorry, Jack.'

I put up my hand. I wished I hadn't said anything. 'That's why the police want to talk to her . . . to us,' I explained.

I watched some emotion from the past wash over Henry's face. He looked like he was trying to work something out, a difficult sum.

'Don't be too hard on her,' he said at last, then put up his own hand. 'I know, I know. I'm her father.'

He gazed down at the coffee things as though they were now only so much strewn wreckage. 'Do you want a drink, Jack?'

He poured two glasses of bourbon from the cabinet by the window.

'Last July. The last time she was here, our annual father-daughter meeting,' he tried to smile, but couldn't quite convince himself, 'do you know what she was telling me, Jack?'

'What was she telling you?'

He handed me my drink. 'How she was utterly in love with you. How she had never loved anyone in the same way before. "Je l'aime, Papa," she kept saying, "Je l'aime."'

Henry remained standing. He paced slowly by the fireplace. 'What I'm trying to say is, this business with her now . . .'

But he couldn't finish that.

'Are *you* telling me I should have just forgiven and forgotten, Henry?'

My father in law turned and looked at me. It struck me that I had perhaps not referred to his past with Gina before. 'You are an astute man, Jack,' he said, and smiled. 'Her name was Denise. No doubt Anne-Marie has told you.'

'She hadn't mentioned anyone in particular.'

Henry looked relieved. I had guessed a long time ago that he had been unfaithful to Gina; Anne-Marie had said as much. But I was sick of it all – him, Anne-Marie, me (Rachel's kiss still reigned wet and warm in my mind). Couldn't any of us control ourselves? I took a swig of Henry's bourbon. 'That's why you and Gina got divorced,' I said.

Henry looked away.

'Something else, then?'

He didn't answer. He got up and went to refill his glass. As I looked at him standing by the window (he is fifty-eight), I thought it would be easy to dismiss Henry Parrot as just another divorcé approaching retirement. But this morning, there was something else, something about him, as he stood in his apartment, looking out over the avenue de Lorraine, drinking his bourbon. It was clear that he had chosen his life, not without costs but he had chosen it none the less, and that now here was a man who was no longer content with his choice.

I looked around his living room, at the painting above the mantelpiece, his Turkish rug and maroon-leather furniture. From what I'd gathered from Anne-Marie, the year her parents filed for divorce, when they were all still living in the capital, she had begun to cause havoc at her school in Arcueil. It was that summer that Gina made the decision to move them to England.

My gaze fell suddenly upon a framed picture of my wife, which stood on a small table at the end of the sofa. It shocked me to have my thoughts materialise in front of me, especially as in this picture it was the older Anne-Marie, just after we were married, still under a year since her mother's death, no longer the rebellious schoolgirl, or the studious undergraduate I had met drunk at a party on her twentieth birthday.

'They're hers,' Henry said.

Slowly I became aware of the room again, the empty glass in my hand.

'Anne-Marie. You were thinking of Anne-Marie. Those are her paintings, behind you.'

Still sitting, I turned around and looked up at the two pictures I had glanced at earlier – the lake and the forest.

'I took them out a year or so after Gina died,' Henry said. He walked around the sofa and stood in front of them.

'That's Brocéliande forest. I used to take Anne-Marie

there when she was a girl and I was researching my first book. We used to go at the weekends mostly, and would sometimes stay at a guesthouse there. Or if we were only going for the day, we'd get up early, make up flasks and sandwiches, and drive out of Paris when it was still dark. Anne-Marie used to like that.'

He glanced at me to gauge what effect his story was having. I could see he knew that I was trying to connect his words about the young Anne-Marie with the woman I knew as my wife.

'We played such games,' he said. 'Gina came, too, in the beginning. Then things changed. If I was researching my book she'd say it was far better if I went on my own. But she never stopped Anne-Marie going with me. Anne-Marie liked the make-believe of it all. Brocéliande's quite a journey from Paris. Sometimes we'd continue to the coast. Anne-Marie loved the sea.'

'She still does.'

Henry looked lost for a moment. My words had brought him back to the room again, the presence of his son-in-law. 'I remember standing on the beach with her so distinctly,' he said. 'It's funny how some things you can't recall at all, but others you remember so precisely. I bet you scientists have a theory about that. I remember standing with her, looking out at the Atlantic. She must have been seven or eight. It was in the days of our trips to Brocéliande. She never grew tired of the stories I'd tell her. But then she got older, Gina started taking her into town. She'd take her one place and I another. With Anne-Marie, it was like we were bargaining for time with her, trying to instil ourselves in her. It was as if Gina and I had nothing for us any more, nothing to say to one another. I met her on a beach, you know. She had my sandals. When I met her—' He broke off, avoiding my gaze, and stared at the painting above the mantelpiece. I wondered how many people had stared at that painting, and for what reasons. I was discovering things about Anne-Marie, as if she was one of her own jigsaws: pieces of her had been missing all along, and now I was finding them, one by one.

Outside the window, clouds hung heavy; the sky was turning a brilliant grey. Winter was coming, and soon the trees would be stripping themselves bare. It was almost midday.

'What's at Brocéliande?' I asked.

Henry's breath caught. Before he looked up, I saw his reflection in the silver tray on the coffee-table. 'Arthur is,' he said. *Arthur*. He let the word settle slowly on the objects in the room. 'Arthur's at Brocéliande. My books are there.' His tone became detached and textbook-like: 'Brocéliande is supposedly an enchanted forest. It's not far from Mauron and St Meen. Rennes is the nearest city. The rock there is six million years old. Red slate. Granite. Quartz. They say the earth is wounded from what the French call the times of the Cyclops and the fire of the earth.'

He smiled. 'More myth-making.' Then his forehead furrowed, as if he was pushing aside a memory. 'Brocéliande is the heart of the Arthurian myth in France. In the French myths it's the forest where Viviane trapped Merlin, where he built her the invisible palace, where the Lady of the Lake gave Arthur Excalibur and where Lancelot was born. It is also the centre of French Grail history.'

My father-in-law was dragging this out of the great closet

of his life. For him it was all painfully familiar. 'None of this is really of any consequence,' he said deliberately.

'What you mean is that, to a young girl, it was a whole other world.'

'Exactly.' He paused. 'When I published my book, it was as if an era in our lives had ended.'

I turned back to Anne-Marie's paintings and gazed into the depths of her forest. Suddenly I wanted her to be there with me. I wanted to see her. I wanted to put my hand on her face. What had I done? Would she ever let me touch her cheek again? I had to know. I needed her now more than ever.

Henry misinterpreted my look. 'They're very old of course,' he said, 'She must only have been twelve or thirteen when she did them. They were some of her first paintings.' He stared at the picture of the lake. 'They are the only ones I have,' he added sadly. 'I built her an easel once, when she was a girl. It had a magpie on it.'

He turned to me. 'I don't suppose she's started painting again?'

'No.'

He took my glass from me and returned to the cabinet, but I shook my head when he raised the bottle. He looked at his own glass and changed his mind, then returned to the sofa and lit a cigarette. 'I used to have those paintings in my room,' he said, 'I only moved them in here this year. I think it shocked Anne-Marie on Sunday that I had them up at all.'

I met his eyes. They weren't such a piercing blue as I had first thought, yet there was still a brightness about them. I was running out of time. 'Henry, where is Anne-Marie?'

His hand with the cigarette began to shake again. His smoking was reminding me of my mother, but I couldn't think about her now. I forced myself to concentrate on my father-in-law who, once more, was on his feet. 'Anne-Marie hasn't been here since yesterday afternoon,' he said. 'I'm not certain where she is. She said she'd telephone, but she hasn't.'

'She didn't say anything?'

'She said . . . some things. She wasn't specific. Tell me, Jack, is she in danger?'

'She might be.'

'This business, does it have something to do with her past?'

'No. What do you mean?'

'But it's serious?'

'Yes.'

Henry's features tensed. 'The police don't think she knows anything about Sebastian Martinez's death, do they?'

I felt my blood first stir, then surge. I tried to keep my voice from breaking. 'They want to talk to her. He was murdered, you see.'

'Murdered?'

'Yes. Henry, listen to me. It's important that I see her. Did she give you any idea of where she might be going? Didn't she say anything?'

Henry was pacing furiously now. He looked ridiculous, as if he was trying to play some part in a black-and-white film. He was frightened. 'She kept talking about when she was younger. She kept asking these questions. Such questions.'

He sat down quickly. 'It was so . . . strange. She looked

terrible. She wouldn't sit down the whole time, kept walking around and asking me things. About Gina and me. Things I've not talked about for years.'

'The divorce?'

He nodded.

I didn't say anything.

'Sometimes people just don't know how to express their love,' he said. 'They clam up somehow. I was so young when I met Gina. We both were. I did love her then, Jack. I know the first moment I loved her. We were in this restaurant and I was rabbiting on about this thesis I was writing – King Arthur and everything – I was trying to impress her by reciting some Tennyson, and then she just reached forward and took my hand. I'd been telling her about my father – he died in the war, you see, that's why I'd gone to Normandy in the first place – and she said that just like Arthur maybe my father, too, was safe, sleeping on some island somewhere. I knew I'd never forget it. She was so pretty, Jack. It was her idea, you know, to turn all that stuff I was working on into a proper book. When we were married, even when we had Anne-Marie, we were always trekking all over the place to research something or other. It was fun at first. Until she began to think I cared more about the figures in books than I did about her. More about Denise.'

'Is this what you told Anne-Marie?'

'She asked me why we were divorced. If it was her fault.'

'But she knew about the affair?'

'Oh, yes. But she wanted details. She wanted to know . . .'

'Why you were unfaithful.'

He stubbed his cigarette out.

'Denise worked for the publisher who acquired my book,' he said.

'And Gina didn't forgive you.'

'When she died—' But he broke off. His voice had abandoned him. He looked at me, and a wave of something that might have been fear or loneliness or regret folded over his face. 'I still loved her,' he managed to say at last, 'It wasn't serious between Denise and me. It didn't last.' He looked directly at me. 'You love Anne-Marie, don't you?'

Now it was my hand that started to shake.

'Paimpont,' Henry said, 'I think she's in Paimpont.'

'Paimpont?'

'Brocéliande forest. She talked about it yesterday. There was a part of it she used to like when she was a child, a little way on from Merlin's tomb, where the trees form a kind of tunnel . . .' My father-in-law paused again. When, at last, he met my eyes, there seemed to be tears in his own.

'How long will it take to get there?' I asked.

He straightened on the sofa. 'Five, six hours. But only if you drive.' He stood up. 'You'll take my car.'

When he left the room, I looked at my watch. It was twelve thirty.

Henry returned with a set of car keys, a mobile phone and a road atlas. He cleared the coffee things to one side of the table and opened the atlas. 'We're here. You must take the E50 out of Paris. Paimpont is here, see? You can stay on the main roads most of the way, round Chartres, Le Mans and Laval, until you reach Rennes. Brocéliande is about two miles out from Paimpont. You can get directions in the town. The guesthouse we used to stay at was called Relais de Brocéliande. I think it's a hotel now. I'd come with you, only . . .'

'It's best I go alone.'

Henry seemed relieved. He looked a little drunk, and old suddenly. I wondered how long it had been since he was in Brittany, strayed from the safety of the avenue de Lorraine, even.

'You have a phone?' he asked.

Concern for his daughter was visible now all over his face. I noticed how thin his cheekbones had become. 'It won't work here,' I said.

'Take mine.' He handed me the mobile and wrote his home number on a scrap of newspaper. 'Ring me. You promise?'

'I promise.'

Outside, the street was empty. I backed Henry's Mazda out of the communal garage, while he directed me. It had begun to rain. I wound the window down, kept the engine running.

My father-in-law stood beside the car, unsure of what to say. I put my hand through the open window and grasped his. 'Thank you, Henry. I'll call you, I promise, as soon as I find her.'

'She loves you,' he said. Then he pulled himself up. 'Good luck.' He glanced back at the house. As we left his apartment, we had heard the telephone. He'd left it ringing.

'Will there be others?' he asked now.

'There might be.'

Something in his face altered. 'And they will be police, won't they?'

'Yes. They will.'

I nudged the car out into the street. Soon, in the rear-view mirror, Henry became a silhouetted figure in the morning drizzle. The smaller he became, the larger my own fears loomed and multiplied again. As I drove along the E50, out of Paris and into the rain, it wasn't my father-in-law I was thinking of but Sebastian Martinez tumbling away from me down into the foyer. I was thinking of the body of Sebastian Martinez suspended in mid-air from a line on the end of a winch, his skin bright white, his clothes heavy like sacks dripping, like a fish on a hook.

22

Where are you, Anne-Marie?

By the time I reached Rennes my nerve was failing me. Driving drained my concentration. I'd never got used to travelling on the right-hand side of the road and it had been over a year since I'd had to. Signposts were no problem, the turns I could manage: it was the roundabouts I had to think about. More than that it was the motorways: moving to the left to overtake seemed the most illogical thing in the world. It had also been a while since I'd driven such a distance. My mind kept alternating from one fixation to another – Anne-Marie, Martinez, my mother's convalescence – and I was aware of how tired I was. Henry's bourbon hadn't helped. Once more, images of Martinez stretched out in the autopsy room made me think of Gina, and now, as the Tarmac sped towards me, I pictured her driving home that night from her party, pulling out to overtake, then her head-on collision. I kept seeing a mangled green Laguna absorbed for ever by a removal lorry on the A52.

I pulled into a service station and drank two espressos. It was a quarter past four. Paimpont wasn't far now. Sitting by the window, with the atlas Henry had given me open on the table, I worked out that I had to leave the motorway at the next junction.

I walked back across the car park. The sun shone

brightly, showing little sign of more rain. I had just less than three hours before it got dark, if I was lucky.

Rennes came and went quickly, below me at first as I turned off the motorway, then behind me in the mirror as I headed along the N24. I felt like I was entering the back of beyond; there was nothing but bare fields of corn, a few white houses, one with balloons in the window, the odd farm building. I was scared I was going to miss my turn, but I found it, picking out the sign easily on the grass verge. Eventually, a sharp S-bend sent me into the trees, which all at once lined the road on either side of me. This was Brocéliande.

I know now from my guidebook, Maguire, that the Forêt de Brocéliande is best seen in the spring. It consists of seven thousand hectares of private property with just six hundred owned by the National Forestry Office. During the hunting season some parts of the forest are closed. What's hunted is stag, deer, wild boar and small game. The forest contains nineteen lakes, including the one in Anne-Marie's painting, near château de Comper. Some of the trees in the forest are very old – beeches, oaks, birches, chestnuts, alders and many conifers. More recently pines and firs have been planted, but the bulk of the forest remains cropped vegetation, gorse, broom and heather. The ground in the lower forest is rich in iron ore and still bears scars from the metal-working industry; there are monastic forges dating from the thirteenth century, and a fifteenth-century arms factory. It's the enormous amount of wood consumed by this industry that has moulded the appearance of present-day Brocéliande: less mature timber, and lots of coppices.

It was coppices that lined the road as I entered Paimpont, punctuated now and then by neat cottages with stone walls and black slate roofs. The road was wide and smooth, eventually levelling out at a junction, a set of staggered crossroads. The road on my right narrowed and passed through a stone archway, set in a row of three-storey houses, which, if they hadn't looked so new, might have been a part of the old town wall. I stared in front of me, through the windscreen. The main road passed another house and then a hotel on the left, before heading off into the country again.

I drove up to the hotel, swung round into the car park and cut the engine. I was tired and my feet ached from the driving. Sure enough, a sign above the door read, 'Relais de Brocéliande: Hôtel et Restaurant,' just as Henry had said. The walls of the hotel were the same brown and yellow stone that all the houses here seemed to be made from; it had a sweeping roof and empty flower-boxes under its windows. In front of the entrance there was a cobbled area with plastic tables and chairs and yellow umbrellas, surrounded by a low, well-kept hedge.

Can that really only have been this afternoon, Maguire? I've lost all sense of time! It seems an age ago that I arrived, strung-out, exhausted, at the door of that hotel where I booked myself a room and took a shower, frightened that I didn't have time for such a thing. But I wanted to wake myself up. I needed to get a grip again. For I was thinking of you, Maguire. I thought, if you were coming, you might arrive today. You'd have talked to Rachel, and June would have told you I wasn't at work. You'd be on your way to see Henry. They would have flown you out first thing this morning, perhaps even last night. It might already be too late.

I hurried back downstairs. I really needed Anne-Marie now. I would explain everything. She would know what to do.

An elderly man sat at the bar, drinking cider. Two French couples were eating in the restaurant, the women very careful with their paper napkins, the men talking in firm, confident tones, as if to say it was their country.

The woman who had booked me into my room smiled cordially. She wore a waistcoat with a white shirt and blue cravat. 'May I help you?' she asked in English.

I didn't even attempt French. 'Can you tell me if an Anne-Marie Stone is staying here?'

'One moment, please.'

The attendant disappeared through a door behind the bar, while I waited nervously. She could be here right now, I thought, in a room somewhere, around the corner of the bar. What would I say to her?

The attendant returned with another woman, who had long brown hair that hung down around her spectacles.

'Good morning.' Her English was impeccable. 'My name is Nicole Raine. I'm the manager. Who is it you are looking for?'

'Anne-Marie Stone.'

'We are not usually allowed to give out such information, but since we have no record of her, I will tell you. No, she hasn't stayed here.'

'Thank you for your help.'

I turned to go.

'Monsieur?'

'Yes.'

'This woman you are looking for, she is your wife?'

The other woman smiled behind her.

The sun remained bright on the street outside, but I floundered along the pavement as though I'd lost my way. I stood still on the corner and tried to think. I felt like a man out walking who had hiked too far in the wrong direction. I had been so certain Anne-Marie would be there, as her father had said. So much so that I hadn't let my imagination, stretched as it was, entertain the inkling of doubt I'd felt while driving west to Rennes. Now that inkling blossomed. Where was she? Where on Earth? I thought I'd lost her, Maguire, along with all sense of what I was doing. I had driven my father-in-law's car across France, probably itself against the law, to find a small Breton town with an enchanted forest. Had I mislaid my mind? She could have been anywhere, perhaps still in Paris. By then, for all I knew, she might have been back in Derby. But I couldn't turn back now. Brocéliande was all I had: it was what I was pinning my last hope on.

By the time I spotted a sign for the Syndicat d'Initiative, pointing me in the direction of the arch I'd seen earlier, my disappointment had spilled over into ardent desperation. From that point onwards I knew what I was doing.

Passing underneath the arch, I found myself in a narrow street, lined with the same brown and yellow brick houses, some of which were restaurants, but mostly shops selling Arthurian merchandise. All of them had flowers in boxes under their windows and were flying the French flag. A sign on the side of one of the houses informed me I was on the rue du général de Gaulle. At the end of the street stood the thirteenth-century abbey, and a war memorial served as a roundabout where the rue du général de Gaulle and the avenue du Chevalier Ponthus converged. A plaque on the side of the monument, a grey pillar with a bronze soldier, said: 'La Commune de Paimpont. À ses enfants morts pour la France. 1914–1918.' I guessed little had changed in Paimpont over the years. The whole place felt as though it was caught in a time capsule.

That was what I wanted, Maguire, to be sealed off permanently in that French village, safe from the outside world, whose officials were, even then, closing in to apprehend me. Stability: isn't that what most of us wanted, deep down at the heart of things? For centuries mankind believed in a universe that was fixed and unchanging. For Jews, Christians and Muslims, Maguire, this universe had been created by God at some finite time in the not-so-distant past. For those Greek philosophers who did not believe in divine intervention, humans and the world around them had existed, and would continue to exist for ever. All our beliefs and early cosmologies agreed on a universe that was static, due most likely to an apparent human need to believe in eternal truths of one kind or another.

However, in the twentieth century our view of the universe changed for ever, with profound implications. In order to understand these implications we need to go back three hundred years, to a man now regarded by history as the father of science: Sir Isaac Newton, who, in 1687, first proposed a theory of universal attraction.

Newton's *Philosophiae Naturalis Principia Mathematica* is one of the most important works ever published in the sciences. In it he introduced the concept of a universal attractive force, which he called gravity, a force that reached out through space, affecting the motions of the planets as well as smaller objects that could be observed on Earth, such as, famously, the fall of an apple. One of Newton's laws states effectively that every body is attracted to every other body by a force that is directly proportional to its mass. In other words the more massive the bodies and the closer they are, the stronger the force attracting them. It was Newton's laws that Einstein, confronted in his own time with the problems posed by a finite speed of light, would consider when formulating his own theory of relativity, giving rise to our modern views of space-time.

However, until the time of Newton, and for two hundred and thirty-odd years after him, scientists continued to believe that the universe was essentially static and unchanging, despite the implications of universal attraction. Even Newton himself, who fully realised what his theory implied, reassured himself of a static universe by getting bogged down in notions of infinity, proposing that there existed an infinite number of stars distributed uniformly over an infinite region of space. Einstein, too, altered his general-relativity theory to bring it into accord with a static universe, such was his refusal to believe it could be otherwise. But both Newton's theory of universal attraction and Einstein's theory of general relativity predict a non-static universe. If the universe were static, it would contract under the influence of gravity: the stars, which attract each other, would at some point all fall together. The universe must, therefore, be expanding. Science was still not willing to consider this, however, until in 1924 the American astronomer Edwin Hubble proved through observation that ours was not the only galaxy. Furthermore, Hubble found that the further away a galaxy is, the faster it is moving away from us.

When I was a teenager, I spent the money I earned helping my grandmother on the market (she began to pay me a little for this when I turned thirteen) on a subscription to the weekly *Star Gazer*. Week by week for a year they gave away 'a page of space,' showing the position of all the known galaxies, until, by the end of the year, I had covered my small ceiling with what I then naïvely considered to be a map of everything. With such a map, I thought (then on the threshold of adulthood), I would know exactly where I was. I could learn who I was. I might find my way.

That was what I needed this afternoon, Maguire. A map.

The Syndicat d'Initiative stood in the abbey grounds; indeed, the building was once a part of the abbey itself. It was small inside, cool and dusty. Everything was made of wood – the floor, the desk, the shelves. There were brochures and leaflets everywhere.

I went in just before they closed for the day. The man at the counter looked no older than eighteen.

'Bonjour. Parlez-vous anglais? Do you have this in English?'

'Yes, Monsieur.'

It's the book I have before me now: *France Today: The North West*. There's a Union flag in the top right-hand corner, a chapter on Brocéliande, and a large map.

Outside the Syndicat d'Initiative, I opened the map and scanned it, remembering Henry's words. Marked with a red arrow, I found Tombeau de Merlin. It was about five miles up the D71.

I doubled back to the hotel for the car. It was only a ten-minute drive, but as I followed the curves of the deserted road, a new fear seized me: a sudden unparalleled concern for Anne-Marie. Why had she not stayed with her father? And again – over and over – if she wasn't here, *where* was she? I glimpsed the flash of a lake through the trees on my left. It was still light and didn't look as if it would rain again. The road wound on. The forest continued to unfold like an endless puzzle all around me.

If the universe is expanding, Maguire, then logic declares there must have been a time when everything was closer together.

Before Edwin Hubble provided observational evidence of an expanding universe, the only scientist willing to consider the full implications of general relativity was the Russian physicist and mathematician Alexander Friedmann. He proposed that the gravitational attraction between the galaxies would eventually cause the expansion of the universe to slow down and stop. The galaxies would then start to move towards each other and the universe contract. Luckily for us, with the knowledge we have so far, it appears there is not enough density in the universe to stop its expansion, so it seems we are safe from reaching a point where the universe will not be able to balance itself against its own gravity. What Friedmann's work showed, though, was that there must have been a time when the universe was infinitely dense and small, a point ten to twenty thousand million years ago when the distance between the galaxies was zero. This was what we now refer to as the Big Bang. From singularity theorems, especially the work carried out by physicists such as Roger Penrose and Stephen Hawking on the behaviour of the singularities contained in black holes, we know that at such a point the curvature of space-time would be infinite, and at that point all our laws of science would break down. In 1970 Hawking and Penrose wrote a joint paper proving that a Friedmann-like model of an expanding universe must have begun with such a singularity: they proved that the universe must have had a beginning in time.

If so, then who began it? Is there, after all, a God? A Supreme Being? *Are* our destinies pre-ordained?

The Tombeau de Merlin and the Fontaine de Jouvence were signposted off the main road.

I pulled over into a gravel car park just inside the trees. There were no other vehicles. In Henry's glove compartment I found a torch. It would be getting dark soon.

It was cool and shadowy in the forest, like in the Syndicat d'Initiative. I didn't need my map after all: everything was well signposted from here, a real tourist route, the paths wide and worn from use. I took the one for Merlin's tomb, and slowly grew accustomed to the tick of the forest.

Soon I passed a large clearing on my left, whose sides had been cut out of the hillside. It was circular, surrounded by what was left of a stone wall. It looked like the remains of a small amphitheatre. In the centre, the ground was charred, where I imagined many fires to have been. The wall itself was covered with painted slogans, names and graffiti. Some of these looked like old cave drawings – stick figures, faces, genitalia – as if the clearing had been witness to some obscure fertility ceremony. There were cigarette butts and beer cans in the bushes and black burn marks on the stone. I wondered how long the land had been national property, and whether this clearing had been here when Anne-Marie was a girl.

The path I was on wound past the clearing and back into the trees.

And it was then I remembered something, Maguire, something from those earlier hours of Sunday morning. I had been walking on a path through grass, only it hadn't been a gravel path like this one, it was Tarmac, like a pavement. It was . . . I was . . .

But it was gone. A bird fluttered loudly out of a nearby tree. I listened to its wings flap and fade away. A few loose leaves settled at my feet. I walked on.

According to my book, what has become known as Merlin's tomb is the remains of a Neolithic gallery grave. But when I rounded the corner and saw it for myself, I found it wasn't like the picture in my book at all. The clearing seemed man-made: the surrounding trees had been chopped down. The tomb just looked like two stone slabs leaning on one another, back to back, in the middle of a well-trodden path, each slab slightly less than the height of a man. A thin trunk sprouted between them, straight up into the air, its puny branches littered with paper, cards and notelets, silver and gold foil – memorabilia from a thousand fans. One of the rocks had fallen slightly, or been moved since the picture in my book had been taken, creating a crevice. This, too, was filled with papers. I stepped closer. Pieces of foil glittered like leaves in the branches. I picked up one of the cards. It said, in English:

'To Merlin. Please make Mark Hammond love me. From Jenny Brighton.' Another said: 'Come back to us, Enchanter, the world needs you.' And all these were tied to the tree with ribbons or pieces of string: letters, signatures, prayers.

Don't you see, Maguire? Our need to believe. Any old mythology. All those particles rushing through the silence of space, and yet how, when it comes down to it, we are prepared (yes, even I) to throw it all to the wind in order to have faith again; to believe that we are not just meant to decompose in the worm-ridden earth, that we were made for better things, that we are, in fact, *made*, and that 'better things' includes the notion of 'true love.'

The clearing around Merlin's tomb was surrounded on three sides by a wire fence. The path I'd entered on was the only way to or from it. I thought of Henry's words, 'a part of it she used to like when she was a child, a little way on from Merlin's tomb, where the trees form a kind of tunnel.' I was grasping at straws now, I knew. But it was all I had, all I could do. Except turn round and go back. But to where? Paris? England?

I turned the map in my hand. According to my book, the lake where Merlin built his palace for Viviane, the one Anne-Marie had painted, was one of the lakes surrounding château de Comper. I worked it out. The château was out on my left, in part of the forest that was fenced off. I picked my way to the wire. There was no one about. I climbed over.

At first, I couldn't see a path. The trees were thick and close together. But then I detected a kind of trench in the ground, like an empty stream bed, grown over with vegetation. I began to follow it. After ten minutes the clearing behind me was completely closed off. In front of me, my route opened out into more of a path. I had a feeling that nobody had been this way for years. I could get lost here, I thought. I felt like I was approaching the core of something that had nothing to do with the scraps of blue sky I could see momentarily through holes in the trees' canopy; it was something concerning the earth, like the centre of a nest.

Behind me, I could no longer tell where the trees ended and where anything else began. Previously there had been faint patches of light, like the light in a railway tunnel growing narrower and narrower. But now even they were gone. I kept going, until finally I found I had to start bending down. The canopy of branches above me was becoming lower and lower. I couldn't see the sky through it any more. I pressed on, until the only way forward was on my hands and knees. I crouched down and peered through the brambles. There was a kind of tunnel ahead, just wide enough for me to crawl through.

After five minutes of thorns scratching my face and hands, I emerged into a tiny haven in the undergrowth. Here I could stand up again. In front of me was a small pool, surrounded by four slabs of stone, a bit like a well. There was enough room for me to walk round it comfortably. It was like being in a tiny alcove built of trees, a living cave.

I stared into the pool. In the shadows of the trees the water looked so black it might have been oil. I looked up. Here, at least, there was a small gap in the canopy, letting in the afternoon light.

What now? I sat down on one of the stone slabs and put

my hands into my pockets, where I was surprised to find the notes from my lecture. I read them through: an outline of the history of twentieth-century physics – determinism, general relativity, quantum mechanics . . . My handwriting was unfamiliar: it seemed to reach me as if from the other side of the solar system. I stared at the white band of skin on my ring finger, and remembered Anne-Marie's ring, which you'd presented to me at the station, Maguire. At the time I'd assumed she must have given it to him, but now it didn't seem to make sense. Her wedding ring. Why would she do that?

Was I surprised to see her, a few minutes later, emerging head first from the undergrowth on her hands and knees? I don't know. Maybe. So you *have* been here, was my first thought: Henry had been right. But what did that mean? Why Brocéliande? The questions were queuing in my mind even then as she got to her feet, untangling the leaves from her hair.

'You found it,' she said.

I understood that this was my moment. This was what I'd hoped for, an opportunity to explain myself, husband to wife, before you arrived, Maguire, with your accusations, your full forensics report and autopsy-table photographs. Long had I agonised over how best to begin. How did a husband inform his wife of the death of her lover, and how he, her husband, was wanted by the police, only he couldn't remember, couldn't recall . . .? But now that she stood in front of me, in this peculiar room of trees (she was wearing jeans and her brown suede jacket), something else worried me, something I was beginning to feel would render all previous concerns redundant.

The diameter of the pool was only two metres or so. If we both reached out we could almost touch one another. It was the way we had stood at the beginning, facing each other across her bed-sit in Belgrave Road. And I was feeling now as I did then: that there was something in Anne-Marie's eyes, as their brown turned to amber in the dying light, that I couldn't quite place.

I said her name aloud; the sound waves carried and were absorbed by the trees. There might not have been another person for a mile. The hum of the forest, the birds and the insects busy in the walls about us, seemed a silence of its own, as if it was waiting only for a human voice to break it, as if it was inviting a confession. Only it wasn't me who began to speak.

23

At fourteen, Anne-Marie believes she knows every inch of Brocéliande forest. Her father takes her to other places too, all over the north of Brittany, to research his book on King Arthur. 'That's what we're doing, Anne-Marie,' he says, striding between the trees. 'Research.'

And what was that book about, after all his playing at happy families, after all the old myth-making? Infidelity. Yet Anne-Marie is too young to understand, too naïve at fourteen to notice the way her father behaves with a certain woman from Rapporteur Livres, who is only five years older than Anne-Marie, and who buys her a lipstick. Her name is Denise. 'Anne-Marie, this is a friend of mine, Denise. She's going to help publish my book.'

And her mother doesn't have a clue, when the book was her idea in the first place, her idea to transform all those endless notes and academic essays of her husband's into something substantial and coherent. But she finds out soon enough, and later that year, after the divorce, she takes Anne-Marie to England. And why England? Because she has nowhere else to go. She can't go to her parents. Because she can't look anyone in the eye. And Anne-Marie is causing havoc at St Mary's.

Yet in England it all seems very far away. Anne-Marie's father remains in Paris. His books become successful, and are translated into twenty languages. Anne-Marie's mother never forgives him. Why should she? He and Denise don't even last the length of the divorce proceedings. But, then, that's not the real reason.

'Jack, I'm so sorry I hurt you.'

Anne-Marie had sat down on the stone slab across the pool from me. In different circumstances we might have been two lovers meeting by a well, but not there: there the atmosphere felt oppressive, walled in as we were by the trees. Yet it was still light. Looking up, I could see a single patch of blue-grey sky through the only gap in the canopy, but I knew it would be dark soon enough.

Across the still pool, Anne-Marie seemed a galaxy away. Her jeans were muddy from where she had crawled through the undergrowth. She'd pulled her brown suede jacket tight round her, as if she was cold, and was sitting with her knees drawn up to her chin. Now, for the first time, she looked up at me. 'I never meant to,' she said.

Her voice sounded small and vulnerable. I wanted to hug her but I couldn't bring myself to stand.

'I didn't think you cared any more,' she said.

I bit my tongue.

'I wanted to show you that I was wanted. That day . . . I don't know what happened. I don't know why I did it. Suddenly I just did it. It was all so wrong. Sebastian was wrong. Poor Sebbi.'

I winced at his name. I stared into the water, not wishing to hear what she was going to say next, for I knew now she would tell me everything. Isn't that what I had wanted?

'I'm sorry, Jack, but I must.'

I turned away. How could this be harder than what I

was shrinking from telling her? Didn't she realise the man was dead? I should have been holding up my hand to stop her. I should have said, firmly but gently, 'Anne-Marie, listen, there is something I must tell you.' But I didn't. I gazed at the one gap in the undergrowth, the opening to the tunnel we had both crawled through, our only way in and out. I didn't say anything.

When she first sees him, the meeting to discuss the exhibition, he has with him some sketches. She's been thinking about her own painting recently. I'm the only one who ever believed in her painting, but she feels so alone, with things as they are between us, and her father wanting her to go and visit. And it's typical, just her luck, that she has to go in on her day off to cover one of the students' shifts. I have already left for the museum. The house seems so quiet when I'm gone. She remembers standing in the bathroom, her skin pale in the mirror. Later, she heads out, wondering how obvious it will be that she's been up all night crying.

All the way to work the sky is a hazy grey-blue, but cloudless, like a single promise that, whatever else happens that day, it will be clear and dry, and all she can think of is how she will be trapped indoors in her box, selling tickets. Though she prefers this to being at home. (Did I know she thought about leaving?) She thinks not just of what is happening to us, but also, of what is happening to her, Anne-Marie. How often has she watched the world flounder through its old routine? How many times have she and I stumbled through ours? What are we doing, me with my work looking after toy trains and engines, her selling tickets for plays we have never been able to afford? Where are our friends? Where are we going, we who were going to change the world?

And then he walks in, just a tall man with a brown beard, who doesn't look very Spanish. But his arms are full of drawings. All those pictures. How many hours, days, years has he put into them? How many experiences are on display there? And he is going to exhibit them for everyone to see. He is actually *doing* something, creating something where there was nothing before. She doesn't know how famous he is. He just has a way of firing her up about her own painting again. Of course she knows what he wants. He can pick anyone. She has no idea he will fall in love with her. Maybe he doesn't. She doesn't know. It's his pictures that intrigue her. Those small sketches, the trees and the forest, they remind her of this place. And suddenly this man is asking her to come and see the rest of his work. Oh, she knows what he wants, all right. She gives him a ticket for *Twelfth Night*, and he holds her hand throughout. That's all, just holds her hand. She and I are hardly speaking. She's busy organising the exhibition and I'm preparing my talks for the museum.

Then one afternoon he asks her back to his flat for coffee. That's when she realises how famous he is, from how much that flat must be costing. He tells her about his life, how he was born and grew up in Madrid, how in 2000 he won the Miró Prize. His friend Darmony is with them the first time, and his agent, Kirker. But the second time she goes alone. She is supposed to be picking up the last of his paintings, to take them to the theatre. He tries to kiss her. She won't let him. 'I'm married,' she says. But the next evening she and I have the argument over the bottle of wine, and she cries herself to sleep. She thinks we're finished, that I don't want her any more. So that's when she does it, not meticulously planned; she just thinks she'll invite him to our house this time. She has a vague notion about showing him some of her old paintings, of finally fetching them down from the attic. She knows I'm due back from the museum at eight, so she tells him to come at six. She just wants us to meet, that's all, for me to be jealous. She hadn't planned to sleep with him.

But when the time comes, she thinks, Why not? She just thinks, Why not? What will happen? Let's see what will happen, then. And I come home early, that's what happens. And afterwards, when I've left, she has nothing to say to him. She has nothing to say to either of us. She feels sorry for us all. She just feels this incredible sorrow for everything. How can I forgive her? How can I love her the same way again? So she books her ticket for Paris, like we've discussed. Run away, she thinks, run home to Papa, after all these years. Because he is all she has. Because her mother's burnt body has been scattered in the Trent.

How little she knows then, the night of the exhibition, that by the morning the flight she's booked to Paris will be a necessity. The last thing in the world she expects is for me to show up at the opening, to punch Sebastian like that, in front of everyone. It's ridiculous, hilarious, the way he falls down the stairs, and me turning to her as though I think I'm some knight in shining armour. She wants to laugh and hug me. She's jealous of how drunk I am. That's what she wants: oblivion. When we'd first met, we would have laughed at ourselves. But not now. She is angry and proud of me. So I do want her after all.

'I felt sorry for myself,' she said.

She pulled the collar of her jacket tighter round her neck and held it there. The temperature had dropped.

'I didn't know what to do. How were we supposed to get over this, to go back again, you know?'

In the shadows, I could tell she was crying because she kept bringing the suede sleeve of her jacket to her cheek.

And there was something else. Something she had said was making the individual hairs on my neck start to rise. Nothing ever goes backwards, I thought. Why this need to go back all the time? I thought of her standing at the top of the theatre steps, screaming, 'Get out! Get out!' with Martinez in a heap below.

I took a deep breath and, for the first time, I met her eyes. 'I didn't think you loved me any more,' I said. 'I thought you wanted him. You told me to get out.'

She was crying steadily now, but made no effort to stop her tears. She smiled through them. 'What I really wanted to do was follow you out,' she said, 'stuff the lot of them.' She paused, and wiped her eyes, then stared hard at the ground. 'But I didn't. How different everything could have been.'

The forest maintained its ministry, keeping its arms round us.

'How different everything could have been,' she repeated. She gazed into the black pool. 'The real reason wasn't Denise. It was me.'

*　　*　　*

Sunday afternoon. Anne-Marie, her father and Denise have been having lunch at the Relais de Brocéliande. Anne-Marie doesn't know her father and Denise are lovers. She doesn't know that the argument they have outside in the car park, while she waits patiently in the back of her father's car, is a lovers' quarrel. In her English lessons at school, Sister Agatha has presented the class with a piece of Charles Dickens to translate. It is an extract from *Great Expectations*. This is what Anne-Marie has on her lap to read in the back of the car, while her father and Denise spar with one another outside. Denise has on a pair of blue pedal-pushers, finishing just below the knee; she wears a sports top made of Lycra, a white tube that barely covers her small, pointy breasts. She has her blonde hair in a long plait. She is shouting something at Anne-Marie's father, and every time she turns her head just a little too sharply, that long blonde plait whips round in the air like the tail of an insect.

'That's what they looked like from the car, circling each other on the Tarmac like that. Like two animals,' Anne-Marie said.

There was anger in her voice.

She winds up the windows. She can't bear to hear people fighting. She can see Denise's lips mouthing, 'Gina.'

Does she have a first inkling then, as she sits in the car reading, that there might be something going on between her father and Denise, something a good deal more than friendship? She can't remember. But Denise doesn't come back over with her father, doesn't get back into the passenger seat in front of Anne-Marie, so they can finish their trip to Brocéliande, the three of them, like they'd planned. Instead, Denise storms off across the car-park to her own car and drives away. Her father gets into the driver's seat and swears; he says something about the dangers of drunk-driving, about not being surprised if Denise gets herself killed, about him never expecting to hear of his daughter doing anything like that ever, and does she understand? Yes, she says. But she doesn't. And she doesn't think it wise for her to mention that he has drunk a lot more than Denise. Her father starts the engine and they drive off. She asks if they are still going to Brocéliande. He says, 'Of course we are.' But he doesn't seem as enthusiastic as before. Later she gets the feeling that he is just going through the motions for her sake. He asks her what she is reading. She says, 'Charles Dickens.' He doesn't say anything. He isn't an expert on that.

They park by the side of the road opposite the path to Merlin's tomb. He suggests they should go for a walk. Perhaps he realises that he really shouldn't be driving after all: he needs to sober up. She begs him to take her here, to the small, secret clearing with the pool. He looks at her as if to say: Aren't you too grown-up for this yet? Pretending to hunt for some make-believe sword? She tells him he has promised. 'All right,' he says. So they crawl along the thick tunnel of trees, down on their hands and knees, and afterwards sit side by side on one of the stone slabs, catching their breath. Anne-Marie is fourteen. She never finds out what her father and Denise have argued about, but Denise must have upset him because she can tell he is angry. She has spoilt their plans. Perhaps they'd hoped to get rid of her for a while – 'Stay and read your *Great Expectations*, Anne-Marie.'

'It should have been her, don't you see? It should have been Denise, not me.' Anne-Marie paused, but didn't look up. She was staring wide-eyed into the depths of the inky pool. She wasn't talking to me any more: she was talking to anyone who was listening. I felt the same sensation I had had at the morgue, when we had gone to identify her mother's body. I was there and I wasn't there. She was talking to me as if I were only a wave of probability. 'Perhaps I should have reacted quicker,' she said.

But she is tired and too stunned at first to realise that the hand he has placed so lovingly, so fatherly, on her knee, as if to pat it, is slowly slipping upwards under her patterned skirt. The tips of his fingers brush the cotton of her knickers.

'Papa.'

Anne-Marie rocked back and forth on the stone slab opposite me, clutching her knees.

'"Come on, Anne-Marie, what's the matter with you?" That's what he said. I started to cry, and he stopped.'

Everything stops. Then her father cries too – loud, hot tears. 'I'm sorry,' he says. 'I'm sorry, I'm sorry, I'm sorry!' And she does feel sorry for him. She wants to hug him, but he won't touch her again, not even to hug.

*   *   *

Anne-Marie looked up sharply. 'He didn't rape me, you understand. He touched my leg. He touched my knickers once. And he cried.'

She explained this carefully. Her voice wasn't shaking now: it was firm and deliberate.

But back at home, when her mother asks what the matter with her father is, and she tries to explain, it's no use. Don't I see? She was the reason, not Denise. The divorce. England. She remembers that night clearly, how sorry she feels for him, how she wants to stop her mother's shouting. And how later, when it gets dark, she lies awake in bed, lies wide awake and terrified that he will come in the night and touch her. But he doesn't.

'Everything's the same as before, the same as it was then,' she said, 'Where we sat. Where he cried. The same, but different.'

I looked across at my wife, whose gaze was searching out her husband in the dusk. It was I who had tears in my eyes now, Maguire. My Anne-Marie. I couldn't believe what she was telling me. I felt myself thrust back to the staircase in Woolrych Street when I was eight years old and my mother first told me about my father. Taking in those words was as though I had been expecting them my whole life. But this was different: Anne-Marie's words clawed and chipped at me as they fought their way in. This couldn't be real; this couldn't be happening.

I brushed my tears away. How could I tell her about Martinez now?

'Oh, Jack.'

Anne-Marie got to her feet, a little awkwardly, and edged her way round the pool. She sat down beside me and took my hand. Now she seemed the one in control. In fact, she looked relieved, as if, used to her burden so long, she had finally passed it on. And I took it heavily. I clutched her hand. It was surprisingly warm and clammy. I was aware that my own was cold.

I struggled to ask her what had happened next, putting off my own cruel revelation.

'We left him, Maman and I. We left him alone in Paris with Denise and his books, and we came to England.'

I was unable to meet her eye. 'And Gina . . . Your mother never forgave him?'

'Why should she?' Anne-Marie paused. She squeezed my hand, a little too hard. 'I thought I'd forgiven him. Until Sebastian grabbed me under the bridge.'

'What?'

I slapped into a cold wall of nausea. Once more I felt as though gravity had abandoned me, only to be reapplied abruptly. I was no longer there: I was somewhere outside this little clearing, out there among the trees, peering in.

She turned suddenly to face me. 'I swore I would never let any man get to me, take advantage of me in any way. Do you understand, Jack?'

She was gazing deep into my eyes with a look of the Anne-Marie I knew. There she was.

'You were so different, Jack. That time in my room, when I pretended to paint you, wondering, could this be the one? And you were, Jack. You are. You were so innocent.'

24

That was it, Maguire: the world slipped away from me; the forest appeared to collapse, pitching sideways. Slowly, everything in those woods stiffened in time: the branches of the trees stopped swaying; the clouds froze in the sky; insects ceased their endeavours in the undergrowth; and a strange silence reigned. Then everything began again: the world accelerated. And, for an eternity, all I could think about was Henry. My father-in-law, with whom this morning I'd sat taking coffee. Who had once . . . But it wasn't anger I felt: it was more surprise at my lack of it. And sadness. What I felt was an immense sadness for all of us: Anne-Marie, Henry, Martinez, myself. And now a new fear was working its way through me, a terrible dawning. Exhausted, I sat bolt upright on that stone slab, with my wife's hand gripped in mine. I hardly had the stamina, let alone the stomach, for what she was telling me now.

Closing time, Saturday night, and the last few people are leaving the theatre, making their way down from the bar and out through the foyer. There is a general consensus among the staff that, once the food from the buffet has been cleared away, everything else is to be left until morning. Anne-Marie has joined the catering staff, going from table to abandoned table, ferrying the empty plates and leftover food to the kitchen and removing the dispos-able tablecloths. She has tied back her hair for this purpose. She now feels restricted in her black dress; her ankles are aching from her high-heeled shoes, and she wishes she had brought something more appropriate to change into.

'Can't you leave all that?' Sebastian says.

He is standing in the doorway to the auditorium, wearing the black suit trousers and white dress shirt he will die in. For a moment he looks a little like a waiter. Anne-Marie smiles at this. He still has a patch of dried blood on the front of his shirt, from his nosebleed.

'Yes, leave that 'til morning,' Anita says, appearing at the top of the stairs, with the artist's coat. 'Go on, get off home. We'll clear all this tomorrow.'

'Okay,' Anne-Marie agrees.

Wiping her hands on a napkin, she suddenly feels worn out. She goes downstairs and fetches her jacket and handbag from her office. She finds Sebastian waiting for her in the foyer, where more drinks tables have yet to be cleared. He has a bottle of wine in his hand.

'Have a drink with me,' he says.

'You look like you've had a few already.'

'You look like you could do with one.'

She considers it; considers him.

'I don't think so. They're locking up now.'

She can see the front-of-house manager coming down the stairs, jangling a bunch of keys.

'Then we'll take it with us,' Sebastian says, sweeping up a corkscrew and two glasses from the nearest table.

'Are you two planning to stay here all night as well?' the front-of-house manager says, grinning.

'Okay, okay, we're going,' Anne-Marie says. 'Have a good weekend, John.'

'You too.'

She walks out with Sebastian and they stand for a moment on the kerb. It has stopped raining; the road is wet, but she is not particularly cold.

'Look, I'm sorry about tonight,' she says. 'Jack had no right. I didn't even think he would come. Are you okay?'

Sebastian touches his nose, and looks down at his stained shirt. 'I'll be all right,' he says. He winks at her. 'It's not the first time.'

'I feel guilty.'

'Then have a drink with me.'

She looks at the bottle in his hand, and sighs. She must explain things to him, once and for all.

'Okay. One drink.'

The river is his idea. They take the path behind the bus station and stroll along the bank towards the Lombes bridge. The pubs have closed. In town people are queuing for taxis or staggering on to clubs; shouts carry faintly on the breeze, but for the time being the riverbank is deserted. The noise of the weir further down-river is far greater than the sound of the city behind them.

It starts to rain again. They hurry to shelter under the bridge. Here the river looks black; it sits beside them as still as a millpond. Without saying anything, Sebastian starts to open the bottle of wine. Anne-Marie shivers. She only has her leather jacket on over her dress, not the best thing to have chosen. Now she wishes she had brought her winter coat. It had seemed mild earlier, but now, with the rain, the temperature has fallen. She thinks of the girls they passed in town, in their short skirts and crop tops.

The cork pops. 'Allí!' Sebastian says.

She holds the two wine-glasses while he pours. He is unsteady on his feet. Watching him squeeze the cork back into the bottle, she wonders how much he has had. He trades the corkscrew with her for a glass.

She smiles at him. 'To you. A wonderful exhibition.'

He places the bottle on the ground and puts his free hand on her waist. He raises his glass.

'To us,' he says. He looks around them. 'It appears we are stranded, at least for the moment.'

The rain patters on the path, and drums and sloshes on the bridge above. Drops drip steadily from the stone ceiling, while Anne-Marie just stands there, her glass in one hand, the corkscrew in the other, wishing there was some way to wriggle free. She steps back, forcing Sebastian's hand to fall from her waist. 'It went really well,' she says, 'the exhibition and the play. You must be pleased.'

But Sebastian isn't interested in those things. He talks about the day they made love. 'You were wonderful,' he says. 'Are wonderful. I could have lain there with you forever. If only your husband . . . But that's okay. I'm sure he is a good man, and we must do the right thing by him. What are your plans?'

'What plans?' She takes a small step back, towards the stone wall of the bridge behind her; her high heels click on the cobbles.

Martinez steps towards her. 'It's okay, you shouldn't worry. Things will be all right. We could get a place together, here in Derby. I like this city. Kirker won't be keen, but I can deal with him. I think I love you.'

It is the last thing she expects from him, the last thing she wants. She doesn't know what to say, so she doesn't say anything.

But he keeps talking anyway, as the rain gushes, about all sorts of things, like the possibility of him getting a house permanently, of having a proper exhibition in the Midlands, of them even painting together. 'Would you like that?'

'No.'

She steps towards him. 'Listen, Sebastian.'

'Sebbi.'

'Sebbi. We need to sort things out.' She pauses. 'I'm not in love with you.'

He stares at her. Then he smiles. 'Until this moment I think, perhaps, I've never been in love my whole life.'

It is like listening to someone talk about someone else.

'I love you,' he says again, raising his voice this time, above the rain.

He keeps saying it over and over, searching her face for the response he wants. He is making sweeping hand gestures as he speaks, spilling his wine onto the cobbles, while behind him the river waits in the dripping dark.

She doesn't want to be there any more. She wants to go home. 'I want to go home.'

But he doesn't listen. 'Come here,' he says. He steps forward. He tries to kiss her. 'Come on, Anne-Marie, what's wrong?'

'No, Sebastian.'

She struggles, but he won't let go. 'No!' Her shout echoes around the stonework of the bridge.

He begins to panic. 'Be quiet! What's the matter with you?'

He pulls her against him, but she resists, pushing hard, spilling her wine on his shirt. Then, suddenly, she pops free, and when he tries to grab her again, she thrusts out both arms in front of her to stop him.

'No, no!'

She doesn't hear his wine-glass smashing on the cobbles when he drops it. It's the change in his voice she hears: it plummets; he sounds as if he's gargling. She notices that she still has the corkscrew in her hand, and that now it is sticking in his throat. She pulls it free, for it looks so horrid impaled in him like that. The blood comes slow at first, just a small stain spreading on his skin, but then it spurts, almost reaching her shoes, and pours down the front of him, and seeps though his shirt. He is trying to say her name – Anne-Marie – but he can't say anything anymore. She can't move. She can't even let the corkscrew drop out of her hand. She just stands there on the cobbles, watching him flounder in front of her. She notices the pieces of glass on the path. There is now a long line of blood. He is staggering backwards on his heels, both hands to his throat.

It might be minutes; it might be seconds. She doesn't know. But eventually something clicks inside her. Her feet feel free again. She realises that she is still holding her own wine-glass in one hand and the corkscrew in the other. The horror tears into her. She drops them.

'Sebastian!'

She moves towards him, but he isn't there.

There is a splash. She remembers the splash. She feels wet, and looks down to find her dress is soaked. When she looks up, when she steps forward to look along the river, there is just the top of his head bobbing in the darkness, moving away from her under the bridge in the rain.

She stands still and shivers. The water is cold. The blood on her hands is warm. She forces herself to run a little way down the path beyond the bridge, but he is gone. It's pouring now and too dark to see. There are no lights along the path here. Briefly she thinks she can make out something floating in the water further off, still moving; only that and the rain and the muffled screaming of the weir.

I'd have thought she would have stood there in shock, but she doesn't. I'd have thought she would have wandered about the riverbank in a daze, but she doesn't. She can still go and phone for an ambulance, or the police. But she doesn't. Something else is taking over.

She looks around her. There is still no one on the riverbank in this weather. She walks back beneath the bridge. The bottle of wine is standing neatly on the cobbles, half full. She picks it up, removes the cork and takes a long, hard swig. She wraps the bloody corkscrew in some handkerchiefs and places it in her handbag. Then, one by one, she picks up the pieces of the two wine-glasses, and does the same with those. She hitches her dress and crouches beside the water, to try to wash the blood from her hands. It is remarkably persistent. This doesn't surprise her: she has heard this. At last she wipes her hands on her dress.

Again she stands and looks around her. Everything seems quiet and still along the river; there is just the sound of the rain and the weir. She picks up the wine bottle and walks back towards the lights. It is Saturday night, and she is not the only person carrying a bottle in the street; she is not the only soaked woman hurrying home in the rain.

'That's all I did,' she said. 'I just went home.'

We were still sitting on the slabs by the pool. Above us, through the gap in the trees' canopy the sun was starting to set. I sat motionless, Maguire, but inside I was hurtling like a cell in my own bloodstream, breaking through all boundaries of space in time. How can I begin to describe to you the utter unbelievability, the awe and the fear, the sheer wonder and despair? This was Anne-Marie, my Anne-Marie. And I'd even been thinking, trying to plug the gaps in my drunken memory, that it could have been me, that I was the one who was capable, that I had wanted to . . . But Anne-Marie? It wasn't possible. What was, just could not be.

'Part of me hoped you would be there, Jack,' she was saying, 'to make everything all right. To undo things. Part of me wished you'd be there, but you weren't.'

Half-way through her story I had dropped her hand. Now she placed it back in mine.

'I remember the clock said it was a quarter past one,' she said, 'and as if none of it had ever happened, as if it was all just a bad dream, even me washing the rest of the blood off in the shower, I went to bed.'

A sharp chill was snaking through my skin, as what Anne-Marie had been telling me finally sank its teeth in. She looked up at me, as if not quite believing it herself. 'I slept,' she said. 'I slept peacefully without interruption, without bad dreams or the police banging at the door.'

She began talking faster. 'You see, he might not have

been dead. That was how I played it out on the plane. He didn't look like . . . I mean he was so alive, upset, angry, talking and everything. Even when he floated away, he looked . . . Well, he looked like he was swimming.'

She fell silent.

Light years later, I squeezed her hand.

I could hear insects busy in the undergrowth around us. What else was I to do?

Without saying anything, she got up, edged back round the pool, and knelt on the stone slab facing me. I watched her gaze down into the inky water. Then she pushed up her suede sleeve, rolled up the sleeve of her sweater below and, without looking at me, plunged her arm deep into the pool as far as the elbow. The water must have been cold, Maguire, but she didn't flinch. She had done this before.

Slowly, through the algae, she pulled out a dripping white plastic bag. She set it down on the stone. I recognised the carrier-bag she had taken on Sunday from beneath our bed and buried in her suitcase. Out of it she carefully drew two items: a bottle of Bordeaux (still half full, with the cork pushed in) and a wooden-handled corkscrew. The pine had darkened from being in the water; the metal still had pieces of the carrier-bag stuck to it, from when Martinez's blood had been warm. She laid out each item on the slab.

She stared into the pool, watching the surface settle. 'When I was a girl, that's where I thought Excalibur was,' she said, 'and that one day, if I was patient, if I was here at the right time, I would see a hand rise from the water, "Clothed in white samite, mystic, wonderful."'

She got up and rejoined me on the other side of the

water. We sat together, staring at the bottle and the corkscrew on the stone slabs opposite. I put my arm round her and she leaned her head against my shoulder. I could smell her usual shampoo.

'Where have you been staying?' I asked, then suddenly burst into tears at the ridiculousness of my question. Was such small-talk all that could remain?

'At the Relais de Brocéliande,' she said. She lifted her sleeve to wipe my eyes. 'It's the hotel where we used to stay before.'

'They told me you weren't booked in there.'

'I used my maiden name.'

'Dufeur,' I said aloud. I had not heard this for a long time.

She took my hands in hers. But, looking down, we were both aware of the wedding rings missing from our fingers. I thought of my own, sinking slowly through the Derwent, where I had indeed discarded it the previous day.

'I threw it in the river,' I said.

Anne-Marie smiled, then nodded. She looked over at the corkscrew and the bottle of wine. That river had a lot to answer for.

'I took mine off that afternoon . . . with Sebastian,' she said. 'But afterwards. After you had seen us, when I thought we were over. It's on the dressing-table.'

But it's not, I thought. It's been sitting in a police interview room and now it's on its way here in a detective's pocket; soon it will be presented as evidence in a court-room. But there seemed little point in explaining all this now. Carpe diem.

I kissed Anne-Marie lightly on her forehead, and we remained sitting with our arms round each other, looking up through the trees at the single patch of sky where the light was still scattering, dispersing through the atmosphere, from yellow to orange to red, until the red dimmed. We watched the way any other couple would. But for us it was a cruel sunset, indifferent and cold.

25

A complicated case then, Maguire, at once so simple and yet not quite so straightforward after all. But you, of all people, should understand that. How much is Henry Parrot to blame? How far back do you go? Anne-Marie has dealt with Henry. You'd be barking up the wrong tree there, even I can see that. She forgave him years ago. Not until Martinez was grabbing her under the bridge did it all come back to her, did she panic. An accident, then. No premeditation. She just did it. The way she slept with him. One second he was alive and another he was dead.

But that won't stop you requiring your answers, will it? I know it doesn't stop me needing mine. All this going back. I can feel myself remaining only slightly on the sane side of the thin line. There's a part of me that cannot deal with this. There is a part of me that doesn't, even now, believe it was her. The events of Saturday night – extraordinary in the extreme – shatter everything I thought I knew. It is terrifying to think that while I was drinking with Rachel at the Thirst, at that very moment a certain corkscrew in my wife's hand was obeying Newton's laws and inserting itself into the base of Sebastian Martinez's throat. And I know it would only take a nudge to make me stumble gratefully across that line. It is only the unpredictability of Anne-Marie, of love itself, fluctuating ceaselessly like a riot beneath all that has happened, everything we've done and do, that stops me. Because now only the uncertainty rings true.

Yet we are still, I expect, as far as the next few hours are concerned, subject to a sureness of sorts. Now that you have us there'll be rights read, warrants and law courts and swearing to tell the truth. There'll be questions of evidence, of a ring with an inscription. By now you'll know that it's Anne-Marie's ring, the one Martinez took from her dressing-table. You'll also know that I lied about being with Rachel Seaga all Saturday night, after assaulting Martinez at the theatre and storming out. You'll have interviewed her. She might even have told you how much I said I still loved my wife. Motive, you see.

And just where exactly was I between three o'clock on Sunday morning, when I left Rachel's, and six when I showed up at Sam's? I still can't tell you, can I? I can hardly remember getting into Sam's kitchen. I have a vague recollection of walking on a Tarmac path through grass. Merrick Park, I imagine, and then what? Out through town? To the river, even? It's likely. And not irrelevant now. Yes, now what's important is that it was I who had both the time and the motive. All it takes when you knock on this door, Maguire, or when Jouette drives me back to the commissariat, is for me to confess, for me to divulge how my wife and Martinez were having an affair. And I bet you suspect that anyway, don't you? How hard have you questioned Anita?

At least that part will be true: her infidelity (it hardly qualifies as an affair) on that one afternoon, Wednesday 29 September, at 18.35, according to the clock by the bedside table, while I just stood in the doorway, coat and bag in my hand, watching my whole world contract to a single point.

Do I forgive her?

She asked this as we sat beside the pool among the trees, listening to the first shouts, and watching the flicker of torches far off through the branches. It had grown dark. A single shaft of moonlight glared through the gap in the trees' canopy. Around us, police were trying to find the entrance that Henry must have described to them, the only way in or out. Each officer would have to climb through one at a time. But we weren't going to resist.

I was wondering if you'd be with them, Maguire: I was trying to work out how fast you could have got out here. Or had the Parisian police questioned Henry? Had Anne-Marie's father broken down and confessed everything? Everything?

But all the shouts were in French. I didn't understand what they were saying.

'They're coming,' Anne-Marie said. 'They're telling us that they're armed.'

I turned and looked far inside her brown eyes and, for the first time, almost fathomed them. Did I forgive her? I, whose memory even then still flitted occasionally to a recent kiss in the back of a rain-pummelled taxi. Who are any of us to forgive?

I took my wife in my arms and kissed her hard, then tenderly, and she kissed me back, taking my face in her hands.

As I got to my feet, I brought Henry's torch out of my pocket, switched it on and edged round the pool. I picked up the carrier-bag. Other torches now flashed through the trees nearby: they were getting closer. I could hear a handful of voices talking to one another, trying to negotiate the prickly tunnel of Anne-Marie's childhood. I looked over at my wife. Without saying a word, I placed the corkscrew and the wine-bottle back in the carrier-bag, wrapped the plastic tightly around the shape of the bottle and tied it off. Then I dropped it into the pool, which appeared blacker than ever in the darkness. The bottle bobbed briefly, then sank, and was gone.

A yellow beam penetrated the clearing: someone was preparing to emerge from the tunnel. I stepped back round the edge of the pool and sat down beside Anne-Marie. She took my hand. I shone Henry's torch on the mouth of the tunnel, where we heard a sudden babble of French: two voices. Anne-Marie said something to them. There was silence for a moment, then the first gendarme risked crawling through unarmed. He stood up, found his gun.

Does *she* forgive *me*?

The second gendarme came through. They searched us, briefly, then took us out, one at a time: one gendarme, then Anne-Marie and me, then the other gendarme, all crawling through on our hands and knees in the pitch black. We might have been children again, only somehow we were playing a very adult game.

Finally we emerged from the undergrowth, out onto the main path, where we could stand. There were more police waiting. Jouette was with them, in his navy suit; he was wearing rubber boots and carried a map. He motioned for Anne-Marie to stay put, but for me to go with him. They had cut a hole in the fence, where we were marched through separately. Merlin's tomb was small and insignificant in the dark. I never had a chance to speak again to Anne-Marie. When we reached the car park they put us into different vehicles. Headlamps flared, engines turned over and we drove out of the forest, through the quiet and contented streets of Paimpont, where people sat eating in the windows of the Relais de Brocéliande, all the way to Rennes.

I expected us to arrive at the commissariat together. But we didn't. Anne-Marie and I were kept apart. I was shown into a small but plush-looking office – Jouette's, I assumed – with green carpet and a wooden desk that matched the bookshelf behind it. It was Jouette who questioned me. On his desk a bright Anglepoise lamp was switched on, which made the bags under his eyes more pronounced. He told me to make myself comfy. He had obviously acquired the word 'comfy' from somewhere. His English was shaky. He had another gendarme fetch me coffee.

When I was sitting opposite him, sipping it, he asked me to confirm my name, our address in England, and whether Anne-Marie Stone, the woman I was brought in with, was my wife. I confirmed all three points. The clock on the wall beside the bookcase said 8.55 p.m. Jouette explained I had been picked up on the orders of the Derbyshire Constabulary, under the charge of leaving the British Isles while under investigation. There was no mention of Martinez. Detectives were arriving in the morning to question us, and we would both be held in temporary custody until then.

Jouette smiled. Did I like my coffee? He must make it clear that this was not his case: it had nothing to do with the French police. I should understand that this was an English investigation, conducted with the co-operation of local authorities. Therefore we were not to be held in the cells here. We would have rooms elsewhere for the night, guarded, of course. We would be handed over to the English in the morning.

I haven't seen Anne-Marie properly again. I know she's here somewhere, though: I caught a glimpse of her being guided to another car as we left the commissariat. Surely they are putting us up at the same place. The French police seem to know little of what's going on. I don't think you have enough evidence yet, do you, Maguire? Otherwise we'd be back downtown and booked – manslaughter or murder. Fleeing the country, that's a bit lame, don't you think? From what Jouette said, it doesn't even sound like an arrest to me. Though we weren't resisting. They carry guns here, you know. This must seem a chore to them. I feel sorry for the gendarme outside, pacing alone in the corridor. Yes, surely they don't have the resources to use two hotels. Anne-Marie must be here. How many rooms away?

There is little time left. The bedside clock says 5.20 a.m. Outside, the sun is coming up, the sky's light scattering again. A patch of it is spreading across the room and onto the bed. Birds are singing. Can you hear them, Maguire?

Love, I would like to say, is the ultimate expression of the need to unite. All that matter rushing through space and time. The ultimate unity. Know love, and you have known the workings of the universe.

Soon the city of Rennes will be waking. Soon you will arrive, Maguire, either via Paris, or straight from the Midlands. You'll say, 'Let's start again, shall we, Mr Stone? Did you see Sebastian Martinez for a second time on Saturday night, after you left the Theatre Royal?'

And I'll say, 'Yes, I did. I killed him.'
I will play the jealous husband faultlessly.

Because you will need your answers, Maguire, your evidence, beyond reasonable doubt.

The way we all do.

Yet, so far, a doubt that is reasonable is all we have in this world of ours. For centuries humans have sought to understand the environment around them. Recent developments in science have enabled us to come the closest we've ever been to finding answers to our oldest questions: why are we as we are? Why do things happen as they do? The ultimate goal of science is to find one theory that will explain the universe in its entirety – a theory of everything. The twentieth century has given us two great partial theories: general relativity, describing the very large structures of the universe, and quantum mechanics, describing the very small ones. These two theories, however, are incompatible. While classical theories, such as Newton's theory of universal attraction and Einstein's theory of general relativity, can explain the orbits of the planets right down to smaller objects we can observe on Earth, they cannot explain the behaviour of the smallest particles. This is left to quantum mechanics, which predicts probabilities for the behaviours of particles within the limit set by the uncertainty principle. The search is now on to unite these two theories, to find a single quantum theory of gravity that will explain everything. Theoretical physicists have already proposed that such a theory may be able to eliminate the need for a singularity at the Big Bang; that is, no edge to space-time and no singularities at which the laws of science break down and, therefore, it could be argued, no need for a Creator. In his no-boundary hypothesis Stephen Hawking proposes that space-time can be pictured a bit like the Earth's surface – finite in extent but with no edge or boundary: a universe that is neither created nor destroyed, but just *is*.

Despite our rapid advances in technology, however, soon everything is going to be either too big or too small for us to get to grips with. We will either know everything – one breakthrough, one grand theory to unravel the workings of the universe – or we will know nothing because there'll be no way of proving it. And, anyway, wouldn't a theory of everything have already predetermined the outcome of our search for it? Why should it let us find it? Furthermore, even if we did make such a discovery, what science has often been inclined to forget, and what human beings ultimately are unable to forget, no matter how hard we try, is that knowing how is never, ever the same as knowing why.

26

Because you are beautiful, Anne-Marie, standing by the sprinkler in the park opposite the Sagrada Familia, more spectacular than the cathedral itself, which we will wander around, held in awe.

We are the last to be admitted. A few tourists pass us in the entrance on their way out.

'Cuarenta minutos,' an attendant says.

'Gracias!' we call through the darkness, and disappear into the shadows and the stone, past the memorabilia and photographs and museum pieces, all those sketches and daguerreotypes of serious-looking men, hurrying down the aisle with your hand wrapped in mine and your eyes blinking up at me as if I'm a part of all this splendour.

And we reach the staircase that winds its way up St Barnabas's Tower, rising over the eastern portal, pausing briefly at the bottom of the steps where there are no attendants, no one saying it is too late to go up. So you say, 'Come on,' and up we go, all one hundred and five metres, until we are standing alone among the clouds, with me wanting you, right there at the top, looking out towards Subadell, with Barcelona stretched before us, the buildings standing to attention in perfect rectangles, the roads all parallel and the sky blushing pink.

'Gracias. Muchísimas gracias!' to the annoyed attendant on our way back down. Past eight o'clock, the night still young, not daring to let us go, as we walk along La Rambla, where tourists are gathering for music, puppet shows, fire-eating and juggling.

And there, opposite the fire-eater, behind a stall brimming with fruit, we find the Frenchman, sitting on a stool by his tiny two-wheeled cart, his rings and brooches and bracelets laid out before him, with just enough breeze brushing across the street, up from the marina, to make the crêpe paper covering the cart start to whisper.

We pick out the rings, the Frenchman asking if we want them engraved, making no attempt to address us in Spanish or English, quite indifferent, with his clipped beard and white hair, his wrinkled face, so darkly tanned it looks like a church pew, and his large hands offering paper and pencil to write down the words. A popular request, no doubt, although he makes no comment, but works on in silence, almost reluctantly, taking his time.

And then that smile on his face when he's finished. Only a brief smile, a suggestion of a smile, but we both see it: a blessing of some kind. For a moment we are captured there, the three of us, me digging in my wallet to pay, you thanking him, and him seeming neither relieved nor displeased to be speaking his own language with a stranger.

A stranger who seems happier than ever, standing beside me among all this activity, with the singing and the dancing and the old men huddled in their shirtsleeves, playing their backgammon, and the old women on benches, muttering and crossing themselves.

'What shall we do?'

'The beach!' you say. 'The beach! I want to see the sea.'

And you might just as well say the moon – I will get you

there. So we unravel the map in the hotel car-park, right there on the bonnet of our hire car. The Premià del Mar, a twenty-minute drive from the bustle of the city, you right there beside me, and nothing else existing. Only a shower coming at last, a storm that's been brewing for days but won't break before morning, yet still, here is a little for us. Pitch black when we eventually pull over, parking so the windscreen overlooks the ocean, the headlamps picking out the rain and losing themselves on the water.

The two of us getting out and walking for the horizon, a mile across the rainswept sand, where the sea seems always just out of reach, so we think we'll never get there, as if it has retreated, or gone on quietly and disappeared into the land. And here you are, a wonder, leaving my side, pirouetting in your white dress left and right, as I shout finally, hoping you can hear me, hoping I can out-shout the sea, 'Marry me! Marry me!'

And then the shape of you, the white ghost of you, returning, taking my hand, silent as a fish. 'Yes! Oh, yes.'

And then gone again, out across the wet sand towards the blackness moving beyond, where I see you suddenly, like a brushstroke, a dot almost rained off the canvas. And then returning, running up to me when the shower stops, so we can stand by the water, dots together. We could be anywhere. The sea could be any. But it isn't. We are six miles from Mataró. This is the Mediterranean, and you are turning, wrapping your arms round me effortlessly, your whole weight against me, your mouth waiting and your eyes like stars. We could be anybody. But we aren't.

Acknowledgments

I would like to thank Professor Stephen Hawking, whose book *A Brief History of Time* not only inspired a significant aspect of Jack's character, but also provided many of the explanations of theories and history of physics in the novel.

My thanks also to Neill Lambert for his valuable advice regarding my use of physics in the book.